Praise for *Oscar Wilde and a Death of No Importance*

"One of the most intelligent, amusing and entertaining books of the year. If Oscar Wilde himself had been asked to write this book he could not have done it any better."   —Alexander McCall Smith

"Wilde has sprung back to life in this thrilling and richly atmospheric new novel . . . The perfect topography for crime and mystery . . . magnificent . . . an unforgettable shocker about sex and vice, love and death."   —*Sunday Express*

"Gyles Brandreth and Oscar Wilde seem made for one another. . . . There is much here to enjoy . . . the complex and nicely structured plot zips along."   —*The Daily Telegraph*

"Brandreth has poured his considerable familiarity with London into a witty fin-de-siècle entertainment, and the rattlingly elegant dialogue is peppered with witticisms uttered by Wilde well before he ever thought of putting them into his plays."   —*The Sunday Times*

"Fabulous. . . . The plot races along like a carriage pulled by thoroughbreds . . . So enjoyably plausible."   —*The Scotsman*

"Both a romp through fin-de-siècle London . . . and a carefully researched portrait of Oscar Wilde . . . Very entertaining."

—*Literary Review*

"Brandreth has the Wildean lingo down pat and the narrative is dusted with piquant social observations. A sparkling treat for fans of Wilde and Sherlock Holmes alike."   —*Easy Living*

"A lively, amusing, and clever murder mystery starring Oscar Wilde— larger than life, brilliant, generous, luxurious—with a new trait: he is now a master sleuth not unlike Sherlock Holmes. . . . Brandreth is steeped in the lore of Wilde, but this doesn't oppress the story which is a cleverly plotted thriller through London's demimonde. . . . Highly entertaining."   —*The Dubliner*

D0051928

"This is not only a good piece of detective fiction in its own right, it is highly entertaining, spiced as it is with Wildean sayings, both real and invented, and the imagined conversations and intellectual sparring between Wilde and Conan Doyle. Future tales in the series are something to look forward to."　　　　　　　　　　　*—Leicester Mercury*

"Excellent . . . I'd be staggered if, by the end of the year, you'd read many better whodunnits. Brandreth demonstrates supremely measured skill as a storyteller."　　　　　　　*—Nottingham Evening Post*

"Wilde as detective is thoroughly convincing. . . . The period, and the two or three worlds in which Wilde himself moved, are richly evoked . . . [This] is an excellent detective story. I'm keenly looking forward to the rest of the series."
　　　　　　　—The District Messenger, newsletter of the Sherlock Holmes Society of London

"Brandreth knows his Wilde. . . . He knows his Holmes too. . . . The plot is devilishly clever, the characters are fully fleshed, the mystery is engrossing, and the solution is perfectly fair. I love it."
　　　　　　　—The Sherlock Holmes Journal

"A skilful and erudite piece of writing and one well worth reading, not only for the plot but for much information about Wilde and his friends at that period."　　　　　　　*—Tangled Web UK*

"It works quite brilliantly. This is the first of a series. You'll want to start the next the day after finishing this one."　　　　*—The Diplomat*

"A witty and gripping portrait of corruption in late-Victorian London, and one of which Oscar Wilde and Arthur Conan Doyle would be proud."　　　　　　　*—Livewire*

"A wow of a history mystery . . . a first-class stunner."　　　*—Booklist*

"Beautifully clear prose . . . We tend to be wary of books that use real-life characters as their protagonists, but we were completely enchanted with this one."　　　　　　　*—The Denver Post*

"Wilde beguiles those inside the novel and out . . . Brandreth writes breezily, effortlessly blending fiction and historical facts in a way that keeps the novel moving."

—*The Atlanta Journal-Constitution*

"An intriguing tightrope walk . . . engaging, ingenious."

—*Newsday*

"Immensely enjoyable, one of the best in the canon of literary mysteries."

—*The Philadelphia Inquirer*

Praise for *Oscar Wilde and a Game Called Murder*

"The second in this wickedly imagined and highly entertaining series . . . an intelligent, jaunty, and hilarious mystery."

—*The Good Book Guide*

"Hugely enjoyable."

—*Daily Mail*

"A cast of historical characters to die for."

—*The Sunday Times*

"A carnival of cliff-hangers and fiendish twists and turns. . . . The joy of the book, as with its predecessor, is the rounded and compelling presentation of the character of Wilde. The imaginary and the factual are woven together with devilish ingenuity. Brandreth also gives his hero speeches of great beauty and wisdom and humanity."

—*Sunday Express*

"Wilde really has to prove himself against Bram Stoker and Arthur Conan Doyle when a murder ruins their Sunday Supper Club. But Brandreth's invention—that of Wilde as detective—is more than up to the challenge. With plenty of wit, too."

—*Daily Mirror*

"Gyles Brandreth's entertainment is an amusing and satisfactorily unlikely story featuring Bram Stoker, Arthur Conan Doyle, a locked room, and Oscar Wilde in the role of the series detective." —*Literary Review*

"The plot speeds to an exciting climax. . . . Richly atmospheric. Very entertaining." —*Woman & Home*

"Sparkling dialogue, mystery piled deliciously on mystery, a plot with pace and panache, and a London backdrop that would grace any Victorian theatre." —*The Northern Echo*

"The acid test for any writer who has enjoyed first-time success is that all-important second novel. Gyles Brandreth, I am happy to report, has sailed through the ordeal with flying colours. . . . Irresistible . . . Elegant . . . Rich . . . Enjoyable . . . A classic Agatha Christie–style whodunit involving some particularly inventive murders with a few well-placed red herrings." —*Yorkshire Evening Post*

"As much imaginative biography as murder mystery . . . Terrifically well researched, it whizzes along." —*Scotland on Sunday*

"What raises this book several notches above most mysteries is the authentic historical detail and the engaging portrait of Wilde. . . . sparkling." —The Historical Novel Society

"Terrific period atmosphere, crisp writing style, and the flamboyant Wilde make this series pitch-perfect. Great entertainment." —*Booklist*

"[*Oscar Wilde and a Game Called Murder*] is the eagerly awaited second volume in Gyles Brandreth's series of detective stories and it doesn't disappoint." —*The District Messenger*, newsletter of the Sherlock Holmes Society of London

Praise for *Oscar Wilde and the Dead Man's Smile*

"One of the most consistently entertaining historical series starring a real-life sleuth." —*Booklist*

"The murders begin. Highly theatrical ones . . . An entertaining and meticulously researched piece of pop fiction about Wilde and his circle." —*The Washington Post*

"Through his excellent writing Brandreth has brought to life 1880s Europe, and his descriptions evoke all the senses as if you were there following Oscar. It is a fun book that introduces you to many interesting characters. . . . A lighthearted and entertaining murder mystery."

—*The Irish Post*

"Gyles Brandreth began his Oscar Wilde murder mysteries in grand style. The second book was actually better than the first, and the third consolidates and improves on that achievement. An exceptionally good detective story, it's also a fascinating historical novel."

—*The District Messenger,* newsletter of the Sherlock Holmes Society of London

"A cleverly plotted, intelligent, and thoroughly diverting murder mystery. This novel is an educated page-turner, a feast of intriguing and lighthearted entertainment."

—*The Good Book Guide*

"An entertaining yarn, easy and pleasing to read—with an extensive set of vivid characters."

—*Gay Times*

"For me this whole series is a guilty pleasure: Brandreth's portrait of Oscar Wilde is entirely plausible, plots are ingenious, and the historical background is fascinating."

—*The Scotsman*

Praise for *Oscar Wilde and the Vampire Murders*

"Gyles Brandreth's Oscar Wilde murder mysteries get better and better. [This one] is positively dazzling. Both witty and profound, it's also devilishly clever."

—*The District Messenger,* newsletter of the Sherlock Holmes Society of London

"Inventive . . . brilliant . . . marvelous . . . glittering . . . graceful . . . intricate . . . enthralling."

—*Booklist*

"Oscar Wilde is back in rare form in this clever and intricate mystery that brings 1890s London vibrantly to life. Verdict: great stuff."

—*Library Journal*

Praise for *Oscar Wilde and the Vatican Murders*

"A flight of imagination that partners Oscar Wilde with Arthur Conan Doyle in a deadly pursuit to the heart of the Eternal City merits a round of applause for sheer chutzpah. . . . Literary and theological references merge easily into a skilfully crafted story that goes all the way to meet the standards set by his two eminent protagonists."

—*Daily Mail*

"Hugely enjoyable . . . a story that reminds us just how enjoyable a well-told traditional murder mystery can be." —*The Scotsman*

"Brandreth has become a true artist as he so skillfully writes the dialogue between these two detectives . . . Well done, Brandreth!"

—MysteryNet.com

SEP   2013

Gilpin County Public Libra

ALSO BY GYLES BRANDRETH

THE OSCAR WILDE MYSTERIES
Oscar Wilde and a Death of No Importance
Oscar Wilde and a Game Called Murder
Oscar Wilde and the Dead Man's Smile
Oscar Wilde and the Vampire Murders
Oscar Wilde and the Vatican Murders

BIOGRAPHY
The Funniest Man on Earth: The Story of Dan Leno
John Gielgud: An Actor's Life
Brief Encounters: Meetings with Remarkable People
Philip & Elizabeth: Portrait of a Royal Marriage
Charles & Camilla: Portrait of a Love Affair

AUTOBIOGRAPHY AND DIARIES
Under the Jumper: Autobiographical Excursions
Breaking the Code: Westminster Diaries
Something Sensational to Read in the Train: The Diary of a Lifetime

NOVELS
Who Is Nick Saint?
Venice Midnight

SELECTED NONFICTION
Created in Captivity
I Scream for Ice Cream: Pearls from the Pantomime
Yarooh!: A Feast of Frank Richards
The Joy of Lex
More Joy of Lex
Great Theatrical Disasters

For Michèle

Touchstone
A Division of Simon & Schuster, Inc.
1230 Avenue of the Americas
New York, NY 10020

This book is a work of fiction. Any references to historical events, real people, or real places are used fictitiously. Other names, characters, places, and events are products of the author's imagination, and any resemblance to actual events or places or persons, living or dead, is entirely coincidental.

Copyright © 2013 by Gyles Brandreth

All rights reserved, including the right to reproduce this book or portions thereof in any form whatsoever. For information address Touchstone Subsidiary Rights Department, 1230 Avenue of the Americas, New York, NY 10020.

First Touchstone trade paperback edition May 2013

TOUCHSTONE and colophon are registered trademarks of Simon & Schuster, Inc.

For information about special discounts for bulk purchases, please contact Simon & Schuster Special Sales at 1-866-506-1949 or business@simonandschuster.com.

The Simon & Schuster Speakers Bureau can bring authors to your live event. For more information or to book an event contact the Simon & Schuster Speakers Bureau at 1-866-248-3049 or visit our website at www.simonspeakers.com.

Designed by Aline C. Pace

Manufactured in the United States of America

10 9 8 7 6 5 4 3 2 1

Library of Congress Cataloging-in-Publication data is available.

ISBN 978-1-4391-5375-8 (pbk)
ISBN 978-1-4391-7231-5 (ebook)

OSCAR WILDE

AND THE

MURDERS AT READING GAOL

A Mystery

GYLES BRANDRETH

A TOUCHSTONE BOOK
Published by Simon & Schuster
New York   London   Toronto   Sydney   New Delhi

Oscar Wilde and the Murders at Reading Gaol

Drawn from the previously unpublished papers of
Robert Sherard (1861–1943),
Oscar Wilde's first and most prolific biographer

Principal characters in the narrative

At the Café Suisse, Dieppe, France, July 1897

Sebastian Melmoth
Dr. Quilp

At Reading Gaol, Berkshire, England, November 1895–May 1897

Oscar Wilde, Prisoner C.3.3.
Eric Ryder, Prisoner C.3.1.
Achindra Acala Luck, Prisoner C.3.2.
Joseph Smith, Prisoner C.3.4.
Sebastian Atitis-Snake, Prisoner C.3.5.
Tom Lewis, Prisoner E.1.1.
Charles Thomas Wooldridge, prisoner executed on 7 July 1896
Richard Prince, Prisoner A.2.11.
Constance Wilde
Colonel H. B. Isaacson, Governor of Reading Gaol until July 1896
Major J. O. Nelson, Governor of Reading Gaol from July 1896
The Reverend M. T. Friend, Chaplain of Reading Gaol
Dr. O. C. Maurice, Surgeon at Reading Gaol
Warder Braddle
Warder Stokes
Warder Martin
Wardress from E Ward

In Reading gaol by Reading town
There is a pit of shame,
And in it lies a wretched man
Eaten by teeth of flame,
In a burning winding-sheet he lies,
And his grave has got no name.
And there, till Christ call forth the dead,
In silence let him lie:
No need to waste the foolish tear,
Or heave the windy sigh:
The man had killed the thing he loved,
And so he had to die.
And all men kill the thing they love,
By all let this be heard,
Some do it with a bitter look,
Some with a flattering word,
The coward does it with a kiss,
The brave man with a sword!

FROM *THE BALLAD OF READING GAOL* (1897)

Author's Note

My name is Robert Sherard and I was a friend of Oscar Wilde. I met him first in Paris in the spring of 1883. He was twenty-eight years old and already famous—as a poet, wit, and raconteur, as the pre-eminent "personality" of his day. I was twenty-two, an aspiring poet, a would-be journalist, and quite unknown. Oscar and I met for the last time, again in Paris, in 1900, not long before his untimely death at the age of forty-six. During the intervening seventeen years I kept a journal of our friendship.

Oscar Wilde and I were not lovers, but I knew him well. Few, I believe, knew him better. In 1884, I was the first friend he entertained after his marriage to Constance Lloyd—the loveliest of women and the most cruelly used. In 1895, following his incarceration, I was the first to visit him in prison. It was in a letter from gaol that my friend did me the signal honour of describing me as "the bravest and most chivalrous of all brilliant beings." In 1897, on his release, I travelled to meet him in

France. In 1902, I tried to do justice to his memory as his first biographer.

The book that you are holding is one of six volumes I have compiled covering hitherto unknown aspects of the extraordinary life of Oscar Wilde. This volume, in particular, describes episodes from his darkest years, and for that reason, at the outset, it is worth reminding the reader that, before his downfall and imprisonment, Oscar Wilde was a happy person. Indeed, happiness was the essence of the man. Oscar Wilde was *fun*—fun to be with, fun to know. He loved life: he *relished* it. "The only horrible thing in the world is *ennui*," he said. "That is the one sin for which there is no forgiveness." He loved colour and beauty. "To me beauty is the wonder of wonders," he declared. He loved laughter and applause. When a friend suggested to him that the reason he wrote plays was a desire for immediate applause, he agreed. "Yes, the immediate applause . . . What a charming phrase! The immediate applause . . ." He loved the English language. He loved to use it. He loved to play with it. He savoured words like "vermilion" and "narcissus." He took much pleasure in letting a name like "Sebastian Atitis-Snake"—or a title like "the Marquess of Dimmesdale"—roll off his tongue; none in saying, baldly, "John Smith" or "The Duke of York." He had his own way with words. Whatever annoyed him, he described as "tedious." Whatever pleased him, he called "amazing."

When I wrote my original account of Oscar's life I told the truth—but not the whole truth. A short while before his death, I revealed to my friend that I planned to tell his story after he was gone. He said, "Don't tell them everything—

not yet! When you write of me, don't speak of murder. Leave that a while." I have left it until now. I have been preparing these volumes during the winter of 1938 and the spring and summer of 1939. I am old and the world is on the brink of war once more. My time will soon be up, but before I go I have this final task remaining—to tell everything I know of Oscar Wilde, poet, playwright, friend, detective . . . avenging angel.

The material that follows is based on Oscar's own account of what occurred during the twenty-five months between 25 May 1895 and 25 June 1897. What you are about to read he told me in the late summer of 1897. Three chapters—the Introduction, the Interlude, and the Conclusion—are written entirely by me. The rest is Oscar's own narrative and, for the most part, I have been able to use his own words because I took them down (as best I could) at his dictation—directly onto my new Remington typewriter. It was to me that Oscar remarked, "The typewriting machine, when played with expression, is no more annoying than the piano when played by a sister or near relation."

RHS
September 1939

Prologue

London, 25 May 1895

From the Star, *final edition*
OSCAR WILDE GUILTY
Sentenced to 2 years' hard labour
Jubilant scenes in street

At the end of a four-day trial at the Old Bailey, Oscar Wilde, the celebrated playwright, was tonight found guilty on seven counts of gross indecency and sentenced to two years' imprisonment with hard labour.

Addressing the court, the trial judge, Mr. Justice Wills, 77, declared, "It is the worst case I have ever tried." The judge said it was impossible to doubt that Wilde, 40, had been at the centre of "a circle of extensive corruption of the most hideous kind among young men." Passing the severest sentence allowed by law, he said, "In my judgement it is totally inadequate for such a case as this."

In the dock, the guilty man was seen to sway as sentence was passed and called out to the judge, "And I? May I say nothing, my lord?" Mr. Justice Wills gestured to the warders standing at the side of the dock to take the prisoner away. Wilde, white-faced, appeared to stagger before being escorted to his cell beneath the court-room. He was then taken to Newgate Prison near by, where the warrant authorising his detention was prepared, and later, by prison van, to Pentonville Prison in north London.

Outside the Old Bailey, the news of the guilty verdict was greeted with scenes of jubilation. There was loud applause and cheering from the crowd that had gathered and, when the detail of the sentence reached them, a small group of street women danced a jig in the gutter, one of them shouting, "Two years is too good for 'im." Another provoked laughter saying, "'E'll 'ave 'is 'air cut regular now."

It is understood that Wilde's most recent comedy, *The Importance of Being Earnest,* will continue to play at the St. James's Theatre, but that the author's name will be removed immediately from the playbills and programmes in deference to the sensibilities of audience members.

Constance Wilde, 36, the unfortunate wife of the guilty man, was not in court to witness her husband's ruin. It is believed that the authoress and her two sons, aged nine and eight, are now travelling on the Continent.

*

"NAPOLEON" POISONER NOT INSANE

Life Sentence for Attempted Murder

At Reading Assizes today, the man who claimed that he had attempted to murder his wife under the delusion that he was the Emperor Napoleon of France, and that she was the Empress Josephine and had been unfaithful to him, failed in his plea of not guilty on grounds of insanity and was sentenced to life imprisonment.

Throughout his four-day trial, Sebastian Atitis-Snake, 37, an unemployed chef of Palmer Road, Reading, addressed the court in broken French and stood with his right hand tucked into his waistcoat in the manner of the late Emperor. Passing sentence, Mr. Justice Crawford, 69, told the accused, "You have attempted to make a mockery of your own trial in the hope of confusing the jury. You have failed. The gentlemen of the jury are not fools and you are not insane. It is clear, from both the police evidence and from the expert medical witnesses we have heard, that you are, at best, what is termed, in common parlance, a 'confidence trickster,' and, at worst, a cold-hearted and calculating would-be killer."

The judge said that there was no evidence of any kind that Mrs. Atitis-Snake had been guilty of adultery. "By all accounts your poor wife is an entirely blameless young woman. Her only misfortune was to meet you when she was just eighteen years of age and recently orphaned. She had a little fortune, amounting to £5,000, but no family and few friends. You were fifteen years her senior and, doubtless, by means of telling her a string of the fantastical falsehoods that appear to be your stock-in-trade, you persuaded her to marry you. Having secured her fortune, you quickly tired of her youth and beauty and decided to dispose of her. You attempted to murder this innocent creature by serving her a dish of poisonous mushrooms—disguised as what you termed an *omelette de campagne*. Had you killed her, you would have been charged with murder and would now be facing the death penalty. As it is, the poor woman lies in a coma in a nursing home. As I understand it, there is hope, at least, that one day she may recover. Her future is uncertain. Yours is not. The sentence of the court is that you be imprisoned for the rest of your natural life and be kept to hard labour."

*

THE QUEEN'S BIRTHDAY

Her Majesty Honours Henry Irving

Her Majesty Queen Victoria has marked her seventy-sixth birthday by conferring a knighthood on actor Henry Irving, 57. Sir Henry, as he will now be known, is the nation's most celebrated Shakespearean player and the manager of London's Lyceum Theatre. He is the first actor in the history of the theatre to receive such an honour and today professed himself "truly humbled" by Her Majesty's recognition. "This is a mighty day for actors everywhere," he said. "May it be long remembered."

Introduction

Dieppe, France, 24 June 1897

It was six o'clock in the evening, but the bright summer sun still stood high in the sky.

On the pavement outside the Café Suisse, in the shade beneath the blue- and white-striped awning, at a round table covered with a red- and white-checked cloth, a large man sat on a small chair nursing an empty glass. He had been seated there for an hour—for two, perhaps. At five o'clock, with narrowed eyes—hooded but amused—he had scrutinised the passengers from the paddle-steamer—the *Victoria* from Newhaven—as, bags and baggage in hand, porters in tow, they had trooped by on their way from the quayside into the town. He had raised his straw boater to one of them. The man he had thought he recognised had not caught his eye.

Now the parade had passed and the hubbub had subsided. Apart from the retreating figure of the *curé,* a bustling black beetle in a biretta, the street was deserted. From the docks he could hear the faint rumble of barrow wheels on cobblestones and the occasional cry of a stevedore. Near by, beneath the stone archway alongside the café, a stray dog yapped, rolling over and over in a pile of newspapers and cabbage leaves—the detritus of market day.

The man had a large, long, well-fleshed face: a prominent nose; full lips; uneven, yellow teeth; a pasty, putty-like complexion; lank, thinning, auburn hair. He was smoking a Turkish cigarette and gazing vacantly ahead of him. He wore a cream-coloured linen suit, a white shirt, and a loosely tied bottle-green cravat. There was a button missing on his jacket and he had no money in his pocket, but he looked not uncontented. When the *curé* (whom he knew) had paused at his table to wish him a good afternoon, they had exchanged a few pleasantries (in French) and, with some ceremony, the large man had raised his glass to the priest—and drained it. Now he was ready for another drink.

As he turned round to look for the waiter, he saw instead a smiling stranger emerging from the café, coming directly towards him with outstretched arms. The beaming individual—a pale-faced man of middling years and middling height, slightly built and sandy-haired, bespectacled and smartly dressed—was carrying a pair of wine-glasses in one hand and a bottle of champagne in the other.

"Is this a mirage or a miracle?" murmured the large man, throwing the butt of his cigarette into the street.

"It's a Perrier-Jouët 'ninety-two," answered the stranger, turning the bottle in his hand to show off the label. He glanced back, over his shoulder, towards the café. "The boy is bringing out some ice." With a little flourish, the stranger placed the champagne and the glasses on the table, pulled down his shirt-cuffs, pushed his spectacles up his nose, and inclined his head in a small bow. Abruptly, he brought his heels together so that they clicked. "May I join you, sir?" he asked.

"I should be utterly appalled if you did not."

The stranger laughed and drew up a chair. He sat down. He moved, the large man noticed, with a dancer's grace. The wine was already uncorked. With studied concentration, the stranger filled both glasses to the brim and handed one to the large man, who gazed upon the pale-gold bubbles with evident delight.

"This is my favourite drink in all the world," he said.

"I know," replied the stranger. "A second bottle is being chilled. I thought we might enjoy it later with a little lobster mayonnaise."

The large man closed his eyes and, with one hand, brought the champagne to his lips. The other hand he rested gently on the stranger's arm. "Thank you," he whispered, as he took a second draught.

"The pleasure—and the honour—are both mine. I am glad to have found you. It has not been easy."

The large man opened his eyes and looked directly at the stranger. The man wore a thin moustache and a tiny beard. As a rule, he was mistrustful of those who covered their faces with hair—what did they have to hide? But these facial adornments were barely discernible—and the cold yellow wine was wonderful. "You have been looking for me?" he enquired, pleasantly.

"Yes, and now that I have found you I hope that you are behaving very well."

"I am feeling very well," replied the large man, narrowing his eyes.

"That is not quite the same thing. In fact, the two things rarely go together."

The stranger's voice was soft. He had the accent of a gentleman, but there was something unnatural about his way of speaking—affected, almost effeminate. And his skin appeared to be covered with a thin coating of powder. "Are you an actor?" asked the large man. "Do I know you?"

"I am an apothecary," replied the stranger. He reached into his waistcoat pocket and produced a small visiting card. He passed it across the table.

The large man took the card and brought it close to his eyes. "Your name is Dr. Quilp? And you are an apothecary?"

"And a writer—among other things."

"I am a writer, also," responded the large man, still studying the stranger's card. "That's all I am, alas. I have a friend who is a medical man as well as a writer—Arthur Conan Doyle. You know who I mean, of course?"

"The creator of Sherlock Holmes."

"Exactly. Dr. Conan Doyle and I have shared the odd adventure over the years and he has instructed me in the Holmesian Science of Deduction and Analysis. He has taught me some of the great man's tricks. He has impressed on me the importance of observation and the significance of detail." Smiling, the large man returned the stranger's visiting card. "I have to say, Dr. Quilp, that your hands are rougher than those one would expect to find upon an apothecary."

"I have my father's hands," replied the stranger, smoothly. He pocketed the card and then spread out his fingers on the table and gazed down at them. "My father was a blacksmith."

"And your mother?"

"She was a lady," said Dr. Quilp, simply.

The large man took another sip of champagne and contemplated his host. "You clearly know me, sir. But do I know you? You seem familiar to me, but I am not sure why. Have we met before?"

"You have seen me, I think—watching you."

"Watching me?"

"Observing you. I wanted to make sure that it really was you. I did not want to approach the wrong person."

"And cause embarrassment?"

"Your appearance might have changed."

"It has changed."

"And photographs can be deceptive."

"Not only photographs . . ." The large man tilted his head to one side as he considered his new-found friend. "For how long have you been 'observing' me, Dr. Quilp?"

"I have been here in Dieppe since the beginning of the week. I arrived on the day of your children's party."

"My little fête in honour of Queen Victoria's Diamond Jubilee? Fifteen children came, you know. I had only invited twelve—the garden at my lodgings is so small. And I hate crowds."

"It seemed a very jolly party."

"It was the happiest party of my life. We had strawberries

and cream, apricots, chocolates, cakes, and *sirop de grena-dine*. I promised every child a present and they all wanted musical instruments—tin trumpets and accordions. We sang songs and played games—and they danced for me."

"I know. I was watching from the roadway."

"It was you, was it?" said the large man, emptying his glass. "I saw you. I thought it was a policeman in plain clothes. I am glad it was only you."

"It was a happy gathering."

"It was perfect. At seven o'clock, as the children departed, I gave each one a little basket with bonbons in it and a little cake, frosted pink and specially inscribed: *Jubilé de la Reine Victoria*. As they went on their way, they all cried out, '*Vive la Reine d'Angleterre! Vive Monsieur Melmoth!*'"

"I know," said Dr. Quilp. "That's how I learnt your new name."

"Ah yes," said the large man, "my name." He sat forward and felt in his coat pocket. "I have a card, also. It is very like yours. Almost identical, in fact." After a moment's rummaging, he produced his calling card and handed it across the table. He inclined his head. "Sebastian Melmoth, at your service."

Dr. Quilp smiled. "It is a fine name."

"Inspired by a fine novel—*Melmoth the Wanderer*. The novel was written by my great-uncle by marriage on my mother's side, so it's a family name in a way. I know Melmoth's a mouthful, but it feels appropriate—don't you agree?"

"I meant that Sebastian is a fine name."

"Sebastian is a *beautiful* name. It is my favourite Christian name—for saints and sinners."

The boy from the café had arrived at the table bearing an ice-bucket and a fresh bottle of champagne. Dr. Quilp refilled their glasses. "I collect Sebastians," continued Monsieur Melmoth, "of all kinds. I knew a murderer called Sebastian once."

"Tell me about him," said Dr. Quilp, raising his glass to his companion. "I love tales of murder."

"Don't we all?" replied Melmoth, raising his glass, also. "There's the scarlet thread of murder running through the colourless skein of life, and our duty is to unravel it, and isolate it, and expose every inch of it . . . according to my friend Conan Doyle."

"Tell me about this murderer named Sebastian," insisted Dr. Quilp.

"He was but one of the murderers I've known. I have been in prison for the past two years. I take it that you knew that, Dr. Quilp?"

"Yes," replied Quilp, lowering his eyes. "I did know that."

"In politics one meets charlatans. In prison one meets murderers. I met several. Sebastian Atitis-Snake was one. I liked his name—every element of it. Charles Wooldridge was another. I am writing a poem about Wooldridge."

"About the murder he committed?"

"About the day he died. He was hanged in Reading Gaol—a year ago, when I was there."

"Tell me your story, Mr. Melmoth."

"You appear to know my story, Dr. Quilp."

"I know what I have read."

"And what you have researched? I sense you have been assiduous in your researches."

"I want to know about your time in prison. The *world* wants to know about your time in prison."

"The world's a huge thing."

"Yes, and would pay handsomely to read your story, Mr. Melmoth."

"The world can read my poem."

"I think you'll find that prose is better paid."

"Ah, so it's about money?" The large man sat back and laughed. He lit a cigarette and gestured with it towards the champagne bottles. "This is all about money. Finding me, tracking me down, plying me with Perrier-Jouët . . ."

"It's about telling your story, Mr. Melmoth—in your own words, in your own way."

"And sharing the proceeds with you, Dr. Quilp?"

"I'll be your scribe, if you'll allow me."

"I can put pen to paper myself, you know."

"But will you?"

Melmoth drew slowly on his cigarette and smiled. "You are right, Dr. Quilp. Left to my own devices, I might not. I never put off until tomorrow what I can put off until the day after."

"And if you do, you'll do it in the form of a 'prose poem' or a verse drama or—"

"—Some such overwritten nonsense." Melmoth completed Quilp's sentence, laughing. "You appear familiar with my work, dear doctor. Did you not enjoy *The Duchess of Padua?*"

"If we're to reach the widest audience, Mr. Melmoth, we need something that the widest audience can readily comprehend. We need a human story simply told. That is where I hope to be able to assist you."

"A human story!" The large man quivered with amusement. He reached for the second bottle of champagne and replenished his glass. "So, Dr. Quilp, it turns out that you are not so much an apothecary as a journalist."

"I am a writer, Mr. Melmoth. If you will tell it to me, I will record your story in plain English—that is all."

"I am an artist, Dr. Quilp. Art should always remain mysterious. Artists, like gods, must never leave their pedestals."

"Two years ago, Mr. Melmoth, you fell from yours."

A lone seagull screeched in the sky. Melmoth, smiling, contemplated his glass and, suddenly, his eyes were filled with tears. "Yes, passing strange, was it not? How did I let that happen?" He turned away from the table and looked towards the archway, where the mongrel was still playing among the old newspapers and cabbage leaves. "The gods had given me almost everything, Dr. Quilp—as I think you know. I had genius, a distinguished name, high social position, brilliancy, intellectual daring. I made art a philosophy, and philosophy an art. I altered the minds of men and the colour of things. There was nothing I said or did that did not make people wonder. I awoke the imagination of my country so that it created myth and legend around me. I summed up all systems in a phrase and all existence in an epigram."

"And then you were brought to the Old Bailey," replied Quilp. "And put on trial. And found guilty of gross indecency. And imprisoned. We don't need high-flown phrases for any of that, Mr. Melmoth."

"Is that what you are after?" asked Melmoth, turning back sharply. "The story of my foul crimes and misdemeanours—the lurid details of my lewd offences recounted in language that's anything but high-flown?"

Quilp laughed awkwardly. "No. The details of your offences would be far too scandalous. No publisher—beyond the backstreets of Paris—would be able to print any of that."

"But you want the story of my downfall, don't you? The story of the downfall of Oscar Wilde. You must have Oscar Wilde in the title!"

Dr. Quilp widened his eyes, but said nothing.

"There," continued the large man, drawing slowly on his cigarette, "I have dared to speak the name . . . I am allowed to do so. It was once mine. No longer. I am Sebastian Melmoth now."

Quilp felt inside his jacket pocket. He produced a pen and a cheque-book. Carefully, he laid them on the table, one upon the other. "Mr. Melmoth, I want the story of your time in prison—nothing more and nothing less. I want the story of what it was like, of those you met there. I want it told chronologically, simply, unadorned."

Melmoth gazed upon the pen and cheque-book and smiled. "An unvarnished tale—in the tradition of Bunyan and Defoe?"

"If we're to make a proper fortune from it," said Dr. Quilp, "more in the tradition of Arthur Conan Doyle and

Edgar Allan Poe. Readers look for a touch of murder nowadays."

Melmoth extinguished his cigarette. "I'm no murderer, Dr. Quilp." He looked carefully at his interlocutor. "At least, not yet."

"But you've considered murder, I imagine?"

"Who has not?"

"And you have known murderers—men like Sebastian Atitis-Snake. Men who have killed—and hanged for it. Atitis-Snake was found guilty on the same day that you were, I believe."

"So he told me."

"He was the man who claimed to be the Emperor Napoleon?"

"He was."

"Tell us his story, as well as your own." Quilp poured out more wine. "*Oscar Wilde and the Murders at Reading Gaol*—by Sebastian Melmoth. There's a book we can sell around the world. Readers want murder."

Melmoth put out his hand and with his forefinger lightly touched Quilp's pen. "And I want money. I admit it. I *need* money. I have none of my own—none at all. I am dependent on the generosity of friends and the kindness of strangers. And on a small allowance from my dear wife— which she threatens to withdraw if she does not approve of the company I keep. I am in urgent need of funds. And I take it, Dr. Quilp, that you are, too. The suit that you are wearing is new, I notice—and from an excellent tailor. The fragrance that you are wearing is a particular favourite of mine—and costly."

"Tell me your story—tell me of the murderers you have known—and we shall be as rich as Croesus."

"I only wish to be as rich as Conan Doyle."

"He is paid a pound a word—and his murderers are creatures of fancy. Yours are real. Tell me your story, Mr. Melmoth. Begin at the beginning. Tell it all—spare me no detail—and we shall have Perrier-Jouët night after night."

What follows is the story that he told.

25–27 May 1895

Newgate

*E*verything about my tragedy has been hideous, mean, repellent, lacking in style.

If I begin at the beginning, the very moment that I stepped from the dock at the Old Bailey was both grotesque and absurd. As I was jostled down the stairwell from the vast and echoing court-room to the warren of half-lit corridors and soulless cells that lies beneath, I stumbled on the worn stone steps and lost my footing. I lurched forward and reached out to catch hold of the warder who led the way. But my grasp failed me. Arms flailing, knees buckling, like a marionette whose strings have suddenly been cut, I tumbled downwards to land in a crumpled and humiliated heap at the stairs' foot.

The warder coming down the steps behind me laughed. "One moment it's Oscar Wilde, the next it's Clown Joey." It was this man's jostling that had propelled my fall.

I lay, motionless, my face pressed hard and flat against the cold, black ground. I closed my eyes. I held my breath.

In that ghastly moment I did not so much want to die—given the circumstances, that would have been too grandiose an aspiration—I simply wanted to vanish into thin air: to dematerialise, to "cease," to be no more.

"Up," bellowed the voice of a second warder. This was the man who had been leading the way. "Up," he barked again. I heard him turn. With the toe of his boot, he prodded me sharply in the small of my back. "Get up. Now. *Now.*"

With difficulty, and without assistance, I pushed myself to my knees and then to my feet. As I began to brush the dust from my clothes, the first warder said, "We've not got time for that."

The second added, smiling as he spoke, "You'd be surprised how many fall down these stairs. But there's no point. Take my advice, Wilde. Accept your fate. Don't fight it."

That night, for certain, I could not fight it. I had not the strength. I emptied my mind and let the warders march me where they would. They took me through a labyrinth of tunnels and corridors, passageways and guard-rooms. They were taking me, I later realised, on the subterranean route from the lower depths of the Central Criminal Court in the Old Bailey to the dungeons of Newgate Prison near by. At every turn on the journey there were gates to be unlocked and locked again. I remember that the warders whistled as we went—sometimes singly, sometimes in unison. It is, of course, good for a man to be happy in his work.

I recollect, too, that for an hour, at the end of our meandering, I sat alone in a windowless cell, in pitch darkness, waiting for I knew not what. It was an hour that passed,

I know, because when, eventually, I was brought, blinking, from the cell, I took out my pocket-watch to see the time.

I was still holding the watch—a fine half-hunter, a souvenir of my American lecture tour, and happily not broken in my fall—when, a moment later, pushed abruptly through a final doorway, I found myself standing in another cell, this one lit by gaslight. Facing me, seated behind a wooden table, I saw a large, bald man, dressed, astonishingly, in evening clothes.

"I am the deputy governor of Newgate Prison," he said. His voice was lyrical, high-pitched, and fluting. His accent was distinctive. He was evidently a Welshman. I did not discover his name, but his remarkable appearance I will not forget. His face was spherical and shiny, like a polished apple. His lips were full and ruddy; his nose was small and pug-like; his eyebrows were as black and thick and wild as bramble bushes. They danced up and down like Cossacks as he spoke. "You may keep the watch until Monday morning, Wilde. Return it to your pocket now and place your hands behind your back."

"Thank you, sir—"

"Do not speak unless I invite you to do so."

"I—"

"Do not oblige me to repeat myself. You are not here to make conversation. You are here because you have been found guilty of seven offences under the Criminal Law Amendment Act of 1885 and consequently are sentenced to two years' imprisonment with hard labour."

I bowed my head, not so much in shame as because the drama of the moment seemed to require it.

"Look at me when I'm speaking to you," said the Welshman sharply. I looked up at once. The deputy governor's eyebrows were lifted high. "Before we pack you off to gaol, Wilde," he went on, almost amiably, "there are formalities to be seen to. A warrant authorising your detention is required. I have it here." He searched among the papers on the table and brandished a foolscap document before me. "Paperwork must be done, a great deal of paperwork, and I am the man who will do it."

"Thank you, sir," I said. "I'm obliged."

I sensed the warders standing behind me stirring, unsettled by the impertinence of my interjection.

The deputy governor raised a hand to reassure them, but kept his eyes fixed on mine. "You are right to thank me, Wilde," he continued, mellifluously, easing his chair away from the table and revealing a starched white waistcoat stretched to the limit of its capacity. "Because it is a Saturday night I have been obliged to come in specially to deal with your case. I was on my way to the opera. Madame Patti is giving her Gilda. You know her voice, I'm sure."

I inclined my head by way of acknowledgement. "To me," said the Welshman, eyebrows dancing, "her voice is one of the wonders of the world. Her staccatos so precise, her legatos so smooth, her trills so . . ." He hesitated.

"Solid," I ventured.

The deputy governor emitted a high-pitched laugh and slapped his hand on the table in front of him. "I knew you'd know her voice. She earns a thousand pounds a night and has it paid to her in pieces of gold before she makes her entrance. That puts a spring in her step when she takes to the stage, eh?"

"Perhaps you will catch the second act?" I suggested, leaning forward, lost in the lunacy of the scene now being played around me. The warder at my shoulder pulled me back.

"I don't need to," said the deputy governor, smiling. "I know how *Rigoletto* ends. Don't we all?" He glanced between the warders mischievously and then returned his gaze to mine. "And Madame Patti will sing again, no doubt . . . whereas you, Wilde, will only be imprisoned this once, I trust." He sat back in his chair, folding his short arms across his fine stomach. "I am on duty tonight because I choose to be. You might have been dealt with by the prison clerk, but when I heard that your case was due to be concluded today, in the event that you should be found guilty I asked to be called. I am a collector of fine sopranos—and exotic prisoners. I am Newgate's archivist. This is London's oldest gaol. We've had them all in here over the years, the notable and the notorious. Casanova, Ben Jonson, Captain Kidd . . ." He looked about him with proprietorial satisfaction. "This was once John Bellingham's cell. He assassinated a prime minister, you know."

I felt, absurdly, that this last remark required some aphoristic response. My mind raced as I made to speak, but he raised his hand to silence me. "We have work to do." He pulled his chair up to the table and took up a pen. He leafed through the documents before him and brought one to the top of the pile. He raised his eyebrows to me once more. "I am sorry to see you here, Wilde, but I am glad to meet you. I know who you are. I am an admirer of your writing. I took my wife to see one of your plays last year—*An Ideal Husband*. I took her for our wedding anniversary. The irony of the title was not lost on her. She is a spirited woman. I hope you are a spirited man, Wilde. The next two years will not be easy for you."

He dipped his pen into the inkwell. His voice remained light and lilting, but his manner now became more business-like. "You will be in my charge for just two nights. On Monday morning at break of day you will be taken from here to Penton-ville Prison to serve your sentence. Until then you can remain in the clothes you are wearing—and you can keep your watch. Tonight, you will be given a beer with your evening meal. Enjoy it. It will be your last taste of alcohol for some time."

"May I smoke?"

"Whatever cigarettes you have on you, you may smoke— whilst you are here. On Monday, you will be required to hand over your cigarette case and all your other possessions to the authorities at Pentonville. Do you understand?"

"I understand."

He held his pen over the first of the documents and looked at me enquiringly. "Name?"

"You know my name, sir."

"You must say it."

"But you know it."

"You are a prisoner now, Wilde. Someone else has writ-ten the rules." He put his pen to the paper and prepared to write. "Name?" he repeated.

"Wilde."

"Christian names?"

"Oscar Fingal O'Flahertie Wills."

"For your own sake, I'll just list the first." He wrote down my name. "Place of birth?"

"Dublin."

"Date of birth?"

"Sixteenth October 1854."

"Next of kin?"

"I have a wife, Constance, née Lloyd."

"Constance Wilde."

"She may have changed her surname. I do not know. She spoke of it—to safeguard the children. The ignominy . . ."

"What is Mrs. Wilde's address?"

"I do not know. She has gone abroad, I think—with our sons."

"Do you have other family? Brothers, sisters?"

"I have a brother, Willie, but he's not to be relied on. He has been defending me all over London—and you see the result. Willie could compromise a steamroller."

The deputy governor smiled. "Are your parents living? I must list a next-of-kin."

"My mother is living. She will vouch for me. Lady Wilde, 146 Oakley Street, Chelsea."

"Thank you." The deputy governor wrote out the name and address. "Occupation?"

"My mother is a saint."

"*Your* occupation, Wilde."

"Poet."

"You have not met the governor of Pentonville, have you, Wilde?" He glanced up at me, his eyebrows twitching. "I shall put you down as 'author.' It will be best." He turned over the document and scanned it, sighing gently as he did so. "Height?"

"Six feet two inches."

"Build?"

"I—"

"I shall put 'Large,' if you'll allow me." I nodded. The Welshman scratched away at the paper. "Distinguishing features?" he asked. "Pray don't answer," he said quickly. "I shall put 'None.'" He laid down his pen for a moment and looked up at me. "You will be given a full physical examination on Monday, but I take it that you are in good health?"

"I am dead already," I answered.

"No, Wilde, for you this is a living hell, perhaps, but you are not dead."

"I am dead in all but—"

"Silence. Do not indulge yourself. Let us complete these formalities in good order, then I will bid you good-bye. Once our interview is concluded, I will not see you again. I regret that the prison regulations do not permit me to shake you by the hand. Perhaps at some future date we will meet in happier circumstances. Between now and Monday morning you will be locked in your cell and left undisturbed. Do not brood on your fate, Wilde. Do not give way to self-pity. Sleep. Let the time pass. Imagine your sentence is an opera by Wagner. It does not seem possible now, but it will come to an end."

I believe that was the last occasion that a man made a joke in my presence for two years.

2

27 May–4 July 1895

Pentonville

On the following Monday morning—27 May 1895—I was confronted by the full horror of my fate. I was a man who had known princes—and soft sheets—and sweet perfumes. I had drunk the best champagnes and dined on lobster and fresh caviar. At six o'clock that morning I woke in my prison cell at Newgate and smoked my last cigarette. At seven o'clock, I was given breakfast: a tin cup of watery cocoa and a piece of dry bread. At eight o'clock, in hand-cuffs, escorted by two warders, I stepped from the gates of Newgate Gaol into a windowless prison van and was driven the four miles from the Old Bailey to Barnsbury in North London. At nine o'clock I stood in the wash-house of Her Majesty's Prison, Pentonville, naked and ashamed.

"Bend over," commanded the senior warder in charge of my reception at Pentonville. His name, as I recall, was Warder Harrison. He was a stocky man, with a rat-like face and thick, wiry hair, jet black. His voice was harsh—it was the voice of a hard-drinking man—but his manner, though curt, was at all times correct. He was not cruel beyond the requirements of his calling. He knew the rules and lived by them. His examination of my body was meticulous. With a wooden rule, he prised apart my buttocks. "No blades, no knives, no contraband," he said. "Stand up." With the same rule, he held down my tongue as he peered inside my mouth. "Poor teeth," he said. He put down the rule and stood behind me, taking my cranium in both his hands. He pulled back my head and ran his thumbs upward from the nape of my neck towards the crown. "No lice. Good. Bathe yourself thoroughly. Use the carbolic soap."

I stepped into the waiting bathtub. The water was cold and the colour of dung. I washed myself while Warder Harrison stood watching. "You are overweight, Wilde. The treadmill will be to your benefit." I said nothing. What could I say? "You'll be on it six hours a day for the first month—twenty minutes on, five minutes off. It's useful exercise—the equivalent of climbing six thousand feet of hillside daily. You'll be a fit man before you're through."

I stepped out of the tub and the warder handed me a small brown rag with which to dry myself. "There's your uniform," he said, pointing with his rule to some garments that hung like a shroud from a peg in a corner of the washhouse. As I saw them I thought at once of Dürer's drawing of Christ's body taken down from the cross and wrapped in a winding cloth. As I donned them I thought of Watteau's paintings of Pantaloon and Scaramouche. The prisoner's garb is a costume, not a set of clothes. It makes him both a figure of tragedy and a figure of fun—a zany of sorrow, a shabby clown whose heart, we know, is broken.

I put on the uniform. The jacket and trousers were made of coarse grey serge, rough to the skin, and decorated from ankle to collar with a pattern of broad black arrows—the sign that the garments, like their wearer, are the property of Her Majesty. "Put on the cap," ordered Warder Harrison.

I put it on and was enveloped in darkness. The cap had a soft peak that hung down like a mask or veil.

"There are slits for you to see through," said the warder. "Can you find them?"

I adjusted the cap until my eyes found the narrow slits, each one no wider than a penny, no deeper than a farthing's rim. I half closed my eyes and the warder's face came into view.

"Outside your cell you will wear the cap at all times. If you fail to do so, you will be flogged. Do you understand?"

I bowed my hooded head, but said nothing.

"We work what's called the 'separate system' here," Warder Harrison explained. "We keep you prisoners apart—at all times. You cannot communicate with one another so you cannot contaminate one another—or make trouble. You have separate, solitary cells. You lead separate, solitary lives. You may not speak to another prisoner—ever. You may not see another prisoner's face."

"I will go mad," I said from behind the mask.

"You will be silent at all times," said Warder Harrison.

• • •

My life at Pentonville was hell. For four weeks I endured the torment of the treadmill. Hour after hour, day after day, thirty-two of us silent, nameless, faceless wretches were caged within a gigantic wooden wheel, pacing, pacing, pacing—to no purpose beyond our own humiliation.

When my month on the treadmill was up—and I had lost two stone in weight—Warder Harrison told me I was "fit enough now to take on useful work." For ten hours each day I was set to picking oakum, pulling hemp fibres from old tar-soaked rope. I made a poor fist of it. My fingers bled too readily.

Through all these weeks I spoke to no one and no one—beyond the prison chaplain—spoke to me. The chaplain, a good man, no doubt—God moves in a mysterious way—came to my cell to bring me the only two books the prison regulations would allow me: the Bible and John Bunyan's *The Pilgrim's Progress*. As he handed over the precious volumes, he enquired, "Did you have morning prayers in your house, Wilde?"

"No, sir," I said, "I am sorry. I fear not."

"You see where you are now," said the chaplain. "Reflect on that."

My days were hell—and my nights were worse. Within our prisons three permanent punishments are authorised by law: 1. Hunger, 2. Insomnia, and 3. Disease. I could not sleep because in prison, until a man's spirit has been broken, and been seen to be broken, he has no mattress to sleep on: his only bed is a bare board set on the floor of his cell, covered with one sheet and two thin blankets. I shivered all night long. And I lay bent double in agonies of hunger. The smell and sight of the prison food turned my stomach. For days I could not eat and when I did eat something—thin gruel for breakfast, bitter bread and black potatoes for lunch, suet and water and yet more gruel for supper—it produced in me violent diarrhoea.

When it was built, in the 1840s, Pentonville Prison had been equipped with a water closet in every cell, but these had been removed because the drains became so often blocked and the prisoners used the drainpipes to communicate with one another. Each water closet was duly replaced with a small tin pot. By day, a prisoner might empty his slops into the prison latrines. By night—from five o'clock in the evening when he would be locked into his cell, until morning—he had to live with them. My cell—like every other—was thirteen foot long, seven foot wide, and nine foot high. Because of my diarrhoea, the stench within it was indescribable. On three occasions, the warder who unlocked me in the morning became violently sick as he opened my cell door.

I confess it. Out of my nature came wild despair; an abandonment to grief that was piteous even to look at; terrible and impotent rage; bitterness and scorn; anguish that wept aloud; misery that could find no voice; sorrow that was dumb. At Pentonville, in the black summer of 1895, I passed through every possible mood of suffering. Better than Wordsworth himself I knew what Wordsworth meant when he said:

Suffering is permanent, obscure, and dark
And has the nature of infinity.

One day—it was Wednesday, 12 June 1895—a man came to see me in my cell. I knew from the regulations that Warder Harrison had read out to me on the day of my arrival that I would not be allowed any visitors until I had served three months of my sentence, so who was this man?

"I am a friend," he said. "We have met before."

I turned my head away.

"My name is Haldane," he said. "I am a Member of Parliament and a member of the Home Office committee investigating prisons."

His name meant nothing to me.

"The prison chaplain," he went on, "tells me that you are depressed, and will not listen to any spiritual comfort. He would you were more patient. Prison calls for patience."

"I could be patient," I said, still not looking at the man, "for patience is a virtue. But it is not patience you want here: it is apathy. And apathy is a vice."

"You are a brilliant man, Wilde," said my visitor. "You have not yet used your great literary gift to the full because you have not yet found any great subject of your own. You have wasted your genius in a life of pleasure. You have squandered your youth wading in the shallows and have become enmeshed among the weeds. But, I wonder, could your misfortune now prove your salvation? May you not find your great subject here?"

Still I said nothing, though in that moment I knew that what the man spoke was true.

"I am sorry to find you here," continued Mr. Haldane, "and sorry to find you in this state of mind."

I remained silent, so he turned to leave, and he stretched

out a hand and touched me on the shoulder. "I am a good friend of good friends of your wife," he said. "I can tell you that your wife is well. She is coping. She is in Switzerland and wants you to know that she is thinking of you—and so are your boys."

He pressed my shoulder and, as he did so, the tears poured slowly from my eyes. "Do my sons know where I am?" I asked.

"They know that you have gone away. They do not know where."

"Do they know why?"

"No."

He put out his hand to shake mine and glanced around the cell. "Do you have books here, Wilde?"

"I have the Bible—and *The Pilgrim's Progress*."

"You should have others. A writer must have books to read. I will arrange it."

The tears now tumbled down my cheeks. I tasted the salt and it was sweet as, together, Haldane and I drew up my reading list. We were circumspect in our choices. We settled on fifteen volumes, among them the *Confessions* of Saint Augustine, Mommsen's *The History of Rome,* and Cardinal Newman's *Two Essays on Miracles.*

Haldane's visit was to me a miracle. In the hell-hole that was Pentonville, in the depths of my despair, I was visited by an angel—who was also a Member of Parliament! God's ways are mysterious indeed.

Mr. Haldane was true to his word and later that very day ordered all fifteen books on my behalf at his own expense. The books arrived at the prison before the week was out, but the governor of Pentonville—indignant at Haldane's intervention—refused to let me have them, on the grounds that it was forbidden under the provisions of the Prison Act of 1865.

Haldane appealed at once to the Home Secretary, who agreed that I might be allowed the books. Haldane also arranged for my removal from Pentonville to another prison where he hoped the regime might assist me on what he termed my "road to recovery."

His hope was confounded. On 4 July 1895, I was moved from the north of London to the south, from HM Prison Pentonville to HM Prison Wandsworth. It was at Wandsworth that I first encountered Warder Braddle.

Thomas Braddle was one of the cruellest men I ever met. He was a man whom I would willingly have murdered and rejoiced in doing so.

3

4 July–21 November 1895

Wandsworth

*D*id I murder Thomas Braddle? No. I lacked the courage. And the means. And the opportunity. But that I had the motive cannot be in doubt.

Thomas Braddle was a man of about fifty years of age: tall, sinewy, strong, and vicious. His head was large and clean-shaven; his skin was pockmarked and sallow; his face had the look of a skull covered by a square of cheese-cloth pulled tight and tied behind the neck. His mouth was small; he had no lips to speak of; his nose was like a goblin's, pointed and bent. It was the shape of nose that is born either of a street fight or a bout of syphilis.

"Yes, Wilde"—these were the first words he spoke to me—"I am as ugly as I look—and you, it seems, are as pathetic as I'd heard. Take off your cap and stand up straight, man." I did as I was ordered. "Your hair wants cutting. You're not in Piccadilly now."

Warder Braddle was charged with my reception at Wandsworth, as Warder Harrison had been at Pentonville.

He read me the prison rules, as Warder Harrison had done. They were the same rules, but he read them with more relish than Warder Harrison had done.

"Rule Eleven. 'Silence must be observed on all occasions by day and night.' Do you hear that, Wilde?" I said nothing. "Rule Twelve. 'Every prisoner guilty of any of the following offences will subject himself to punishment: talking, shouting, cursing, swearing, singing, whistling, attempting to communicate by signs, by writing, or in any other way.' Do you hear that, Wilde? No writing. There will be no pen and paper for you here."

"May I have my books?" I asked.

"*Books?*" Braddle hissed the word contemptuously. "*Books?* I saw no mention of 'books' on the warrant. It spoke of 'hard labour'—that I recall. I don't believe there was any mention of 'books,' Mr. Wilde."

In my distress, I turned my head away.

"Look at me, Wilde—*look at me*. Where was I? Rule Twelve—that's the one. 'Every prisoner guilty of any of the following offences will subject himself to punishment . . . Unnecessarily looking around or about at any time . . .' Have a care, Wilde. 'Looking out, or attempting to look out, at window or door of a cell . . . Not folding up clothing in a proper manner . . . Not washing feet twice a week, prior to using water to clean the cell . . .' Do you wash your feet, Wilde? I don't believe you do. You stink, man."

"I have dysentery," I murmured.

He took a step towards me and sniffed about me like a dog around a lamp-post. "Is that it? Or is it the stench of corruption? I know what you are, Wilde. I followed your case. You're a sodomite, Wilde. You take boys and you ruin them—for your pleasure."

"I deny it."

"Silence!" barked Warder Braddle. "Rule Eleven—have you forgotten it already? 'Silence must be observed on all occasions by day and night.' *On all occasions.* Do you know what happens if you break the rules at Wandsworth Gaol, Wilde? You get beaten. And it hurts." He put down the rule book and unbuttoned his jacket pocket to inspect his watch. "It's coming up for ten o'clock. As happy fortune would have it, I can show you how much it hurts right now. Put on your cap, Wilde."

He called another warder in from the adjoining room. "We're going to show our new prisoner his first flogging. If it makes his hair stand on end, so much the better. It'll be all the easier for you to cut afterwards." He laughed. "We'll get the best view from Landing B. A flogging's not a pretty sight—except, of course, it might be to Mr. Wilde. The lad's only fourteen."

The two men marched me from the guard-room, across a yard, along a series of stone-walled corridors and, eventually, up two steep and narrow flights of metal stairs. As we marched through the prison I heard nothing but the clang and echo of our steps and the rhythmic rattle of Warder Braddle's heavy breathing. I saw no other prisoners. I looked neither to left nor right, and in my hideous prison cap could barely see the way ahead.

"Stop," ordered Warder Braddle, at last. "Look over the rail—down there." It was like looking down from the deck into the hold of a ship. Two floors beneath us, in a patch of sunlight at the end of a long corridor of cells, stood a heavy wooden chair. Bent over the chair, face forward, secured to it by his arms and legs with leather straps, was the boy who was to be beaten. His buttocks and back were stripped bare. He was so thin that even I, in my hooded cap, standing thirty feet above him, could see each individual rib.

Standing in front of the youth, about a yard from his head, were two older men: the prison governor and the prison surgeon. Standing behind him were two warders: one held the instrument of torture.

"It's the cat-o'-nine-tails," said Warder Braddle, holding the back of my head so that I could not look away. "Have you seen one before? The prisoner is being flogged for in- solence and insubordination, but because he's a boy, aged between ten and sixteen, it's the small cat he's getting, not the large one. The handle is the same size, but each of the nine cords is just two feet in length. You'd not be let off so lightly, Wilde."

Down below, the governor checked his time-piece. "Proceed," he said. "Twelve strokes."

"Sir!" replied the warder, raising the flail high above his head. "One!" The man brought it down onto the boy's back with a terrible force. "Two . . . three . . ." He counted out the strikes and the governor nodded his acquiescence to each one. I closed my eyes as the blows fell on the tethered child. The boy's screams were horrible—and piteous—like the cries of a pig being unskilfully slaughtered.

". . . Ten . . . eleven . . . twelve."

Warder Braddle at my side called down to the prison governor. "I think the last one went missing, sir, don't you?"

I opened my eyes and saw the governor look up at Braddle and smile. "One more, then," he ordered. The warder with the cat thrashed the boy's bloodied back once more.

While I was in Wandsworth prison I longed to die. It was my one desire.

On 26 August 1895—after three months of incarceration—I was permitted my first visitor. Robert Sherard, the bravest and most chivalrous of all brilliant beings, came to see me. Twenty minutes was the time allotted for the visit. We stood five feet apart, in a vaulted room, divided by two rows of iron bars. In the narrow passageway between the rows, Thomas Braddle stood, keeping watch. As Robert talked—and smiled—and chided—and did his valiant best to lift me from my misery, the warder looked on contemptuously. When our time was up, and Robert went on his way, Braddle sneered, "Not really worth the bus fare, was it, Mr. Wilde?"

On 21 September 1895, my wife, having travelled from Switzerland for the purpose, was my next visitor. In the gloom of the vaulted visitors' room, we could barely see one another. In our mutual distress we scarcely spoke—and what poor Constance said I strained to hear above the hideous sound of Braddle's breathing as he stood guarding the void between us. I told my gentle, unhappy wife of my sense of shame—and my regret. I told her that for the past few years I had been mad and begged her for her forgiveness. Through her tears, and through the iron bars, she gave it—freely. She told me that when I came out of prison, we would be reconciled. She put her hand between the bars and made to reach me. "No," cried Braddle, sharply, stepping forward and pushing back her outstretched arm. "No contact is permitted. And I am surprised, madam, that you should want to touch pitch."

Braddle's cruelty knew no bounds. It respected neither person nor place. When, faint with hunger, and weak from dysentery, in the prison chapel one morning, I fell to the ground, Braddle called out to the chaplain as he was coming to my aid. "Don't, sir. The man's a malingerer and a sodomite. The two often go together. Leave him be. I'll get him to his feet." When I did not move, Braddle, with his boot, kicked me in the head, again and again, until I did. Once blood began to trickle from my ear, he said, "We seem to be getting through to him at last."

Suffering is one very long moment. One cannot divide it by seasons. One can only record its moods, and chronicle their return. In prison, time itself does not progress. It revolves. It seems to circle round one centre of pain. In prison, there is only one season: the season of sorrow. The very sun and moon seem taken from one. Outside, the day may be blue and gold, but the light that creeps down through the thickly muffled glass of the small iron-barred window beneath which one sits is grey and niggard. It is always twilight in one's cell, as it is always twilight in one's heart.

Three sharp rays of sunshine pierced the pervading darkness of my months at Wandsworth Gaol.

The first was when my wife came and offered me forgiveness.

The second was in November, when I was taken by

prison van from Wandsworth to the Court of Bankruptcy. I had debts and no means to pay them. Books, paintings, jewels—all that I had once had was gone. My humiliation was complete; my penury official. I was in the gutter and no longer looking at the stars. After the hearing, as I was escorted from the court-room, handcuffed, between two policemen, I passed along a corridor lined with men who had come to witness my pathetic passage. Some had come to stare, and some to jeer. Alone among them was a friend. He had travelled from another country to be there, journeyed for days for this one moment in that dreary corridor. As I was led past him, my head bowed, slowly and gravely my friend raised his hat to me. It was an action so sweet and simple that it hushed the whole crowd into silence. Men have gone to heaven for smaller things than that.

And the third shaft of sunlight came in November, also—later in the month, on the eighteenth, the feast of Saint Odo. That was the day when I learnt that I was to be moved from Wandsworth Gaol in London to Reading Gaol in Berkshire. Mr. Haldane, Member of Parliament and ministering angel, had visited me again—and secured my books—and seen my wretchedness—and deemed another move advisable. Reading was his recommendation.

During my final weeks at Wandsworth, because of the damage done to my ear when I had fallen in the prison chapel and my continuing bouts of dysentery, despite the protestations of Warder Braddle, I had been transferred from my cell on B Wing to the prison infirmary. The infirmary comprised eight separate cells set around a guard-room that also served as the prison doctor's surgery. There I had a mattress to my bed and food that I could stomach. By day, I still picked oakum, hour after hour, in solitary silence, but by night, at last, I slept.

I continued to have dreams, of course—fearful nightmares from which I would wake in a cold sweat, crying out in terror. It was one such that apparently woke me in the early hours of Monday, 18 November 1895. With what sounded like the clang of a mighty cathedral bell, the iron door of my cell burst wide open and there, silhouetted in the doorway, stood Thomas Braddle, his naked arms stretched out towards me, his face aflame.

"I have returned, Wilde. You can't escape me. I have been where it seems that you are going. I have been to Reading Gaol, by Reading town. It is a pit of shame. I've been there, Wilde. I have told them all about you. You'll not escape me. I've made sure of that."

He shambled through the door and came, haltingly, towards my bed. "Look!" he cried. He had thrown off his coat. He thrust his naked arms towards me. "Look!"

I gazed on him in horror. He had the appearance of a man flayed alive. Over his whole body his skin glistened, raw and red. His flesh bubbled like a cauldron. I looked up at his pockmarked face: it was a mass of scarlet blisters. Mucus ran from his goblin's nose. Bile, the colour of absinthe, spewed from his tiny mouth.

"My lips burn," he cried. "My skin scalds me. My urine has turned to blood. You have done this to me, Wilde. You have infected me. You are diseased, Wilde. Curse you, man."

He raised his right arm to strike me. I saw that he had a bottle in his fist. I covered my face with my hands, but the threatened blow did not fall. The effort of the assault over-whelmed him. He slumped, suddenly and hard, onto the stone floor at the foot of my bed, the bottle smashing onto the ground beside him.

This was not a dream. Within moments it was evident: Warder Thomas Braddle was dead.

4

20 November 1895

Clapham Junction

I stood inside my locked cell and listened, hunched against the door, with my ear adjacent to the spy-hole. I dared not look through it.

Rule 12. Every prisoner guilty of any of the following offences will subject himself to punishment: . . . Looking out, or attempting to look out, at window or door of a cell.

Braddle was definitely dead. I heard the chaplain read a prayer.

"Absolve, we beseech Thee, O Lord, the soul of Thy servant, Thomas Braddle, from every bond of sin, that being raised in the glory of the resurrection, he may be refreshed among the Saints and Elect. Through Christ our Lord. Amen."

I heard a rattle of keys and a door open and close. There were footsteps and murmurings and then two other voices spoke. It was the prison governor and the prison surgeon.

"Was he found here?"

"No, in the cell, with the prisoner. We pulled him out, but it was too late."

"He died as he fell?"

"Or moments after. There was nothing to be done."

"By God, he's a hideous sight."

"He was never very pretty," said the doctor quietly.

The governor laughed. "Cause of death?" he asked.

"He had a weak heart."

"He looked so strong."

"Appearances can be deceptive. His heart was weak. His respiration was poor."

"But these foul eruptions on his skin—like boils . . . And the mucus . . . Revolting. His uniform's covered with vomit."

A fourth voice spoke. It was farther off. "He complained of the colic, sir."

"What?"

"He said he had a pain in his abdomen, sir. As though his guts was on fire—that's what he said. And his throat burnt—like a furnace."

"When was this?" asked the surgeon.

"Last night, sir—late."

"He wasn't on duty yesterday?" enquired the governor.

"No, sir. It was his day off."

"But he's in uniform."

"He'd been over to Reading, sir, for the day—to the gaol."

"A busman's holiday." The governor appeared amused.

"Gaoling was in his blood, sir."

"Yes."

"And he got back late?" asked the doctor. "How late? After midnight?"

"Yes, sir. More like two or three, sir."

"You were on duty?" asked the governor.

"Yes, sir. I was on the main gate. He came, asking for the doctor."

"Why didn't you call me?"

"It was the middle of the night. And I think he'd been drinking, sir. He brewed his own. A strong brew. He wasn't in a fit state, if you know what I mean. I told him to come up here to wait till morning. I thought he'd sleep it off."

"Did he look like this then?"

"It was the middle of the night, sir. I couldn't rightly see. He was in a bad way, but I thought it was the drink."

"Why didn't you send him home to his wife?" asked the governor.

"He didn't have a wife, sir. He lived alone, in digs by the station. He was a bit of a loner."

"He was a good officer," said the governor. "He knew his duty—and did it."

"Yes, sir."

"He was a hard man," said the surgeon, "with a weak heart. They go suddenly."

"We'd better get him to the morgue," said the governor. "When will you do the postmortem?"

"At once. It's best."

"What will you find, do you suppose?"

"Not a great deal. He's spewed up most of it."

The governor laughed. "Natural causes?" he said.

"No reason to doubt it. An abdominal rupture—a burst ulcer, most likely—some kind of intestinal explosion triggering a cardiac arrest. Certain men are inclined to produce ulcers."

"What kind of men?" the governor asked. I sensed that he smiled as he spoke.

"Hard men who live alone—and drink more than they should. And brew what they drink themselves."

"Ulcers—within and without. Not a pretty sight." The governor raised his voice. "Cover him up and take him to the morgue."

I heard feet moving. There must have been more men in the room than I had realised. I heard furniture being moved and grunts of effort as Braddle's body was lifted up and shifted away.

"I'll speak with the prisoner now," said the governor. "It's Wilde, isn't it? Braddle's 'sodomite and malingerer.'"

"Yes, sir. I don't think he knows much. He was cowering on the bed when we arrived."

I moved quickly across the cell and stood by the far wall. I heard the keys turn in the locks to my door. I held my cap in my hand and cast my eyes to the ground.

"Good day, Wilde," said the governor, stepping into my cell.

I looked up and stood to attention. I said nothing. The prison governor looked about the cell. His eye caught sight of the shattered glass around my bed. "What's this?" he asked.

"Glass, sir. A broken bottle. Warder Braddle was holding it when he fell, sir."

"Why had he come into your cell, Wilde?"

"I don't know, sir."

"You've no idea?"

"No, sir."

"Perhaps he was looking for the doctor. This is the infirmary. Perhaps he needed to lie down. He was unwell—that's evident."

"Yes, sir."

"Did he speak to you, Wilde?"

"Yes, sir, but . . ." I hesitated.

"But you don't recall what he said?"

"No, sir."

"Not a word?"

I hesitated. "No, sir."

"You were half-asleep?"

"Yes, sir."

"As I supposed." With his foot the governor spread some of the shards of glass about the floor. "Warder Braddle did not like you, Wilde—we both know that. But he was a good man. He knew his duty and did it."

I said nothing. The governor looked at me, smiling. "Do you have any complaints to make against him, Wilde?"

"No, sir."

"None at all?"

"None, sir."

"I am glad to hear it. It's best not to speak ill of the dead." He nodded and turned to leave. "Clear up this glass before you take your breakfast. I am sorry your night was disturbed."

"May I ask a question, sir?"

The governor turned back to look at me. "It's not about Warder Braddle?"

"No, sir."

"Ask your question."

"Am I to be transferred to Reading, sir?"

"You are, Wilde. I assumed you knew that."

"I had heard something. I wasn't sure."

"Yes, Wilde, you are leaving us very shortly. I am sorry that Wandsworth has not suited you. Ours is a prison for men who are men—if you take my meaning." I said nothing. The governor smiled. "Do you know much about Reading, Wilde?"

"I believe Jane Austen went to school there."

"Is that so? No doubt that is why Mr. Haldane felt you'd be more comfortable there than here." He laughed. "Clear up the glass, Wilde—and don't cut yourself. Good day."

"Good day, sir."

On Wednesday, 20 November 1895, I was transferred from Wandsworth to Reading Gaol. Of all the days of my incarceration it was the most humiliating. I was taken by train. From two o'clock till half past two on that day I had to stand on the centre platform of Clapham Junction in convict dress, and handcuffed, for the world to look at. I had been removed from the prison infirmary at Wandsworth without a moment's notice being given to me. Of all possible objects I was the most grotesque. When people saw me, they laughed. Each train as it came up swelled the audience. Nothing could exceed their amusement. That was, of course, before they knew who I was. As soon as they had been informed, they laughed still more. And one man chose to spit at me. For half an hour I stood there in the grey November rain surrounded by a jeering mob.

For a year after that wretched afternoon I wept every day at the same hour and for the same space of time. That is not such a tragic thing as possibly it sounds. For those who are in prison, tears are a part of every day's experience. A day in prison on which one does not weep is a day on which one's heart is hard, not a day on which one's heart is happy.

I had been naïve to be elated by the prospect of Reading Gaol. Now that my tormentor Braddle was no more, what would Reading have that Wandsworth lacked? From the moment that I first saw the place, from the window of the railway carriage as the train drew in at Reading station, I felt a cold hand grip my very soul.

Reading Gaol is built like a fortress. It has high stone walls, broad ramparts, and tall turrets at each of its four corners. Its architecture would do credit to the imagination of the Brothers Grimm. It is a castle of despair.

On arrival, I was escorted through the outer gates, across a courtyard, through more gates, into the main prison building, and then along an echoing corridor to the prison's central hub: the inspection hall. Four wings of cell blocks radiated from the hub, like points on a compass, and from the inspection hall at the centre, the warders could see the door of every one of the prison's two hundred and fifty cells.

On a dais at the centre of the hall, seated on his throne— a high-backed oak armchair—was the king of the castle, truly master of all he surveyed: the prison governor. His name was Lieutenant Colonel Henry Isaacson. I came to know him well. He had the eyes of a ferret, the body of an ape, and the soul of a rat.

I stood a yard in front of him, handcuffed and desolate.

He leant towards me to address me confidentially. "Prison is for punishment, Wilde," he began. "I believe in the power of punishment. I believe in the discipline of discipline." He clasped his hands together and cracked his knuckles—noisily. "I am proud that the Prison Commissioners have chosen Reading Gaol as the one most suitable for you to serve the remainder of your sentence in," he went on complacently. "I trust you will profit from your time here. Live by the Lord and abide by the rules and you'll not go wrong. I am a stickler for the rules, Wilde. You should be clear about that."

He sat back and considered me with his small and beady eyes. I sensed at once that he did not like what he saw. The feeling was entirely reciprocal, of course, but I doubt that my eyes betrayed me: they were too full of tears.

"Tonight," he said, "you will sleep in the infirmary. To-morrow, the surgeon will see you. Then you will be taken to your cell. You will be on C Ward. Look to your right. There it is. You will be on the third floor, up on the gantry, there on the left—in the third cell, C.3.3. That is where you will dwell while you are here. C.3.3.—that is how you will be known while you are here. C.3.3.—that is your name now, Wilde. You will answer to no other."

"And I, my lord," I thought, *"I—Oscar Fingal O'Flahertie Wills Wilde—am I to say nothing?"* I said nothing.

"You will wear your number on your uniform at all times. When you are not in your cell, you will wear your cap at all times. You will remain silent at all times. You will not communicate in any manner whatsoever with any other prisoner. Should you attempt to do so, you will face the consequences."

The governor shifted his ungainly body in his chair and cracked his knuckles. I sensed the interview was coming to an end. "Warder Stokes will escort you to the bath-house now. He will take you via the punishment block, C.3.3. All prisoners are taken there on the day of their arrival. The wise ones—and they are few, alas—never see the punishment block again." He nodded to one of the warders standing at my side. "The prisoner needs a hair-cut," he added.

"Must it be cut?" I cried. "You don't know what it means to me."

The governor looked to Warder Stokes. "See to it."

In the bath-house there was a mirror. When Warder Stokes had cut my hair, I caught sight of my shorn head in the looking-glass. It was Humpty Dumpty gone to seed. I put on the hideous prison cap and screwed up my eyes to witness my reflection through the slitted eyeholes. I laughed—that I might not weep. The horror of prison life is the contrast between the grotesqueness of one's aspect and the tragedy in one's soul.

In the infirmary cell that night, my first night at Reading Gaol, I lay half waking, half sleeping. In my mind's eye, I saw Constance and our boys. I saw my darling wife as she was when I had first known her, with her slim figure and her violet eyes, with her heavy brown hair and her wonderful ivory hands—hands which drew music from the piano so sweet that the birds stopped singing to listen to her. And I saw our boys playing together in Kensington Gardens, chasing their wooden hoops, running, laughing, strong, and free. But as I ran to join them, they vanished—and when I turned to look for them I found myself on the platform at Clapham Junction, standing in the rain, handcuffed, unable to move, surrounded by a jeering mob.

I closed my eyes against the pain. In my head I heard the scrape of metal and the harsh clatter of the pulling back of bolts. My eyes opened as the blackness of the cell was broken. A small envelope of light shone in the middle distance. I saw eyes looking at me from behind the barred hatch in my cell door. They were the eyes of Warder Braddle.

5

21 November 1895

Warder Stokes

*I*n the morning, at break of day, I was brought breakfast by Warder Stokes. He was a thin young man, with reddish hair and greenish eyes. He had broken teeth and a kindly, freckled face.

"Why do you do this?" I asked.

"You mustn't ask questions," he said, handing me my tin dish of oatmeal gruel.

"You don't belong here," I said. "Why do you do this? Tell me."

"I do this because my father did it. And his father before him."

"Is that your father's uniform you're wearing?" I asked. "It's not your own."

"How do you know?" He looked at me suspiciously.

"It *is* your father's uniform."

"Are you some kind of detective? How do you know?"

"It's worn and shiny at the elbows. Some of the buttons

are old and tarnished and some of the buttons are brand new. And it's too big for you."

"Was you in the police?" he asked sharply. "Are you a bent copper?"

"I am a friend of the man who invented Sherlock Holmes," I said with some dignity. "Have you heard of Sherlock Holmes?"

"Eat your breakfast," ordered the warder, handing me a spoon.

I smiled up at him. The simple fact of his youth and his freckled face had lifted my spirit. "So 'turnkeys' come in families," I said, "like royal princes and barristers' clerks."

"Eat," he replied. "And when you've eaten, clean the cell before chapel. Chapel muster's at nine."

"Am I not to see the surgeon this morning?" I asked.

"The surgeon's not well," said my youthful warder. "He will see you later—or tomorrow."

"The prison surgeon is unwell!" I cried, choking on my gruel. For some reason, the notion amused me vastly. "Physician, heal thyself!" I said.

"Quiet!" ordered Warder Stokes. "You must not speak."

"Physician, heal thyself . . . It is a line from the Bible . . . That must be allowed—surely?"

"I don't know about that."

"It's from the Gospel according to St. Luke, chapter four, verse twenty-three . . . The governor would permit it, I am certain." I looked up at my freckled guard. "Do you read your Bible, Warder Stokes?"

The young man made no reply.

"Can you read?" I asked. I felt the tears pricking at my eyes. "Let me teach you to read while I am here. Please, God, let me do something useful."

Warder Stokes said nothing, but took my spoon from me and my bowl of half-eaten gruel and departed.

I sat at the foot of my narrow bed and lowered my head and tried to say a prayer. It was in vain. Once more, unbidden, the crowd from the platform at Clapham Junction filled my mind's eye. But now, curiously, I began to feel more regret for the people who laughed at me than for myself. To mock at a soul in pain is a dreadful thing. In the strangely simple economy of the world, people only get what they give, and to those who have not enough imagination to penetrate the mere outward aspect of things and feel pity, what pity can be given save that of scorn?

As I sat there, alone in my cell, gazing down at my torn and callused hands, I realised that I must—somehow—find a way to get something out of my punishment beyond bitterness and despair. Until my imprisonment, all my life I had taken praise as my right and pleasure as my due. Now my fame had turned to infamy: to me pleasure and praise were now equally denied. If I could but learn to accept this— to accept all that had happened to me—might not those moments of submission, abasement, and humiliation—at Wandsworth, at Clapham Junction, here at Reading Gaol— lead me, in time, to a better, sweeter, *happier* place? All the spring may be hidden in the single bud, and the low ground nest of the lark may hold the joy that is to herald the coming of many rose-red dawns. So, perhaps, whatever beauty

of life remained to me would be contained in my moments of surrender.

Suddenly, I spoke out loud—in a stentorian tone that would have done credit to Henry Irving: "Sweet are the uses of adversity . . ."

"Silence!" called Warder Stokes. He pushed open the door of my cell. "C.3.3.—silence!"

I stood, reproved. "You are quite right, Warder. I was out of order. That was not the Bible. That was Shakespeare. They say, of course, that Shakespeare may have had a hand in the King James translation, but even so . . ."

"Chapel," commanded Warder Stokes. "Put on your cap."

Almost amused, I donned my hood of humiliation and meekly followed the warder as he led me from the infirmary, through two sets of iron gates, down two flights of steep stone steps, and through a further gate into the prison courtyard. As we crossed the damp, grey flagstones, from beneath my cap I glanced about me. "Is that the chapel?" I enquired.

"That's the gate-house."

I halted in my tracks. "In the November mist, I mistook it for the west front of a Gothic cathedral. And those are turrets, I see now—not bell towers."

"The governor lives in one," vouchsafed Warder Stokes. "The chaplain in the other."

"They live like princes," I declared, gazing up at the twin towers. "I wonder which of them has laid claim to Rapunzel?"

"Move," ordered Warder Stokes.

I began to walk again. "Who guards the rampart between the towers?" I enquired.

"That's the roof of the gate-house," said my keeper. "The warders who guard it are armed. If you try to escape, they fire."

"It must command tremendous views," I said, turning back to look at it.

"It was where they put up the gallows in the old days."

"In your father's time?"

"Ten thousand came to watch a hanging then."

My plays had a following, too, I thought, but I said nothing.

"March on," ordered Warder Stokes.

We crossed the courtyard and passed through further gates. Now, in single files, from all corners of the prison, other prisoners appeared. They shuffled forward, hooded, abject, forlorn. Theirs was the gait of broken men. "And women, too?" I whispered.

"Yes," said my warder quietly. "There are seventeen women here." We fell in alongside them, bedraggled creatures, dressed in long coats of prison grey, bent like witches, veiled like nuns. "You will be silent now," said Stokes.

In the chapel, the women sat in the frontmost pews. Behind them came the debtors and the men on remand awaiting trial. The rest of us—we convicts—filled up the remainder of the stalls, wooden benches that rose, row by row, in banks, tiered like gallery seats at the music hall. Each long bench was divided into individual cubicles, just wide enough for a small man to sit in. The whole construction ensured that all would be uncomfortable and no

prisoner could see or hear or touch another. I found my place—it was marked C.3.3.—and sat in it, in silence, gazing down at my knees once more, listening to the heavy breathing all around me. At the back of the chapel, a man began to whistle. A warder shouted, "Quiet!" Throughout the service, four warders stood at the front of the chapel, with their backs to the altar and their eyes on us. Their presence did not encourage us to incline our hearts to prayer.

Nor, let it be said, did the manner of the prison chaplain, who read out the service as though he understood not a word of it. The reverend gentleman gloried in the name of Friend, but beyond his surname he appeared to me to have no trait or characteristic to suit him to his calling. He spoke the mighty words of the Book of Common Prayer in a dreary monotone, like a man without a heart, let alone a soul.

"It was an arid service that offered me no comfort," I observed to Warder Stokes as he escorted me out of the chapel and back into the prison yard. "Am I to endure this every day and twice on Sunday?"

"Quiet."

"O God, make speed to save me."

"Quiet, C.3.3."

"O Lord, make haste to help me."

"Quiet."

"I am saying my prayers. That must be allowed, surely?"

"You will be silent at all times."

Warder Stokes held no terror for me. He was a young man with crooked teeth and carrot-coloured hair wearing a uniform that was too big for him. He was my gaoler, but might he not also be my friend? I determined in that moment never to address him when we might be observed or overheard. I said nothing more until we had reached the stone steps leading back to the infirmary.

"Where are we going?" I asked.

"You will stay in your cell up here until the surgeon has seen you. He will decide what you're fit for."

"I am fit for nothing," I said.

"It'll either be the pump-house or picking oakum in your cell."

"You don't have a treadmill here?"

"No."

"No treadmill?" I sighed. "What is the world coming to?"

"In the pump-house ten of you work the crank that takes the water round the prison. It's like a treadmill."

"But it serves a useful purpose. It's not like a treadmill at all."

I paused on the stairs to regain my breath. I leant against the wall. Stokes paused, too. "You're not like the other prisoners, are you? We don't get many gentlemen in here."

"You're not like the other turnkeys, are you, Warder Stokes? You don't get many good men in here, I imagine." I turned my hooded head towards him. "Are you happy, I wonder? When we are happy we are always good, but when we are good we are not always happy."

"I don't understand you," he said, walking on.

"I am relieved to hear it," I answered, laughing. As I laughed, I realised I had not laughed out loud for months.

"Shh," hissed Warder Stokes. "You must be silent at all times."

We had reached the top of the stone steps. Warder Stokes unlocked the iron gate that led to the infirmary guard-room. Another warder—an older man—was seated at a table in the centre of the room. He had a tin mug of tea in front of him. He looked up from his newspaper as we entered.

"Who's this?" he asked.

"The new man—arrived last night—from Wandsworth."

"Ah," said the seated figure, pushing back his chair. "The malingerer and sodomite." He gestured towards me with his mug of tea. "Take off your cap. Let's take a look." I did as I was bidden. The warder stared at me. He put down his tea. "We've heard all about you," he said. "There's nothing we don't know." He looked to Warder Stokes. "Why's he up here?"

"The surgeon hasn't seen him yet."

"Does he need to? We know all about this one." He got to his feet and took a step towards me. He eyed me up and down, as though I were a disappointing piece of livestock on my way to market. "There's no sign of the surgeon," he said to Warder Stokes. "I've brought one up from E Ward— E.1.1. Seeping blood."

"Which cell?"

"Number three. I saw number one was taken."

"Much blood?"

"Enough." He turned to look at the clock on the guard-room wall. My eye followed his and I turned to look at the clock, too. "No looking around or about at any time," he snapped. "Hasn't Warder Stokes read you the rules?"

I bowed my head. On the stone steps with Stokes I had laughed. Now, once more, I wanted to weep.

"If you're staying, I'll take my lunch early, Stokes." He sized me up once more. He yawned. "What's this one's number?" he asked.

"C.3.3."

"Up on the third floor?" He looked at me disparagingly. "The exercise should do him good." He picked up his paper from the table, nodded to Warder Stokes, and went on his way.

Warder Stokes pointed me across the guard-room towards the gate that led to the infirmary cells. From beyond the bars we could hear the sound of coughing.

"Where is E Ward?" I asked.

"You don't need to know. You won't be going there."

"Forgive me. I was curious. I apologise."

"It's beyond the pump-house and the punishment block. We passed it just now. It's where the women prisoners are kept. They're only let out to go to chapel."

"Or to come here," I said.

"No, they don't come here. They have their own infirmary." He pushed open the gate to the row of cells. The coughing was close now. "This isn't a woman here. This is a boy. Some of the younger boys are kept over in the women's ward—the privileged ones."

"A boy? How old is he?"

"He's twelve, thirteen, something like that."

"Poor child."

"He broke the law. He's learning his lesson."

"What's his name—his Christian name?"

"Tom."

"Poor Tom."

"Don't worry about him. He gets well looked after. He's Warder Braddle's favourite."

6

21 November 1895

Dr. Maurice

May I ask about Warder Braddle?"

"No."

"Please. I need to know."

"Enough. Into your cell."

Warder Stokes took me by the elbow and moved me briskly along the short row of cells. Mine was the last in the line—opposite that of the boy called Tom.

"Warder Braddle," I persisted. "Is he living?"

Stokes laughed. "He was alive and well when I last saw him."

"I must see him."

"You'll see him soon enough."

"Where is he?" I cried. "Was he here last night? I will go mad. Where is he?"

"Wandsworth, if you must know. I don't know when he's due back, but he'll be here soon enough."

"God almighty—"

"No profanity. You know the rules. Into your cell."

Warder Stokes pushed me into the cell. "Read your Bible," he said. "Calm down. The surgeon will come in due course."

I stood there, in my grotesque prison garb, clutching my absurd convict's cap, looking in desperation at the young man with the crooked teeth and the freckled face. "You are my only friend," I pleaded. "You must save me."

Stokes stood, bewildered and, I now see, embarrassed. "I am not your friend, Mr. Wilde. I am your turnkey. If you want to be saved, you'd better see the chaplain about that." He stepped out of the cell and closed the door.

"You know my name!" I called out.

"We all know your name. Warder Braddle has told us all about you." He turned the keys in the locks. "Be quiet now or I'll have to report you to the governor." With his fist he banged on the back of the door. "You know the rules," he repeated. "Silence must be observed on all occasions by day and night."

I heard his steps retreating along the passageway. I leant back against the cold stone wall of the cell, listening. I could hear the boy in the cell opposite mine—horrible sounds of coughing and retching. I went to my door and put my face to the spy-hole. I could see nothing. I cupped my hands around my mouth and called out the boy's name. "Tom!" There was no reply. I called again, "Tom! Tom! Can you hear me?"

From along the passageway, Warder Stokes shouted: "Silence!" I waited, holding my breath. "Silence—on pain of punishment."

I felt giddy with confusion and despair. I saw the Bible on

the wooden chair beside my bed. I went to pick it up and it fell open at the Psalms. I lay on the bed and turned my head to one side and, as I read the words, I spoke them out loud.

Out of the depths have I cried unto thee, O Lord.
Lord, hear my voice: let thine ears be attentive to the
    voice of my supplications.
If thou, Lord, shouldest mark iniquities, O Lord, who
    shall stand?
But there is forgiveness with thee, that thou mayest be
    feared.
I wait for the Lord, my soul doth wait, and in his word
    do I hope.
My soul waiteth for the Lord more than they that watch
    for the morning: I say, more than they that watch for
    the morning.

I did not hear the surgeon as he entered the cell. I did not register his presence until I opened my eyes and found a bespectacled man with a bird's-nest beard and mutton-chop whiskers leaning over me. He had a hand on my shoulder.

"I have kept you waiting," he said. "I apologise. I had another prisoner to see."

There was a Scottish burr to his accent. He spoke softly and I was startled by the power of his walnut-coloured eyes. They appeared like owls' eyes behind the lenses of his spectacles.

"You are a friend?" I asked, confused.

"I am the prison surgeon," he said. "Dr. Maurice."

"You are a friend," I repeated. "I can tell."

"No," he said, standing up and looking down at me, "but I studied at Edinburgh with your friend, Conan Doyle. We were both students of the great Dr. Bell."

"Arthur's model for Sherlock Holmes."

"Indeed. Observation is everything—that's what Dr. Bell taught us." Dr. Maurice looked down at me intently. He was a tall man, bony and angular. He stood at my bedside with his hands in his pockets, jangling keys and coins, contemplating me with a furrowed brow and what appeared to be kindly amusement. "And you, I've been led to believe, are Conan Doyle's model for Holmes's older brother—the brilliant but indolent Mycroft Holmes."

"So Arthur says—but I have not seen him for a time."

"I imagine not," said Dr. Maurice, "under the circumstances." The surgeon stepped away from the bed—his legs were long, narrow, and stiff, as though he walked on stilts. He bent over to open his medical bag and, from it, fetched a stethoscope. "You'd better rise from that semi-recumbent posture, C.3.3. I am here to examine you."

"You will be my friend," I said. "You must call me by my name, Dr. Maurice."

"While you are here, you will be known by your number, sir. That is the rule—and it has its merits."

"Does it?"

"It does. It reminds us that all men are equal in prison—all will be treated the same, regardless of who they are and where they come from. Now undress."

"What about the women and children?" I asked, standing up to take off my jacket and shirt.

"Men, women, children—once convicted and sentenced,

they are all treated the same here. There can be no favourites." He pressed the cold listening bell of the stethoscope to my chest.

"But Tom, I am told, is Warder Braddle's favourite."

"Do not listen to idle gossip, sir. And do not spread it. The prison rule of absolute silence has its merits, also."

"How is poor Tom?" I asked, turning my eyes towards the cell door.

"If you're referring to the prisoner across the way, the answer to your question is that it's none of your business."

"But it is—surely? We have a Christian duty to love our neighbours, do we not? No man is an island."

"Except in prison—under the separate system." The surgeon gave a small laugh. I realised that if he had studied with Conan Doyle at Edinburgh, he must be younger than he appeared—in his late thirties, at most. He hid his youth behind his heavy beard. "Turn around," he said. "Show me your back." I turned my back to him. I felt his hands on my shoulder blades. They soothed me. I felt the pressure of his fingers as he tapped them—hard—against my rib cage. "Cough for me," he said. I did as I was told. "Now take a deep breath and hold it . . . Now exhale."

"The poet John Donne went to prison," I said.

"And his brother, Henry, died at Newgate—of the bubonic plague . . . Turn around . . . At least, you've been spared that . . . Bend over now, as far as you can . . ." The surgeon growled softly and pulled on his beard. "Stand up—slowly . . . You're unfit—to say the least. You cannot touch your knees, never mind your toes. You have not treated your body as a temple, have you?"

It was my turn to laugh. "I have eaten, I have drunk, I have smoked—so much! I let myself be lured into long spells of senseless and sensual ease . . . And you see the result." I held out my naked arms, I gazed down at my loose and hideous flesh.

"Take down your trousers," said Dr. Maurice. "I must examine your private parts."

I pulled down my ludicrous convict's pantaloons with their obscene black arrows. "Once," I said, "I amused myself with being a *flâneur,* a dandy, a man of fashion . . ."

"I know," said the surgeon, crouching down before me, "Conan Doyle told me—and I read the newspapers and the magazines."

"Look at me now, Doctor."

"I am," he said, examining me. He got to his feet. "I have seen worse," he added, smiling. "But I am a prison surgeon. I have seen the worst." He turned back to his bag to put away the stethoscope. "Where did it all go wrong, do you think?"

"Did Arthur never tell you?" I asked.

"He told me that you had surrounded yourself with smaller natures and meaner minds, that you became a spendthrift of your own genius."

"He is quite correct."

"Conan Doyle is a keen observer—and a good man."

"The best of men," I said, thinking of him, of his firm grip and steady eye, his tweed coat and walrus moustache, his uncomplicated decency, and recollecting the adventures that we had shared.

"He admires you still."

"I admire him."

"*Mens sana in corpore sano*—a healthy mind in a healthy body—that's Conan Doyle's motto. It's not a bad one. It's kept him on the straight and narrow."

"It's kept him out of prison!" I laughed. "But I chose a different path . . ."

"You had everything," said the surgeon, now examining my ears, "but it was not enough?"

"Tired of being on the heights, I deliberately went to the depths in the search for new sensation. What the paradox was to me in the sphere of thought, perversity became to me in the sphere of passion."

"Desire, at the end, is a malady, or a madness, or both."

"I see that now, doctor. I see the error of my ways. I took pleasure where it pleased me, and passed on. I grew careless of the lives of others—my wife, my children, my true friends. I forgot that every little action of the common day makes or unmakes character, and that therefore what one has done in the secret chamber one has someday to cry aloud on the housetop. I ceased to be lord over myself. I was no longer the captain of my soul, and did not know it. I allowed pleasure to dominate me. I ended in horrible disgrace—as you see. There is only one thing for me now, absolute humility."

"Your mind seems to be in perfect working order." I smiled. He nodded towards my prison clothes lying on the bed. "Get dressed now." I pulled on my shirt. He watched me as I did so. "Can I report to Conan Doyle that I have seen you?" he asked. "When he last saw you he thought that you had gone mad."

"It was a temporary insanity."

"I have enjoyed our conversation, sir," said the surgeon, gravely, "but it must be our last. This is a prison. It is a world apart and you who are obliged to live here and we who choose to work here must abide by its rules. It is the only way." He picked up his bag and moved towards the cell door. "There is dry blood around your right ear. Wash the outer ear with care. Does the ear itself cause you much pain?"

"Some."

"Endure it as best you can. I will prescribe an antidote for your dysentery. Take it. Keep yourself clean. Exercise. As you walk around the prison yard, think of Conan Doyle and walk as he would walk—with your shoulders back and your head held high. Eat the food that is provided. You'll get accustomed to it in time. Do not drink anything but the water and tea and cocoa given to you with your meals. If you are offered illicit alcohol, do not touch it. Whoever offers it to you—prisoner or turnkey—refuse it. It is not safe. And take each day as it comes. Your time here will pass."

He pulled open the cell door and called down the corridor: "Warder!" He turned back and looked at me once more with his large owl's eyes. "Good-bye."

"And Tom?" I asked, lowering my voice and turning my head towards the cell that faced my own.

"He is not well," murmured the surgeon. "He has a strong spirit, but a weak chest and . . ." He hesitated. "And other difficulties." His voice trailed away.

"But Warder Braddle will watch out for him," I said.

"Beware of Warder Braddle," said Dr. Maurice earnestly. "Mark what I say. Beware of him."

7

21 November 1895

Warder Braddle

*T*hat evening I was moved from the infirmary to my appointed cell: C.3.3.—the third cell on the third level of the third wing, C Ward.

The cell itself—narrow, dank, and dark, with stone walls painted stone grey—was much like my cells at Wandsworth and Pentonville, but the regime at Reading was different. Supper was served fifteen minutes earlier—from half past five o'clock. The fare, however, was the same: a pint of foul-tasting oatmeal gruel slopped into a tin bowl and delivered through a hatch the size of the mouth of a letter-box, set into the cell door. With mine came what smelled like a saucer of poison: Dr. Maurice's antidote for my dysentery.

Between seven o'clock and seven-thirty a warder would call at each cell to collect any tools that the prisoner might have been using for his day's labour. At 7:30 p.m. a bell was rung to indicate that it was time for bed. At 7:45 p.m., from a central point in the inspection hall, by means of a single lever, the gas-jets in each of the prison's two hundred and fifty cells were extinguished simultaneously.

I lay on my back in the darkness. My ear ached. I closed my eyes and thought of Conan Doyle—of his vigour—and of the unspoiled goodness of the man. I thought of Dr. Maurice—no doubt at home by now, seated by the fireside with his pretty wife at his bony knee. Was he reading to her from *The Adventures of Sherlock Holmes*? I opened my eyes. Six feet above the head of my bed was my window: a hole in the thick wall, six inches deep and eighteen inches wide, barred and blocked with opaque glass. Beyond it shone the moon (the silver moon!), but through the glass I could discern no more than a pale-yellow smudge. I closed my eyes. I could not sleep. I dared not dream. A dreamer, I once said, is one who can only find his way by moonlight—and his punishment is that he sees the dawn before the rest of the world.

What stuff I had said! "A little sincerity is a dangerous thing and a great deal of it is absolutely fatal." What nonsense I had talked! "An idea that is not dangerous is not worthy of being called an idea at all." Had I ever said anything of any worth? "A man who does not think for himself does not think at all." Was that true or merely clever? Was it even clever?

As I lay in my cell in Reading Gaol, I smiled as I thought of Arthur Conan Doyle. I had created the Selfish Giant and the man who sold his soul to retain his youth and beauty. Arthur had created Sherlock Holmes! "How often have I said to you, Watson, that when you have eliminated the impossible, whatever remains, *however improbable,* must be the truth?" I spoke the words out loud—and as I did so I knew that I had solved the mystery of Warder Braddle. I fell into a deep sleep.

I had no idea what time it was when I woke up. It was still night. It was a muffled sound in the distance that woke me. Was it the hooting of an owl? Or the sounding of a bell? Was there a church near by, outside the prison walls? Was it the chime of one o'clock—or the quarter—that I had heard? I pulled myself up and rested on my elbow as my eyes adjusted to the gloom. I looked about my little cell. My furnishings were meagre. Beside my narrow bed, I had one upright wooden chair, a deal table (two foot square), and, in the corner, on the ground, the pan for my slops and a bucket of washing water. Nothing more—apart from the small gong and hammer affixed to the wall by the door to be used to alert a warder in case of emergency.

My ear, I noticed, no longer ached. And my stomach did not churn as insistently as it had done in recent days. I listened to the stillness and felt, curiously, at peace. I was staring immediately ahead, looking directly at my cell door. I could see the outline of the hatch, the spy-hole above it, to the left the locks, to the right the door's heavy iron hinges. As I gazed on it, slowly, silently, the door began to open. And outlined in the doorway the silhouette of a tall, thin man with a large head appeared. Softly, the man stepped into my cell. Carefully, noiselessly, he closed the door behind him and walked, with measured steps, towards my bed.

I looked up at him. "Warder Braddle," I said, quietly, "you have returned sooner than expected."

"You were expecting me?" he whispered.

"I was."

"You know me?" he asked.

"I do," I said.

The man held a box of matches in his hand. He struck a light and, as the blue and yellow flame flared up before his face, I recognised the pockmarked, sallow skin, the lipless mouth, the shining eyes, the goblin's nose. He lit a cigarette.

"And now I see that you are the brother, not the father," I said. "I could not be sure. Your father was a turnkey, too, I suppose—another Warder Braddle. The calling runs in the blood, I know."

"My father died ten years ago."

"And now your brother is dead, too. I am sorry."

"You are not sorry, Wilde." The man sucked on his cigarette. He looked down at me. "You are not sorry. You are the one responsible."

"I am not responsible for your brother's death."

"You killed him, Wilde."

"That is absurd," I protested.

"Don't raise your voice," he whispered fiercely. He stepped closer to my bed and stood looming over me. He had all the features of Thomas Braddle, but was clearly the younger brother. He blew his cigarette smoke into my eyes. "My brother is dead and it is your doing, Oscar Wilde."

"It is not my doing," I said quietly.

"You poisoned him."

"No, his heart gave way. He had a weak heart. An intestinal rupture triggered a cardiac arrest. I heard the surgeon say so."

"Oh, yes, that's what they say. I went to Wandsworth today. That's what they told me, too—the governor and the surgeon—before they buried him. That's what's gone onto the death certificate, you can be sure of that. They don't want any unnecessary trouble. They don't want a scandal. But we know the truth, don't we, Wilde? You killed my brother. You *infected* him."

"This is madness."

"You turned his stomach."

"We were not friends," I murmured. "I grant you that."

"He despised you, Wilde. Do you know what he called you? Do you? Answer me."

"Yes."

"Say it." He bent over and pushed his face close to mine. "Say it, Wilde."

I remained silent.

"Say it."

Still I stayed dumb. Suddenly, the warder raised his right hand and struck me hard on the head. "Malingerer and sodomite," he hissed.

I closed my eyes.

"He died in your cell, Wilde."

My temple throbbed, my ear ached, but I felt strangely calm. This man did not frighten me. "Warder Braddle came to my cell, uninvited," I said, "in the middle of the night. It appears to be a Braddle family characteristic."

"Do not mock me, Oscar Wilde. This is my ward. You are my prisoner. You obey my orders. You are under my command. I shall come here when I please, as I please, and you will do my bidding. My brother is dead. He has gone to heaven, but I am still here and I shall make your life a living hell."

He stood upright, and turned, and tossed the remainder of his cigarette into the bucket of water in the corner of the cell. "This cell stinks, Wilde. You stink." He moved towards the door. He took out his pocket watch and peered at it in the gloom.

"What time is it?" I asked.

"Gone one o'clock," he answered. He pulled open the cell door. "I am on my rounds and I find that all my prisoners are sleeping like babes. Horse thieves and blackmailers, pimps and murderers—all asleep, except for one. Is it your unquiet conscience that's keeping you awake, C.3.3.?"

"All asleep?" I answered. "Is Tom sleeping now?"

"Sleeping? My brother Thomas is dead," snapped the warder. "How dare you speak of him like that? How dare you use his Christian name?"

I sat up. "I did not mean your brother, Warder Braddle—may your brother rest in peace. I meant Tom, the boy who is here as a prisoner—the boy from E Wing."

The warder let go of the cell door. "How do you know of him? How do you know his name?"

"He was in the infirmary today," I said.

"You spoke with him? You will be punished."

"I did not speak with him. I heard him coughing—that is all. He is not well."

"It is a cough," rasped the warder, "nothing more."

"I am glad to hear it. I was concerned. A child should not be in a place like this."

"He is not a child. And he is well enough."

"I was concerned—that is all."

"Concern yourself with what concerns you, C.3.3. Know

your place. Remember who you are—sodomite and malin-gerer." He spat out the words. "Keep clear of that boy. Lay one finger on him and I will kill you with my bare hands. Do you understand? *Do you understand?*"

In the morning, standing on the gantry outside my cell, waiting in line with the other men to take my slops to the latrine, I heard a voice behind me.

"Did Braddle come to you last night?"

I turned my head. "Don't look," said the voice. "Don't answer. Just listen. We can talk later. When breakfast has been cleared and before we muster for chapel, stand by your cell door, put your ear to the hatch, and wait till you hear me call. I will only speak if it's safe. I know who you are and I am glad that we are neighbours."

8

22 November 1895

C.3.2.

*A*t Reading Gaol all men look alike. Our hideous prison garb robs us of our individuality. (It is not called "uniform" without reason.) Our grotesque caps render us invisible. We can reveal who we are only when we speak—and we cannot speak to one another, except on pain of punishment.

As our line trudged back from the latrines to our cells, through the narrow slits in the veil that flapped against my face I studied the man who trudged ahead of me—the man who had called out to me. I tried to look at him as Holmes would have done, with an analytical eye. He was a slim man, not so tall as I am, but clearly fitter, and younger. By convict standards, his shoulders were less stooped than most and his head was held quite high. He moved at a steady pace, not shambling like the others, but treading carefully—gracefully, even. Was he a dancer? No—he held his arms stiffly at his side, with the palm of his free hand open flat and his thumb aligned with his fingers. A soldier, perhaps? A guardsman?

When we were once more in our cells and the doors had all been locked and the clatter of warders' feet on the gantry steps had faded away, I stood, as instructed, with my ear pressed against the hatch in my cell door. The cold metal soothed my ear. I felt exhilarated, almost happy. A fellow prisoner had promised to speak to me! I waited. I waited several minutes, pressing my head against the iron, listening intently. In the far distance, I heard the sound of clanging gates and the faint rumble of wheels on cobblestones. Did I hear a dog barking? Or was it a man's cry? Time passed and silence fell. I went on waiting, standing, leaning against the door, listening, until my back ached and my ear burned. Eventually, I lifted my head from the door, feeling foolish and disconsolate, humiliated. And then I heard more steps, close by—a single pair of boots this time, clattering as they descended the metal stairway outside my cell, moving rapidly away, from the third level to the second to the first. Then, a further silence. I pressed my ear to the door once more.

"Can you hear me?" called the voice. It was wonderfully clear—and light and fluting. I thought, as I heard it, that it was like an angel's voice—strong but gentle, mellifluous, melodious, sweet to the ear. "Can you hear me?" It came again as an echo across a valley.

"I can hear you," I answered. "Is it safe to speak?"

The voice laughed, high-pitched and playful. "Yes, I am always careful. Warder Stokes has just gone down to muster with the rest of them in the central hall. Did you not hear him go? He has a light footstep. You will grow accustomed to the sounds of prison life very soon. You must learn to let your ears be your eyes while you are here. The good news, my friend, is that we have almost ten minutes for our chin-wag now."

"You are Indian," I said suddenly.

"You are very clever," cried my interlocutor, laughing gaily. "It is the sing-song in my voice that gives the game away. How do you do, sir?"

"I am very well," I said—absurdly. I was alone, half crouching, half leaning against the iron door of a prison cell in Reading Gaol, but I spoke as though I were lolling in an armchair in the telephone room at Brown's Hotel. "I am pleased to make your acquaintance."

"And I am honoured to make yours, Mr. Oscar Wilde."

"You know my name?"

"And your reputation, sir."

"I am sorry to hear that."

"It is a fine reputation, sir. You are an artist. And a noted wit. 'I am so clever that sometimes I don't understand a word of what I am saying.' That is my favourite." Through the shuttered hatch in my cell door came a carillon of laughter.

"Can we not be heard?" I asked.

"Only by each other. There are no warders on our floor at present. They will be back to let us out for chapel—not before. Usually we are safe until the chapel bell sounds, but if I hear someone coming before then I will ring my gong and pretend that I have the toothache. We can talk like this every morning. I am so happy to have you as my neighbour, Mr. Wilde. I very much enjoy a good chat."

"As do I, sir," I said, with feeling.

"When I heard that you were coming to Reading Gaol,

I prayed that you would be my neighbour and, by jingo, here you are. Good conversation has been sadly lacking at Reading Gaol."

"It is a happy chance that our cells adjoin," I said.

My neighbour laughed uproariously once more. "It is no chance, Mr. Wilde. It is the work of the gods."

"It is certainly some sort of miracle," I murmured.

"Move your mouth closer to the hatch, Mr. Wilde. I do not wish to miss any of your gems."

I stood back and gazed at the iron door. "I have no gems to offer, alas," I whispered.

"I cannot hear you, Mr. Wilde. Speak up. Are you all right?"

"You render me almost speechless, sir."

"You will have gems again, I know. We have to warm you up, that is all. We have to rekindle the dying embers of your wit."

I laughed and rested my head once more against the door.

"There, sir, you are laughing already. My last neighbour never laughed. He barely spoke. He was a very stupid man. Most prisoners are very stupid men, of course. The clever ones don't get caught."

"How come, then, that you are here?" I asked, smiling as I spoke.

"I was betrayed. It is a cruel world. I pleaded not guilty because I was not guilty, but there is prejudice against my kind. You will not be prejudiced against me—unlike my former neighbour."

"The man who barely spoke?"

"No, not him—he was too stupid for prejudice. The man who was in your cell before him—Atitis-Snake, the poisoner. You may know his name. He would like to think you do. A nasty piece of work—full of venom, like a cobra. And puffed up, like an adder. He believes that he is somebody, because he has been in the newspapers, but he is nobody. I did not care for his conversation. I had him moved."

"You had him moved?" I said, bemused.

"The gods answered my prayers," trilled the voice from nowhere.

"And where is he now?"

"Atitis-Snake? In C.3.5.—just along the landing, but out of earshot and away from me. The gods be praised."

"And the man who was in this cell last?" I asked. "Where is he now?"

"He is dead. We had to make room for you, Mr. Wilde. In his next life, I trust he will prove a brighter spark. He was so stupid."

"And who is your neighbour on your other side?" I asked, almost fearful of the answer.

"C.3.1. is an old man. Decrepit and deaf. When I speak he cannot hear me. When he speaks, I cannot understand him. He has been here for many years. They should move him to a lower floor. He can barely climb the stairs. He will soon be dead."

"And who is next to me—in C.3.4.? Do you know?"

"The dwarf is next to you. But he does not speak. He cowers, poor wretch. He used to speak—too much. He would not be silent, jabber-jabber-jabber all the time, so the governor made an example of him. He was flogged to within an inch of his life. I do not think he will speak again."

"My God," I cried. "If we are caught, will we be flogged?"

My neighbour laughed. "It depends who catches us—and who we have to watch over us."

"You have your Hindu gods," I said.

"Yes, I have three hundred and thirty-three million of them, while you poor Christians have just the one. I have Warder Braddle, also. I am one of his favourites. He does not have many favourites, but he has a few and we are blessed. Warder Braddle is a good man. He came to see you last night, Mr. Wilde, I know. I heard him. He tried to enter your cell silently, but I heard him all the same. Did you make your peace with him, Mr. Wilde? It is important that you should. Did you?"

As my neighbour asked his question, the bell for chapel began to toll and, with it, came the immediate clatter of warders' boots on the metal stairs. "We speak tomorrow," called out my neighbour hastily. I stepped back from my cell door and pulled on my cap of shame. Across the gantry, a prisoner's voice began to sing: "Onward, Christian soldiers, marching as to war!" Other voices took up the chant: "With the cross of Jesus . . ." A warder's voice bellowed, "Silence!"—and silence fell.

When my cell door was unlocked and pushed open, I stepped out onto the landing and glanced to my right. My Indian angel with the girlish sing-song voice was just another convict now, a thin, upright figure dressed in a suit of arrows, hidden behind a veil. His head was held high. He looked directly ahead. I raised my hand towards him in a kind of half-salutation, but if he saw my gesture he gave it no acknowledgement. Beyond him, I recognised the bent and shuffling figure of C.3.1. Yes, I thought, he will soon be dead. I stepped into the line. Immediately ahead of me was the dwarf (I had taken him for an ungainly boy when I had followed him to the latrines at first light); and ahead of him another upright figure—the poisoner, Atitis-Snake, I supposed, though he looked no different from the root.

Along the gantry, down the stairs, through the ward we trudged, past the inspection hall, beneath the archway, and out into the open yard where, in the grey mist of the November morning, our dismal line joined the other dismal lines snaking their way towards the prison chapel. There, in our set places, we stood, and sat, and knelt, and stood, and sat, and knelt, and stood again. Matins in the mouth of the Reverend Friend was a soulless business. At least Colonel Isaacson, before he read the Lesson, cracked his knuckles with a semblance of conviction.

The futility of chapel over, we marched back to our cells. This rigmarole took an hour. It served no purpose. It did good neither to God nor man. But it passed the time. Back in my cell, I sat at my table and laid my head on my folded arms. I shut my eyes and wondered what my neighbours were doing now—at this moment. The dwarf—what was he thinking now? Was he capable of thought—or had all thought been beaten from him at the governor's command? And my Indian friend—what filled his mind? And who was he? I had not even asked his name. And what was his offence? He had pleaded not guilty, but so had I.

My reverie did not last long. With a hollow clang, my cell door fell open. I looked up, bleary eyed. It was Warder Braddle, with Warder Stokes in tow. "Wake up, man," snapped Braddle. "Get up. It says nothing about sleep on your order sheet." He brandished a piece of paper. "It speaks only of 'hard labour.' Get up. Get up now." I shambled to my feet. "Have you picked oakum before?"

"I have, sir," I said, lowering my head. "It is not a task that suits me."

"God Almighty," cried the warder, in a sudden rage. He rushed towards me, letting his paper fall to the floor. With his right hand pressed hard against my neck, he pushed me up against the cell wall and held me pinioned there. I felt the power of the man. I felt his force and fury, but I was not afraid. I closed my eyes. "Look at me," he hissed. "Look at me." I opened my eyes and stared into his. They were small and black and pitiless. "We'll have no malingering here," he said. His fingers clutched my collar, and then he pulled my neck forward and beat my head against the wall.

"I'll put the oakum here," said Warder Stokes, laying the sack that he was carrying on my table.

"You do that," said Braddle, releasing me. "And the prisoner will have it picked by supper-time." He bent over and retrieved the piece of paper from the ground.

My head throbbed. I saw that my hands were shaking. "May I speak?" I said.

"What is it?" asked Braddle. He looked down at the paper that he was holding. "I would have sent you to the pump-house, but Dr. Maurice says you've not got the strength for it."

"My books," I said. "At Wandsworth I was allowed some books. I was told they would be sent after me."

Braddle stared at me in silence. "That's a matter for the governor," he said eventually. "Do you wish to see him? It can be arranged."

"I would be grateful for my books, that is all."

"Anything else?"

"Yes," I said. "My neighbours . . ."

"Your neighbours?" repeated Braddle. He looked at me in astonishment. "What do you mean?"

"The men on either side of me. Who are they?"

"You are a prisoner, C.3.3. You have no neighbours. This is Reading Gaol. We work the separate system here. You are alone."

9

Punishment

*B*ut Braddle was wrong. I was not alone. And just as, every afternoon at Reading Gaol, I wept at the same hour and for the same space of time at the recollection of the jeering mob that had surrounded me as I stood in the November rain on the centre platform of Clapham Junction, handcuffed and in convict dress for all the world to see, so, every morning at Reading Gaol, for ten minutes before the tolling of the chapel bell, I stood against the cold, iron door of my cell, sometimes smiling, often laughing, in a pool of Indian sunlight. Laughter is not at all a bad beginning for a friendship, and it is by far the best ending for one.

On the second morning of our curious intimacy I learnt my neighbour's name. "Are you there, Mr. Wilde?" he called out. "I trust you were left undisturbed last night. Warder Braddle was not on duty, I know."

"I had nothing but my dreams to trouble me last night," I said, "thank you. And, please, do not call me Mr. Wilde. You must call me Oscar."

"Oh no, sir, that would be highly disrespectful."

"My friends all call me by my Christian name," I said, "and I choose my friends with care."

"'I choose my friends for their good looks, my acquaintances for their good characters, and my enemies for their good intellects. I have not got one who is a fool. They are all men of some intellectual power, and consequently they all appreciate me.'" When he had completed the quotation, I heard him clapping his hands with delight. "That is very witty, Mr. Wilde. I told it to my old neighbour and he did not understand a word of it. He was oh so stupid."

"You know my work well," I said, laughing. I was as much amazed as delighted.

"I am very well read and I have a wonderful memory. I am noted for it."

"What is your name, my friend? Please tell me."

"My name is Luck, Mr. Wilde."

"Luck?" I exclaimed. "Is this possible?"

"Your name is Wilde, my name is Luck. The chaplain is called Friend. The poisoner is a Snake. It is interesting, is it not?"

"It is remarkable," I said. "And what is the dwarf called? Do you know?"

"Smith, I think," replied my neighbour, giggling like a schoolgirl.

"And what would you have me call you?" I asked. "Mr. Luck, I suppose?"

"No, sir," he answered seriously. "I have a rank. You should call me by my rank."

"A rank? You are in the army, then?"

"I was—once upon a time. My correct name, Mr. Wilde, is Private Luck."

I held my breath. I did not know what to say. A moment later, a peal of laughter came cascading through the narrow cracks of light in the hatch in my cell door. "It is funny, is it not?" cried my friend.

"It is very charming," I said. "I am so pleased to have made your acquaintance, Private Luck."

"Private A A Luck, late of the Bombay Grenadiers. But you can call me 'AA,' Mr. Wilde. That's what my master called me. My other names are Achindra Acala."

"Sanskrit names," I said.

"Achindra means 'perfect, without fault' and Acala—"

"Means 'the invisible one.' I know," I said.

"You know!" chorused my neighbour gleefully.

"I am very well read," I said, smiling in the gloom of my cell, "and I have a wonderful memory. I am noted for it."

"You are so like my master!" exclaimed AA.

"But I am not a soldier."

"But you are a great man. And a man of letters. Like my master. He admired you very much, Mr. Wilde. He had all your books in his library."

"And did I have all of his in mine?"

"Most likely. Every man of culture and imagination has a copy of *One Thousand and One Nights*."

"Your master was Sir Richard Burton?" I asked, amazed.

"Sir Richard Burton, KCMG, FRGS. Yes," said AA happily, as the chapel bell began to toll, "I was Sir Richard Burton's batman for almost twenty years."

• • •

Was what my neighbour told me true? Or was it, as I suspected, part fact, part fancy? To me it did not matter. That he had a tale to tell and that he chose to tell it to me were all that I cared about. My morning "chinwag" with Private Luck became the moment in the day I lived for. It was my delight—and consolation. The rest was silence.

Speech is what defines a man. Robert Louis Stevenson wrote: "The first duty of man is to speak: that is his chief business in the world." In prison, we may not speak. And conversation—in my experience of life, the only proper intoxication—is not only denied us: in prison, it is a punishable offence. At Reading Gaol, for twenty-two hours of every day, we convicts are locked in our cells. We live alone, in silence. Each morning, we are let out twice: once to file, in silence, to the latrines to empty our slops, and then, a little later, with only slightly less solemnity, to make our way to our daily act of worship. As we walk in line, five paces (no more, no fewer) must separate us from the man in front and the man behind. Each afternoon we are released once more: to take exercise in the prison garden, in a stone-flagged yard set out like a gigantic carriage wheel, with twenty spokes radiating from a central hub. Each sector of the wheel is forty feet in length and, at the rim, the widest point, seven feet across. Hooded and silent, and walking five steps apart, we pace the perimeter, like caged elephants at the zoo. At the centre of the hub, on a dais, stands a warder watching our perambulation.

About six weeks after I arrived at Reading, a second prisoner spoke to me. It was during the exercise hour. As we shuffled around the ring, I heard a voice speak my name.

What direction it came from I could not tell. "Oscar Wilde," said the voice, "I pity you because you must be suffering more than we are." I looked up—foolishly. I looked about me—stupidly. I said, out loud, without thinking, "No, my friend, we are all suffering equally."

Even as I spoke, the warder on his dais was shouting: "C.3.3., C.4.8., step out of line!"

We were arraigned before the prison governor. In the great man's presence, caps had to be removed, so we were escorted into his office separately, one after the other, in order that we might not catch sight of the other's unmasked face.

Who had initiated our illicit conversation? That was what Colonel Isaacson required to know. Whichever one of us had spoken first was the more guilty and would receive the harsher punishment.

The colonel was seated behind his desk. He cracked his knuckles noisily in anticipation of the answer. C.4.8. confessed that he had spoken first—and, when I was called, I confessed the same. The governor was not amused. "I do not understand," he stammered, turning brick red. "C.4.8. says *he* started it. He is to be punished accordingly. He *insists* he started it." I stood my ground. The governor clasped his hands and pressed the knuckles of his thumbs against his chin. "If that's how it's going to be, you will be punished equally. You will both have the maximum the regulations allow without reference to the visiting committee—three days in a punishment cell on a diet of bread and water." He nodded his dismissal.

"May I speak, sir?" I asked.

"What is it?" he growled, looking down at his desk and

affecting to find papers on it that he was anxious to study. "There can be no appeal."

"No," I said hurriedly, "I accept my punishment—"

"That's gracious of you," he sniffed, gazing blankly at the sheet he held before him.

"I wanted to ask about my books, sir."

He looked up. "Books?" His face began to redden once again. He gave the impression that he felt threatened by the very word. "What books?"

"Mr. Haldane kindly arranged for me to be sent some books. He paid for them himself. The *Confessions* of Saint Augustine, a history of Rome, some essays by Cardinal Newman . . ."

"Spare me the details."

"They should have been sent on from Wandsworth."

"Ask Warder Braddle," said the governor, dismissively. He turned back to his papers.

"I have done so, sir, but, alas, I am not one of Warder Braddle's 'favourites.'"

The governor cocked his head to one side and let fall whatever document he was holding. "Say that again, C.3.3. I did not hear you properly. Say that again. I was reading."

"I asked Warder Braddle about my books, sir, but he referred me to you."

"You said something else, C.3.3. What was it?"

"The books should have been sent on from Wandsworth, sir."

"No—it was something about Warder Braddle. Repeat what you said—exactly."

"I said, 'Alas, I am not one of Warder Braddle's "favour-ites."'"

"Yes," said Colonel Isaacson. "I thought that's what I heard you say." He leant across the table and gazed up at me with his ferret's eyes. His face flushed once more. "Warder Braddle has no 'favourites.' Is that clear? There are no 'favourites' at Reading Gaol. We treat all prisoners equally. This is an English prison, C.3.3. We play by the rules. We play fairly—at all times and in all circumstances. Do you understand?"

"Yes, sir."

"One should always play fairly, don't you agree?"

"Yes, sir. One should always play fairly when one has the winning hand."

"What do you mean?"

"I mean nothing, sir."

"You are dismissed. Warder Braddle has no favourites. Nor do I."

The punishment block was below ground, a set of subter-ranean cells—like the wine cellars of a great castle—located beneath the main body of the prison and reached from the prison's inner courtyard by means of a steep and narrow stairway. There were iron gates at the mouth of the stairway and at its foot. The block contained eight cells in all, open-ing off a single low-ceilinged corridor. C.4.8. and I were the only prisoners being held there. C.4.8. was incarcerated in the first cell, nearest to the stairway; I was placed in the last. Halfway along the corridor was an alcove, within which a

turnkey sat on a wooden armchair by a small coal fire. Opposite the alcove, between cells four and five, was a short passageway leading to an open sluice.

For three days and three nights I was confined to my cell. I was kept in total darkness and fed on bread and water. It did not seem to me to be a very cruel punishment. The darkness was a kind of comfort and the bread and water no worse a diet than thin gruel and bitter cocoa. During my confinement I was released from the cell just three times and then only for a matter of minutes. Each morning, after breakfast, I was permitted to carry my pot of slops along the corridor to the sluice.

For seventy-two hours no one spoke to me and I spoke to no one. The duty warder, when he unlocked the hatch in the cell door to pass me my bread and water, said nothing. In the morning I knew when it was the hour for slopping out only because I heard the same warder unlock my cell door and bang his fist against it. He spoke not a word.

Lying in the darkness, I thought of what Private Luck had told me: "You must learn to let your ears be your eyes while you are here." I thought of my friend Conan Doyle—and smiled—and tried to listen with Holmesian perception. There was much to hear—a distant bell; distant cries; footsteps on the stone stairs (some heavy, some light—were those the boots of Warder Stokes?); muffled conversations in the corridor (was that the voice of Warder Braddle?); laughter; a cough; a turnkey pissing in the sluice; the locking and unlocking of gates; the heavy breathing of a turnkey sleeping at his post . . . I listened to it all, by night and day.

The chief effect of the darkness and the silence was that

I lost track of time. On the final morning of my punishment I woke I know not when. I suppose it was the warder's banging on my cell door that roused me, but I do not recollect hearing either the banging or the turning of the key in the lock. That it was the hour for slopping out was clear: my door was ajar, the gloom of the corridor filtered into my cell. I got to my feet, pulled on my boots, and took my pot of slops out into the corridor.

As, blearily, I carried my mess towards the sluice, I heard voices at the end of the corridor. There was laughter and whispering—and the voice of a girl. I peered along the passageway and saw a cluster of figures gathered by the gate to the stairway. The turnkey's alcove was deserted; the fire in the grate was dead. I turned in to the recess that led to the sluice and emptied my slops in the usual way. As I retraced my steps I looked back towards the stairway. There was only one figure standing there now.

"Where's your cap? Get your cap or there'll be trouble."

The figure came along the corridor towards me.

"It's Braddle's watch," he said. "Take care."

As the figure reached me, I realised that he was not a warder, but a fellow convict.

"C.4.8.?" I said.

"No, he's gone. He went last night."

"But—"

"It's Braddle's watch. Braddle does as Braddle pleases."

"Who are you?" I asked, peering down at the man's uniform to find his number.

"C.3.5.," he replied, extending a hand to shake mine. He had the voice and manner of a gentleman.

I felt the grotesque absurdity of the moment. I stood, in a burrow in the ground, dressed in convict's clothes, with a chamber-pot beneath my arm, greeting a man I did not know whose face I could not see. I put out my hand. "I am Osc—" I began.

He laughed. "I can see who you are. You should wear your cap. Braddle will have you beaten if you don't. He's wanting an excuse."

"Where is he?" I asked, looking over the prisoner's shoulder towards the stairs.

"He'll be back."

"Why are you here?"

"I am doing Braddle's bidding. I am a 'favourite.'" He laughed again. "At least, I have been. I am Sebastian Atitis-Snake."

"What a wonderful name," I cried.

"I hoped you might recognise it. We were sentenced on the same day. Our cases were reported in the newspapers at the same time."

"I recollect," I said. "You claimed to be the Emperor Napoleon. That was your defence."

"And you claimed to be Oscar Wilde," he said. "That was yours."

It was my turn to laugh. I knew at once I liked this man. I was about to tell him so when we heard footfall on the stairs. "It's Braddle," whispered my new friend. "Get back to your cell."

10

"It Brings Bad Luck to Kill a Spider"

*W*hat do I remember of my time at Reading Gaol? The answer is simple: almost nothing, beyond the greyness of the place, and the unremitting dreariness of each day, and the sense of desolation that accompanied each night. As I look back now, one month of my incarceration merges into the next, one season is interchangeable with another. From 10,000 hours of imprisonment, all I can recall with any precision are a dozen or so individual moments. One or two are moments of unexpected delight (that curious first encounter with Sebastian Atitis-Snake was one such), but rather more are moments of black despair—and most of those connect in some way with Warder Braddle. Braddle was a monster.

It was Braddle who escorted me back to C Ward following my three days' confinement in the punishment block. As I followed him up the narrow stone steps that led from the subterranean dungeon to the prison courtyard above, I lost my footing and fell forward on the stairs. At once, Braddle turned, stepped back, and crushed my hand beneath his boot. I felt his full weight press down onto my spread fingers; I sensed him hold his breath as he stood waiting for my cry. I made no sound, but, beneath my veil, salt tears trickled down my cheeks.

As we crossed the inner courtyard, we passed the file of female prisoners returning to their ward from chapel. For the first time, I noticed the face of the wardress who accompanied them. Because her uniform was drab, I suppose I had assumed that her face would be equally so. But it was not. I passed within a yard of her and looked into her eyes. They were blue and beautiful. Her eyebrows were unplucked, but her brow was clear and her skin was fresh. Her cheekbones were high and her lips were even. She was not Helen of Troy, but she had about her a touch of Joan of Arc. And, as we marched by, I watched her glance at Warder Braddle and smile at the man.

Was this, then, the woman whose voice I had heard in the corridor outside my punishment cell? Could it be? How was it possible that so odious a creature as Warder Braddle could hold such sway?

"How long have you known him?" I asked Private Luck on the morning after my return to my cell on C Ward.

"Five years," said my neighbour lightly, "since I was sent here."

"And you like the man?"

He gave his girlish laugh. "I understand him. I know his kind—very well."

"Why is he so powerful? He is a brute."

"He is not gentle, but he is our prince."

"Our prince?" Bemused, I stood in my cell, my ear held to the locked hatch in my cell door.

"Only a nine-gun prince, to be sure—but we bow to his authority all the same."

"I do not understand you," I answered.

"This is good." Achindra Acala giggled. "Oscar Wilde is calling to me from his cell and he is saying he does not understand what I am saying. Oscar Wilde, who has so much education, and I, who have none."

"If we bow to anyone's authority here," I persisted, "it must be to that of the prison governor. He is our prince. This prison is his castle."

"No, the governor is our Queen Victoria. She is Empress of India—she merits the one-hundred-and-one-gun salute. But she lives on the Isle of Wight, a long way from Mysore. She never comes to see us in our cells. The governor is Kaisar-i-Hind, but the local princes are still the ones who collect the revenues and administer justice. The governor is the power overseas. Warder Braddle is the power in the land."

"I wish he was dead," I said flatly.

Private Luck clapped his hands. "That can be arranged, I am sure. This is the place for it, by jingo. Reading Gaol must be jam-packed with assassins. The man who tried to shoot Queen Victoria was here on C Ward."

"He is here no longer?"

"They sent him to Bedlam. They said he was mad."

"Perhaps a madman is what we need," I said. "Do you think the Emperor Napoleon would undertake the task?"

Private Luck gave a squeal of delight at the suggestion. "Oh no. Warder Braddle would be our Napoleon's Waterloo. Poor Snake the poisoner could not even kill his own wife, remember? No, no, Mr. Wilde, you need an experi-enced assassin for this assignment."

"Are you volunteering?" I asked, laughing.

"If you would pay me, I would have to consider it most seriously. I shall be needing money when I am released from here. I am not as young as once I was." He said these words with a sudden earnestness and then, as the bell for chapel began to toll, started to laugh once more. I sensed that he was dancing in his cell. "'Tis a lucky day, boy," I heard him cry, "and we shall do good deeds on't."

My morning tête-à-têtes with Private Luck were the only bursts of colour in my day. As the weeks went by, our con-versations grew ever more intimate and strange. He had spent twenty years, he said, in the service of Sir Richard Burton—in India, in Brazil, and, latterly, in England and Austria-Hungary. He had been the great explorer's batman, but, also, he claimed, his "cosy friend." "Sir Richard had a wife, the Lady Isabel, but she did not share his secrets as I did. Sir Richard taught me my Shakespeare, but I taught him the special ways of my people. He loved to learn. He was hungry for knowledge, always. When we spoke together we spoke in Hindustani, so that Lady Burton could not un-derstand. But she understood enough. When he died, Lady Isabel burned the manuscript of the book that Sir Richard had written about me. He had called it *A A's Adventures in the Scented Garden*, after *Alice's Adventures in Wonderland*. That is a clever title, is it not? Sir Richard loved to laugh. When once a doctor asked him, 'How do you feel when you have killed a man?' Sir Richard replied, 'Quite jolly, what about you?' He taught me how to laugh deeply, with the whole body, as well as how best to kill a man."

Private Luck surprised me constantly. Warder Braddle never did. Just as generosity is the essence of friendship, so banality is the essence of evil. Braddle's cruelty was commonplace and predictable. One morning—I can recall the date, 18 February 1896—Braddle entered my cell and found that I had not yet swept it.

"It's filthy," he barked.

"I mind my own dust," I replied.

"It's verminous in here," he said, looking down at the floor.

My eye followed his and, together, we watched as a large spider scuttled out from under my bed. The creature darted forward and then, suddenly, stopped, stranded in the no-man's-land between the warder's boots and my own. Braddle stepped on the spider and crushed it, turning the toe of his boot with a schoolboy bully's bravado as he did so.

"It brings bad luck to kill a spider," I cried, appalled.

The warder said nothing, but raised his head and looked at me contemptuously.

"I shall hear worse news than any I have yet heard," I murmured.

"Is that so?" he answered. "Clean your cell, or you'll hear that the governor has ordered you a beating."

That night, as I lay awake in the black of my cell, I heard the cry of the Banshee beyond the prison walls. And I had a vision—it was a vision, not a dream—of my dear mother standing by my bed with her right hand resting on the back of my wooden upright chair. She was dressed for out-of-doors. I looked up at her and asked her to take off her hat and her cloak and to sit down beside me. She shook her head sadly and vanished from my sight.

It was on the following morning that I learnt that my mother had died. She was seventy-five. No one knew how deeply I loved and honoured her. Her death was terrible to me; but I, once a lord of language (as Private Luck would have it), had no words in which to express my anguish and my shame. My mother was an Irish patriot, a scholar, and a poetess. She and my father had bequeathed me a name they had made noble and honoured, not merely in literature, art, archaeology, and science, but in the public history of my own country, in its evolution as a nation. I had disgraced that name eternally. I had made it a low byword among low people. I had dragged it through the very mire. I had given it to brutes, like Warder Braddle, that they might make it brutal, and to fools, like the Reverend Friend, that they might turn it into a synonym for folly. What I suffered then, and still suffer, is not for pen to write or paper to record.

My mother had died at the beginning of February. My wife, my Constance, always kind and gentle to me, rather than that I should hear the news from indifferent lips, had travelled, ill as she was, all the way from Genoa to England to break to me herself the tidings of so irreparable, so irremediable, a loss. Because of the nature of our interview, we were permitted to meet in one of the prison offices, an upstairs room, with windows—not in a barred and divided cell as we had done at Wandsworth, when Braddle's brother had kept watch and walked between us. This was a room I had not visited before, along the corridor from the governor's own office. Naturally, we were not alone, but our guard was Warder Stokes, who that morning proved a perfect gentleman. As Constance and I sat together at a table in the centre of the room, isolated in a pale pool of February sunlight, Stokes sat apart, as far from us as possible, on a stool by the door, with his arms folded and his eyes cast down.

Constance took my hands in hers and told me what I already knew. I told her of the spider and of the haunting cry of the Banshee and of my vision of my mother at my bedside. She smiled at my story and wept at the same time. She leant towards me and caressed my face and gently swept back and smoothed my unkempt hair. "You are so thin," she murmured. "And your hair is turning grey." I bowed my head. "And, Oscar, I do believe you are beginning to go a little bald."

"When your heart breaks, your hair falls out," I said. "It is well known."

She laughed. "I miss you, husband," she said.

"I miss you, wife. How are our boys?"

"They are well. They are strong and brave. They are your mother's grandsons."

"And do they miss me, too?"

"I think Vyvyan has all but forgotten you," she said teasingly. "But Cyril speaks of you. He has discovered where you are. He read about it in a newspaper."

"Does he know the truth?"

"He thinks you are imprisoned for debt."

I looked away. "And so, perhaps, I am," I said. "The debt I owe to you can never be repaid."

"I am proud to be the mother of your children," she answered. "And they will do you proud."

"Do not spoil them, Constance," I cried. "Bring them up so that if one of them ever should shed innocent blood, he will come and tell you—that you might cleanse his hands for him first and then teach him how by penance or expiation he can cleanse his own soul."

When the allotted hour for our meeting was over, we could not properly see one another as we parted: our eyes were too full of tears.

Warder Stokes escorted us both from the meeting room and left me standing in the vestibule immediately outside the governor's office while he accompanied my wife to the prison gates. I was not long alone. Moments after Constance's departure, I heard footsteps on the stairs and familiar voices in the corridor. They spoke urgently, in hushed tones.

"This *is* madness."

"You leave me no choice."

"What can I do?"

"Keep your word. That's all I ask."

It was Warder Braddle and a prisoner. The moment Braddle saw me, he said, "Put on your cap. Where's Warder Stokes?"

"He is seeing my wife to the gates. She came to tell me of my mother's death." I looked at my persecutor. "It brings bad luck to kill a spider," I said.

"Put on your cap, and face the wall." I did as I was told. "C.3.5., wait here."

Braddle knocked on the governor's door and entered without waiting for an answer.

I did not move. I rested my forehead against the wall and stood in silence.

"I am sorry to hear of your mother's death," whispered Atitis-Snake.

"Thank you," I murmured. "Is your mother living?" I asked.

"I do not know. She vanished when I was a little boy."

"Just as I have vanished while my sons are little boys," I said. "Do you have sons?" I asked.

"No," he said. "I have no children. Just a wife."

"My wife has changed her name," I said. "I have brought shame and ruin down upon her. I loved her once—I love her still—and I have done this. Why? How has it happened?" I turned my head towards Atitis-Snake. "Why did you try to kill your wife?" I asked.

"It was madness," he whispered. "I was mad. I am mad. That is why I have come to see the governor. I am a criminal lunatic. I should not be here. I wish to petition the Home Secretary. There needs to be a medical investigation. I will not die in Reading Gaol." He raised his voice as he spoke and began to beat his fist against the palm of his open hand.

I turned back to face the wall. "Each man kills the thing he loves," I said. "But why?"

"I will not die in Reading Gaol," cried Atitis-Snake angrily.

The door to the governor's office opened. "Silence, C.3.5.," ordered Warder Braddle. "Colonel Isaacson will see you now."

II

Death

*T*he first to die was not Atitis-Snake.

That afternoon, as I sat, depressed, slumped in my cell, with useless, bleeding fingers pulling at tarred threads of oakum, I received an unexpected visitor. I had heard his voice on the gantry. I recognised his gentle way of speaking and the Scottish burr. It was the prison surgeon.

"Medical inspection!" called Warder Harrison, pacing the gantry, unlocking the cell doors. "Stand by your beds."

Dr. Maurice pushed open my door and smiled at me with his owlish walnut-coloured eyes.

"Do men die at Reading Gaol?" I asked, not moving from my chair.

"Men die everywhere," he said. "From death there's no escape." He came into the cell and closed the door behind him.

"Death is close at hand," I murmured. "I know it. I feel it in my bones."

The doctor looked at me, still smiling. "Men do die at

Reading Gaol, now and again—mostly of old age, mostly 'lifers.'" He placed his bag on the ground beside my bed. "Happily, the prisoner I have just seen is not one of those. He's in no danger." He looked at me appraisingly. "And nor, I think, are you."

"You have been with the dwarf?" I asked.

"With C.3.4., yes." He nodded.

"I am glad. The poor dwarf has been beaten again, hasn't he?"

"Why do you say that?"

"It was last night, wasn't it? In the middle of the night. I thought it was the cry of the Banshee that I heard, but now I realise that it must have been that poor man, calling out in agony."

"What did you hear?" asked Maurice. He swayed on his long legs, towering above me.

"It was Braddle who beat him, I suppose. He beats the poor creature for the sake of it."

"Be careful what you say. Do not make wild accusations. You believe that Warder Braddle attacked the prisoner—assaulted him?"

"He has done so before."

"Has he?"

"Braddle likes to pick on the little people. The weaker the vessel, the stronger Warder Braddle shows himself."

"Do you have proof of this?"

"It will be my word against his."

"Do you have proof?"

I laughed. "None whatsoever."

"Then watch what you say."

"How is poor Tom?" I asked.

"The boy is better. Much better."

"Is he still passing blood?" I asked.

Dr. Maurice looked at me gravely and scratched his bird's-nest beard. "You know more than is good for you. Take care." With the forefingers of each hand he brushed back his mutton-chop whiskers and said briskly, "He is much better. His cough has subsided. He's back at work. I passed him just now. He's on the ward here, scrubbing the stairs."

"Is he one of Warder Braddle's victims?" I asked. "He's small enough."

"C.3.3.," said the doctor sternly.

"Oh no. Of course not. For some reason, Tom is one of the warder's favourites. They are a curious crew, these favourites—they come in all shapes and sizes. I wonder what is it, the quality they share?"

"Mr. Wilde," admonished Dr. Maurice, "I warned you before—beware of Warder Braddle. Do not make more of an enemy of him than you already have. Nothing can be gained by it."

I smiled. "Is that why you have called, Doctor, to warn me of the dangers of Warder Braddle?"

"No, I am doing my rounds, and I have come to offer you my condolences. Colonel Isaacson told me of your sad loss—and of your wife's visit."

"Thank you," I said quietly. I felt humbled by the Scottish doctor's kindness.

"I trust Mrs. Wilde is well," he said gently.

"She calls herself Mrs. Holland now . . . And I think

she is well—or as well as can be expected. I have brought desolation upon her."

"Will she forgive you?"

"She does forgive me. She is all goodness. And understanding."

"She knows your nature?"

"She knows that she has always been central to my existence."

"Always?" asked the doctor, widening his round eyes behind his round spectacles.

"Yes," I answered, earnestly, "it was always to her that the cathedral that is my life and work was dedicated. Always."

The good doctor smiled. "But you must confess you allowed individual side chapels dedicated to other saints . . ."

"In accordance with the highest ecclesiastical custom!" I replied. I laughed at myself, and then added, in all sincerity: "The candles that burned at those side altars were never so bright or beautiful as the great lamp of the shrine which is of gold and has a wonderful heart of restless flame."

"You are a fine poet."

"But a poor husband."

"You did not help yourself. 'I can resist everything except temptation.' I recall your line."

"I said it as a joke."

"And then lived the joke—and paid the price."

"If your sins find you out, why worry? It is when they find you in that trouble begins."

The doctor removed his spectacles and, a little self-consciously, polished the lenses with his pocket handkerchief.

"From what I have seen of the world, Mr. Wilde," he said, "it seems that the appetites of the flesh desecrate always."

I sighed and smiled. "Evidently, I should have played more golf!"

"You played golf?" he exclaimed, incredulous.

"I did."

"Oscar Wilde played golf! Well, I never . . ."

"And I played it rather well, I will have you know. Ask Conan Doyle."

Still chuckling, he returned his spectacles to his nose. "I shall," he said emphatically.

"You do not think that I will die at Reading Gaol, Doctor?"

He shook his head and bent down to retrieve his bag. "No, I do not. You will be out of here within eighteen months. And, who knows, from what you say, reconciled with your wife and reunited with your sons—if you can resist temptation . . ."

"And if this oakum does not kill me—or drive me mad."

The Scottish doctor examined my heavy sack of hempen rope and then considered the meagre pile of fibres lying on my table. "How much oakum do you pick each day?"

"A pound," I said. "On a good day."

"That's not much."

"I know. Warder Braddle tells me that the girls on E Ward do better. Six pounds is what I am supposed to pick."

"Yes. You are here for 'hard labour.' That was the judge's sentence, not Braddle's."

"I cannot do it," I said, pathetically. "I will go mad."

"I will speak with Colonel Isaacson," he said, looking

down at me once more. "Perhaps you can be found work in the laundry—or the garden. The garden would be more suitable for a golfing man. I will see what I can do. We don't want you going mad." He placed a kindly hand on my shoulder. "And you are not dying. You lack mental and physical stimulus, that's all."

I looked up at him. "But the angel of death is close by," I said, almost in a whisper. "I can hear the beating of her wings. We are standing in her shadow, Doctor. Who will be the next to die?"

"That's in God's hands, not mine. But men will die, here and the world over."

"But *here*—who is it to be, Doctor?"

He shrugged his shoulders. "Tell me," I persisted.

"There is one two cells away who is poorly . . ."

"Atitis-Snake?"

Dr. Maurice shook his head. "No. He is neither sick nor mad nor old. But C.3.1. is in a bad way. It is no secret. He has been here many years. And he is old. It may be that his time has come. There is nothing sinister in that." The kindly surgeon moved towards the cell door. "I must see him now," he said. "I must finish my rounds. Meanwhile, take my advice. Do not brood on death—and beware of Braddle. Good day to you."

When the doctor had gone, I got up from my table and went to stand beneath the barred window of my cell. I gazed up at it and saw nothing but a rectangle of dull light beyond a rectangle of dirty glass.

"God bless you," said a voice behind me.

I turned and there stood the prison chaplain, the Reverend M. T. Friend. I would describe him, could I remember what he looked like. I recall that he was neither tall nor fair, nor handsome, nor short, nor stout, nor in any way remarkable. He pursed his lips before he spoke—that I do recollect—and his voice had to it a monotonous, plaintive, whining quality. His every utterance was banal.

"Shall we say the Lord's Prayer together?" he enquired.

"No," I shouted, angrily, glaring at him.

"I am sorry to hear it," he answered.

"Go," I cried, "for God's sake, go."

He placed the prayer book that he was holding on my table, alongside my few strands of pulled oakum. "I am doing my rounds and I find that there is a great deal of anger on this ward this afternoon. I am sorry for that."

"Are you surprised, sir?" I cried. "What did you expect to find? Joy? Hope? Gratitude? Look!" I threw my hands up towards my barred window. "Even by day, there is no light in this God-forsaken cell. This is a house of darkness. There is only ever anger or bitterness or despair to be found here. And today you have found nothing but anger. The dwarf is angry. The poisoner is angry. The sodomite is angry."

The chaplain pursed his lips. "I must correct you, C.3.3.," he said primly. "I have just been with C.3.4. He is not angry, nor bitter, nor despairing. He is full of remorse and humility. I left him meekly kneeling upon his knees."

"And C.3.5.?" I raged. "He is angry. I know. I saw him earlier outside the governor's office."

"Then you know the cause," answered the chaplain. "His unfortunate wife—the tragic victim of his dreadful crime— she has died."

"I understood that she was in a coma?"

"Until two days ago. God, in His infinite mercy, has released her."

"Will Atitis-Snake be tried again? Will the poor wretch be hanged?"

"No, no. But it is certain now that he will never be released. And the dawning of such certainty affects a man. I have seen it before. He knows that there will be no earthly remission for his sin. He knows that, without question, he will remain in gaol for the rest of his natural life. He is angry for that reason."

"God help him," I cried.

"God will," said the chaplain, complacently. "That is what God does." He ran his tongue along his lower lip to moisten it. "But you," he continued, "you who are only here for a matter of months—what provokes your anger? What purpose does it serve?"

I stood before the chaplain pointing to the barred window above me. "I cannot see the sky, sir. I cannot even see the clouds."

"Oh, my friend, let me entreat you to desist from such thoughts and not let your mind dwell upon the clouds, but on Him who is above the clouds."

"God Almighty," I cried, suddenly rushing towards the clergyman, who looked at me amazed.

"'He that is slow to wrath is of great understanding,'" he burbled, "'but he that is hasty of spirit exalts folly.'"

"Get out," I cried, taking his prayer book from the table and thrusting it into his hand as I pushed him towards the cell door. I flung open the door and bundled the hapless cleric out onto the gantry.

"'A wrathful man stirreth up strife: but he that is slow to anger appeaseth strife.'"

I slammed shut the door and stumbled, shaking, to my bedside. Slowly, I lowered myself onto my knees and joined my trembling hands together in an attitude of prayer—as I had done every night as a small child in my parents' house in Dublin.

As I closed my eyes, I heard the cell door open once more. From the catch in his breath I knew at once that it was Warder Braddle. "The chaplain has told me what you've been up to." He spoke calmly and barely above a whisper. "You will be whipped for this. It will be fifteen strokes of the birch. It cannot be less."

The cell door clanged shut. I remained as I was, on my knees, my hands clasped before me, my head bowed. It was only a matter of moments before my prayer was answered. Warder Braddle fell to his death just after I had heard the church clock in the distance strike four.

12

A Dying Fall

*H*e fell fifty feet, from the gantry outside your cell, C.3.3., to the ground two flights below.

"He landed on the stone floor—on his back, with his eyes and his mouth wide open. The base of his skull was shattered. His neck was broken and his spine cracked. He must have died in that instant—at the moment of impact."

Colonel Isaacson, the governor of Reading Gaol, sat behind his desk, glowering. His face was brick-red and covered with a forest of wiry black hair. His eyes were small and masked by trailing eyebrows. His body was squat and his long, ungainly arms led to square hands whose backs were covered with yet more black hair and on which the fingers looked like uncooked sausages. He was cursed with a remarkable ugliness which his churlish manner did nothing to mitigate.

Dr. Maurice, the prison surgeon, stood at the governor's right hand—a bearded and bespectacled Adonis beside an ape.

I stood on the other side of the governor's desk, clutching my prison cap behind my back. "Why am I here, sir?" I asked.

Colonel Isaacson cracked his knuckles and leaned towards me. "Two reasons—the first of which is obvious. We are conducting a preliminary inquiry into Warder Braddle's tragic and untimely death. We need to get at the facts— while they are fresh. You appear to be one of the last to see Warder Braddle alive."

"I did not see him," I said quickly.

"The chaplain says that he left your cell a little before four o'clock and encountered Warder Braddle on the gantry. The chaplain says that he spoke briefly with Warder Braddle and saw Warder Braddle enter your cell immediately afterwards. The chaplain is quite clear about this, C.3.3. I know the chaplain well. I doubt that he is mistaken."

"Warder Braddle may have entered my cell, sir, but I did not see him. I heard his voice."

"You heard him, but you did not see him? Your cell was in darkness?"

"No more than usual, sir. My eyes were closed."

"You were asleep?"

"I was at prayer. I was on my knees at my bedside with my eyes closed."

"You were at prayer? I am surprised to hear it," said the governor. "The chaplain led me to believe that when he left you, you were in anything but a religious frame of mind."

"The chaplain is correct, sir. I behaved towards the Reverend Friend with great discourtesy. I apologise. But his religion, I fear, does not help me. The faith that others give to what is unseen, 'above the clouds,' as the chaplain put it, I give to what one can touch and look at. My gods dwell in temples made with hands. Within the circle of actual experience is my creed made perfect and complete."

"Made perfect and complete?" The governor glanced up at the doctor and repeated my words wearily.

"Too complete, it may be, sir," I hurried on, "for, like many or all of those who have placed their heaven in this earth, I have found in it not merely the beauty of heaven, but the horror of hell, also."

"Get to the point."

"What I am saying, sir, is that when I think about religion, I feel as if I would like to found an order of those who *cannot* believe: the Confraternity of the Faithless, one might call it, where, on an altar, on which no taper burned, a priest, in whose heart peace had no dwelling, might celebrate with unblessed bread and a chalice empty of wine."

"And yet, faithless as you say you are, you tell us you were on your knees at prayer?"

"Everything to be true must become a religion. And agnosticism should have its ritual no less than faith. It has sown its martyrs, it should reap its saints, and praise God daily for having hidden Himself from man."

Colonel Isaacson clicked his tongue and turned to look up at the prison surgeon. "I do not think, Doctor, that we are going to find this prisoner as helpful as you thought."

"Mr. Wilde," said Dr. Maurice, pleasantly, "I told the governor of your friendship with Dr. Conan Doyle and of the various mysteries you and Conan Doyle have solved together in your time . . ."

"In younger and happier days," I murmured.

"Not so long ago."

I shook my head. "My mind now, alas . . ."

The doctor raised his hand to silence me. "You are a man of high intelligence, Mr. Wilde," he said. "Your intellect has not been put to use since your incarceration. Perhaps it can be tested now—to your advantage and our benefit."

I was confused. It was many months since any man had addressed me in so civilised—and flattering—a fashion. I hesitated. "With Conan Doyle I merely played at Sherlock Holmes . . . ," I said, suddenly craving a cigarette. "It was a game . . ."

"But you achieved results. According to Conan Doyle."

I closed my eyes. For the briefest moment, I saw myself once more in the Palm Court at the Langham Hotel, mulling over a three-pipe problem with my good-hearted Scottish friend. I drew on my Turkish cigarette and watched the bubbles dance in my glass of iced champagne. Then I heard Colonel Isaacson's knuckles crack and the fantasy passed. I opened my eyes and looked about the governor's dull office. I saw his window covered by bars. "Is this not a matter for the police?" I asked.

"This is a preliminary inquiry," said Colonel Isaacson, irritably. "If it turns out to be an accident there will be no need to involve the police." He looked up towards the doctor once more. "This is my domain. This is my jurisdiction. I am the governor here."

"An accident seems most unlikely," I said, hesitantly,

"given the height of the gantry's wrought-iron balustrade."

Colonel Isaacson looked at me and raised an eyebrow. "Explain."

"I take it Warder Braddle fell over the balustrade?" I said.

"He did," said Dr. Maurice.

"He did not fall down the stairs?"

"He was ten yards from the stairwell," replied the doctor, removing his spectacles and polishing the little lenses with his handkerchief. He smiled at me with kindly, blinking eyes. "Warder Braddle fell over the balustrade immediately outside your cell, Mr. Wilde—that is certain."

"One could not fall over the balustrade by accident," I repeated. "That is certain."

Colonel Isaacson studied my face for a moment before turning to Dr. Maurice. "Had Braddle been drinking?" he asked.

"It's possible," said Maurice. "There was a noxious smell on his breath."

"The balustrade is between four and five foot high," I said. "Drunk or sober, a man couldn't simply stumble and topple over it. He'd have to climb onto it to get over it."

"Could he have done that?" asked Isaacson. "Clambered onto the balustrade and then jumped?"

Dr. Maurice pushed his spectacles up his nose. "To his own death? This was suicide?"

"It is a possibility?" enquired Colonel Isaacson.

"I do not think so, sir," I said, "given what Dr. Maurice has told us."

"What has he told us?"

"That Warder Braddle's eyes were open. When a man jumps to his own death, as a rule he closes his eyes as he makes his fatal leap towards eternity. And he falls as he jumps—forwards, not backwards."

"And this means . . ." The governor sighed and began to drum his fat fingers on his desk.

". . . That Warder Braddle did not topple over the balustrade by accident, nor did he fall unaided. He was pushed. He was thrown to his death."

Colonel Isaacson pushed back his chair and pulled noisily on his knuckles. "Very well. If Braddle was thrown to his death, by whom was he thrown?"

"We are spoiled for choice," I murmured.

"I think not," said the governor, sharply. "Watch what you say, C.3.3. You are a prisoner, a convicted felon—remember that. You are here to assist our inquiry, not to bandy words with us. We are not 'spoiled for choice,' as you put it. Far from it. The field, in fact, is a remarkably narrow one." He turned to the prison surgeon. "How many cells on C Ward were unlocked at the time of the incident?"

"Just five," said Dr. Maurice. "The five that Warder Stokes opened up for me when I arrived at that section of the gantry at around three o'clock."

"C.3.5. to C.3.1.?"

"Yes."

"They remained unlocked while you saw each prisoner in turn."

"Yes. And the chaplain followed soon after me. He was also on his rounds."

Colonel Isaacson opened the drawer of his desk and

took out a foolscap sheet of paper. He took up a pencil and began to draw a sketch of the gantry. He marked out each cell in turn. "C.3.5. is Atitis-Snake," he said. "The man has committed one murder. He might commit another . . ."

"Why would he murder Braddle?" I asked. "He was one of Braddle's favourites."

Colonel Isaacson looked up at me coldly. "Be very careful what you say. There are no 'favourites' in Reading Gaol."

I bowed my head. The governor returned his attention to his diagram. "I interviewed C.3.5. this morning," he continued. "The news of his wife's passing has disturbed him. He told me that he was mad. He said that he was certain of it. I told him that he was not. Perhaps this is proof of his insanity—or intended as such."

"Atitis-Snake is not mad," said Dr. Maurice.

"And he killed his wife with poison," I said. "I recall Dr. Conan Doyle telling me that in his experience murderers rarely, if ever, vary their modus operandi."

Colonel Isaacson studied his sheet of paper. "C.3.4. is Joseph Smith. I know him well."

"Is he violent?" asked Dr. Maurice.

"He's a petty thief. He's been in and out of gaol all his life. He's not notably violent, but he's insubordinate. A stubborn little fellow as these malformed creatures often are. He was given the lash not long ago."

"And Warder Braddle beat him last night," I said.

Colonel Isaacson slammed his pencil onto the desk. "Silence!" He turned again to the prison surgeon. "This was a mistake, Doctor. Why are we allowing this prisoner this licence?"

"Because Mr. Wilde is one of the cleverest men in England, sir."

"One of the cleverest men in England? How comes it that he is serving two years with hard labour in one of Her Majesty's gaols if he is so clever?"

"We can benefit from his experience."

"He has played at being Sherlock Holmes with Arthur Conan Doyle—that appears to be the level of his experience. This is ill advised, Doctor. You will regret it. I already do."

"Bear with me, sir." Dr. Maurice looked towards me earnestly. "Mr. Wilde, do you have proof that Warder Braddle assaulted C.3.4. last night?" he asked.

"I heard cries coming from the dwarf's cell, sir. That is all."

"That is all?"

"That is all."

Colonel Isaacson looked up at me. "Curb your tongue and stick to what you know to be true. Dr. Maurice is showing extraordinary trust in you, for reasons I cannot quite fathom. Repay that trust. Think before you speak. Speak to the point. And do not speak unless you are invited to do so. Is that clear?"

"It is, sir," I said. I stood to attention. "Shall I return to my cell now?"

"When we are ready. We have not finished with you yet." The governor took a deep breath and considered his piece of paper once more. "Are you suggesting, C.3.3., that C.3.4. may have thrown Warder Braddle to his death in revenge for the warder's alleged assault on him?"

"That might have been a motive, sir—yes," I said. "But,

of course, the dwarf could not have killed Warder Brad-dle . . ."

"No?"

"The dwarf is three foot tall."

Colonel Isaacson bared his teeth in a devilish grin. "Perhaps the little fellow had an accomplice? Your cell is next door to his. Your cell was unlocked. It's well known that you had an antipathy towards Warder Braddle. You fell foul of his brother at Wandsworth, didn't you? You and the Braddles have a history. Could you have murdered Warder Braddle? I wonder. From what I have seen of you, I doubt that you have the courage, or the strength, to kill a man—single-handed. But in harness with C.3.4. . . . the dwarf and the sodomite?"

I said nothing, but looked down at the governor's desk as he inscribed my number and my name on his diagram. "C.3.3. Wilde," he said slowly. He studied his sheet of foolscap and then looked up at me and raised an eyebrow. "When you play 'Hunt the Murderer' with your friend Conan Doyle, how many suspects do you like to have on your list?"

I hesitated—and then, even as I gave the answer, I knew that it could only infuriate. "More than the muses," I said, "and fewer than the gods."

"What's that supposed to mean?" Colonel Isaacson tapped his paper with his pencil. "Since Dr. Maurice has persuaded me to play this game, give me a number. How many suspects?"

"Ten," I said.

"Very well. Let us continue." With a black tongue he

licked the tip of the pencil. "C.3.2.," he wrote next. "Luck." He looked up at me contemptuously. "He's another of your kind, C.3.3.—more woman than man and a dozen words when one will do." I held his gaze.

"Does he have a history of violence?" enquired Dr. Maurice.

"Luck? No, not at all. Prostitution and blackmail are his stock-in-trade. He's Indian and inclined to grovel in the presence of authority. In many ways, he is a model prisoner." The governor was looking directly at me. "And let me say it before C.3.3. is tempted to do so. Luck, too, has the reputation of being one of Warder Braddle's so-called 'favourites.'"

My eyes moved back to Colonel Isaacson's sheet of paper. "Which leaves us with C.3.1.," he continued, writing out the name and number. "Ryder."

"He's sixty-eight years of age," said Dr. Maurice, "and not long for this world, I fear. He has emphysema. He can barely breathe. He can barely stand. It won't be him."

The governor looked up at the doctor. "Besides, you were with him in his cell at the moment of Braddle's fall."

"I was," said Dr. Maurice. "I am his alibi."

"And he is yours," said Colonel Isaacson, with a small laugh.

"Yes," said the doctor. "I suppose he is."

A silence fell. "May I ask a question?" I said.

Colonel Isaacson nodded, put down his pencil, and sat back to crack his knuckles.

"Where was the chaplain when Warder Braddle died?" I asked.

"He was in C.3.1.'s cell," said the governor, "with the doctor."

"No," said Dr. Maurice, quickly. "He left a moment earlier—at four o'clock. We heard the clock strike and he said he had to go. He left the cell and almost at once I heard him cry for help."

"Is that what he cried? 'Help!'?"

"Yes, I think so. 'Help! There's been an accident.' He was the first to see what had occurred. As he came out onto the gantry, he heard a sound below—the sound of Braddle's body hitting the ground. He looked over the balustrade and there, fifty feet below, was Braddle stretched out on the stone floor, with the boy at his side."

"The boy?" I said.

"E.1.1.," said the governor. "He'd been on cleaning duty, scrubbing the stairs."

"He saw the fall?"

"He says he saw nothing. They all say they saw nothing."

"He must have seen something."

"He says that he was at the foot of the stairs, on his hands and knees, with his back to the gantry. He says that he heard the sound of Braddle's body crashing to the ground and then turned and ran towards it."

"According to Dr. Conan Doyle," I said, quietly, "the one found closest to the body is very often the one who is closest to the crime."

"The boy is not likely to be a murderer, is he?" Colonel Isaacson smiled grimly as he asked the question. "He could hardly have thrown Braddle over the balustrade. He is even smaller than the dwarf."

"And he could not have run down two whole flights of stairs in the time it took Braddle's body to fall," said Dr. Maurice. "It's an impossibility—even were he fully fit. And he is not."

"And what would his motive have been?" added the governor, still smiling. "Isn't he another of Warder Braddle's alleged 'favourites'?"

"I think you should at least mark him down, sir, as being there at the scene of the crime."

"At the scene of the accident," the governor corrected me. "By all means." He added the boy's name and number to his drawing. "And while I am about it, I shall place the doctor in cell 3.3.1. and the chaplain on the gantry."

"Was no one else present?" I asked. "Or near by? No other warders?"

"On C Ward, Braddle and Stokes were the two on duty," said the governor.

"Who was in the inspection hall?"

"I was," said Colonel Isaacson, "and I saw nothing. And heard nothing—until I heard the chaplain's cry for help."

"Were you alone in the inspection hall, sir?"

"No, of course not. The inspection hall is always fully manned, but there are four wards to be observed and it was four o'clock—when the shifts change. Two warders were coming on duty and another two were going off."

"And you were giving them your full attention?"

"No doubt I was, C.3.3." Colonel Isaacson gazed at me steadily.

"Where was Warder Stokes at four o'clock?" I asked.

"On C Ward," said Dr. Maurice.

"On the gantry?"

"Yes—in the latrine, relieving himself," said the doctor. "He returned a moment after the fall. As I came out of Ryder's cell I saw him at the far end of the gantry."

"So there we have it," said Colonel Isaacson, laying down his pencil. "One victim and *nine* potential suspects. One short of Conan Doyle's requirement. I am sorry about that." Colonel Isaacson handed his sheet of foolscap to the prison surgeon. "What do you think, Doctor? Did the chaplain do it? He appears to be the one closest to the point from which Warder Braddle fell." He smiled. "He is older than Braddle, but just about strong enough, I suppose."

Dr. Maurice considered the diagram carefully. "And Warder Braddle would not have been on his guard with the chaplain—as he would have been had any of the prisoners rushed out at him from their cells."

Colonel Isaacson pushed his chair back from his desk and laughed. "That was not a serious suggestion, Dr. Maurice. Why on earth would my chaplain murder one of my warders?"

"Because he was commanded to do so?" I suggested.

"*Commanded?*" thundered Colonel Isaacson. "Commanded by whom? The Almighty?"

"By whoever has a hold over him," I said quietly. "That at least would provide us with a tenth suspect."

"The game is concluded, doctor," said Colonel Isaacson. "Will you see that the prisoner is returned to his cell?"

C WARD

Latrines   Gantry   Stairway

Warder Stokes

Cells on C.3.

C.3.5. — Atitis-Snake
C.3.4. — Smith

E.1.1. The boy
Warder Braddle's body

C.3.3. — Wilde
C.3.2. — Luck

Chaplain

C.3.1. — Ryder

Dr. Maurice

13

Secrets

I wore the obligatory cap of humiliation as a warder and the prison surgeon marched me back to my cell. As we crossed the prison's inner courtyard we passed a file of women prisoners returning to E Ward from their evening's labour in the prison laundry. Night had fallen, but the February moon shone bright enough and, as she walked close by us, I studied the face of the wardress whom I had seen smile at Warder Braddle. He had been dead four hours at least: she must have heard the news. But if his death had caused her any distress, her beautiful young face betrayed it not. She looked serene.

Once we had reached my cell, Dr. Maurice dismissed the warder and, when the man had gone and the prison surgeon was certain that we were quite alone, he said, so softly that I had to strain to hear him, "Please sit down, Mr. Wilde. I owe you an apology."

"I will sit, Doctor," I replied, "since you ask me and I am

weary, but you should not call me Mr. Wilde—I know that. That is what you told me when we first met."

"I remember."

"I am C.3.3. I am a prisoner in Reading Gaol. You are the prison surgeon. You have authority over me."

"All authority is degrading, Mr. Wilde. It degrades those who exercise it and it degrades those over whom it is exercised."

I smiled and looked down at the dish of cold skilly that had been left on my table for my supper. "I recognise the quotation, Doctor. You know my philosophy."

"I have been reading your work. Conan Doyle encouraged me to do so. He sent me one of your books for Christmas."

"I am flattered."

"It is not flattery, Mr. Wilde. My admiration is sincere."

"But out of place in Reading Gaol, I fear."

"I see that."

"This interview with the governor just now was a mistake. I spoke out of turn."

"You were placed in an invidious position. The fault was mine. I meant for the best."

"I do not know how the governor allowed it," I said. "Or why." The doctor made no reply. In the gloom of the cell I could barely see his face. "You have a hold over him, I am sure. Doctors know secrets."

"I know nothing that would implicate the governor in Warder Braddle's death."

"I am glad to hear it," I said. "Nor do I."

The doctor threw up his hands. "But, Mr. Wilde, ten minutes ago you suggested that the chaplain could have thrown Braddle to his death on the governor's orders."

I laughed. "I spoke for the sake of speaking, Doctor. It is my besetting sin. Colonel Isaacson would be much more likely to order Warder Stokes to dispose of Braddle—and Stokes, being younger and more biddable, would be much more likely to obey."

"But why should the governor want Braddle dead?"

"Because Braddle usurped his power. Braddle threatened his authority. Braddle had 'favourites.' Braddle was a law unto himself. He did as he pleased. That was evident for all to see—and Colonel Isaacson will not have liked that."

The prison surgeon leant forward. "Mr. Wilde, are you seriously suggesting that the governor of Reading Gaol arranged the murder of one of his own warders?"

I smiled in the darkness. "No, I am suggesting it playfully. You proposed the game, Doctor. I am merely playing it. The governor could well have wanted Braddle dead. He might have ordered his murder—or simply put the notion into someone's head. 'Who will rid me of this troublesome turnkey?' Colonel Isaacson did not commit the crime himself—we know that. At the time of Braddle's fatal fall the governor was in the inspection hall—surrounded by witnesses. He did not do the deed, but he might have been its inspiration. Did Stokes do it—when he claimed to be in the latrines? Did the chaplain do it when he was alone on the gantry? Did you do it, Doctor—alone or with the chaplain? It would have been so much easier for two men to throw Braddle over the balustrade than one."

The prison surgeon stood back, affronted. "Why in God's name should I murder Warder Braddle?"

"To please the governor? To appease the governor? To *implicate* the governor, perhaps?"

"This is outrageous, Mr. Wilde."

"I hope so, Dr. Maurice. But do not protest too much. It was you, remember, who first warned me to beware of Warder Braddle. You must have had a reason. What was it, I wonder?"

"The man was a menace," said the doctor quietly. He stepped away from me and stood with his back against the cell wall.

"He was worse. He was a monster. Did you kill him, Dr. Maurice? At four o'clock this afternoon, did you decide to make the world a better place and consign Warder Braddle to oblivion? Was it you who threw him to his doom?"

"I could not have done so," said the doctor slowly. "I was with C.3.1. at the time."

"Ah yes—so you say. But C.3.1. is sixty-eight and at death's door. He is frail and old and easily confused. What is his testimony worth? And, come what may, he will be dead long before Warder Braddle's murderer can be brought to trial."

The doctor threw out his arms in supplication. "I did not kill Warder Braddle, Mr. Wilde."

"I believe you, Dr. Maurice," I answered gently. "And nor did I—though I confess, often, over many months, I wished him dead." I looked up at the prison surgeon, but in the obscurity of the cell I could not see the detail of his features. "Neither of us is a murderer, but someone in this prison is. Warder Braddle did not fall to his death by accident. And you are right, dear Doctor, my mind is atrophying. I want stimulus. I cannot read Dante in this gloom, but I can think—and I will. I shall unravel this mystery for you, if I can. I am one of the cleverest men in England, after all."

The doctor laughed softly and moved towards the cell door.

"Before you go, Doctor, may I ask a question?"

"By all means."

"Where is Braddle's body?"

"In the prison morgue. Why do you ask?"

"Before you leave the prison for the night, find yourself an oil lamp and inspect the body once again, if you will."

"What am I looking for?"

"The unexpected," I said. "Some little detail that you failed to notice earlier in the immediate aftermath of the warder's fall. It's an axiom of Conan Doyle's that the little things are infinitely the most important."

"I'll do you as you ask," he said, pulling open the cell door.

"Thank you."

"Good night, Mr. Wilde."

"Good night, Doctor. The game's afoot."

On the following morning, at the usual time, in the usual way, I stood leaning against my cell door, with my mouth and right ear resting against the hatch, awaiting my daily conversation with my Indian neighbour. It was my custom to let him speak first. His ears were more attuned to the rhythms of the prison than were mine. He could tell, more accurately than I could, when the coast was clear.

I waited longer than I expected. Eventually, I heard his whisper. "Are you there, Mr. Oscar Wilde?"

"I am," I said.

"We must be careful. There may be changes to the roster because of what has happened. If I stop speaking quite suddenly, do not be surprised. For the next few days, we must be on the lookout for trouble. The other warders will be nervous. The atmosphere will be strange."

"Yes," I said. "I understand."

"How are you today, Mr. Wilde? Are you excited?"

"Every death is terrible," I said.

Private Luck giggled. "Even one you desired from the bottom of your heart?"

"Especially such a one."

"I am excited," said Luck. "I am jingle-jangling with excitement still."

"But you were one of the warder's favourites."

"I know." He said it wistfully. "I know."

"Will you not miss his favours?" I asked.

Luck laughed. "I had to work for them—at my age! And they were not so special."

"What were they, these favours?"

He paused. I wondered if he had heard a warder coming. I held my breath. "I was not beaten," he said at last.

"That is something."

"And I got a sausage roll sometimes. And a cigarette.

And the *Daily Chronicle.* That's how I read about you, Mr. Oscar Wilde."

"Warder Braddle brought you the newspaper?" I asked, bemused.

"The other prisoners cannot read and I do not drink. I did not want his stingo. It was disgusting. He brewed it himself. He was drunk yesterday. That made it easy."

"He was drunk, was he?"

"He was very often drunk, Mr. Wilde."

"Perhaps, then, he died happy," I said. "I hope so."

"I hope so, too," replied AA. "Let's drink to that." He laughed at his own joke. "And are you happy now, Mr. Wilde?" he went on. "I hope so. I did my level best for you. You don't have to pay until I am released, of course. You know that, don't you? That will not be until next year, but I will need an I-owe-you now—so there is no misunderstanding. What will you pay me? We did not agree on an exact price, but you are a gentleman. You will pay me fairly, I know. I think one hundred pounds is right. Do you agree?"

My mouth was dry. My heart pounded. "I do not know what you are talking about," I whispered.

"I killed Warder Braddle for you, Mr. Wilde. I did as you asked. You must pay me. One hundred pounds is fair."

14

Madness

*T*his is madness."

"This is business, Mr. Wilde. I do not think one hundred pounds is too much to be asking. You are a rich man."

"I am a ruined man," I protested, pressing my head against my cell door in desperation and disbelief. "I am a bankrupt. Did you not know that?"

"You have a rich wife, I know. She came to see you yesterday. She will pay. It is not for a year."

"I cannot pay you."

"You must, Mr. Wilde. It is a debt of honour."

"How could you do this terrible thing?"

"With courage and skill, Mr. Wilde, although I say so as shouldn't. Braddle was drunk and the coast was clear. I seized the moment. I ran out of my cell and I pushed him over the fence. A nice clean killing, Sir Richard Burton would have said."

"This is very terrible." I said it again and again, as the bell for chapel began to toll. "Terrible and wrong."

"It is what you wanted. It is our secret. You will pay me one hundred pounds and everything will be hunky-dory."

In the days and weeks that followed, I kept Luck's secret. What else could I do? With whom could I share it? And to what purpose? And each morning when we spoke, as we continued to do, while Private Luck sometimes referred to the I-owe-you that he was expecting from me, discussing the ways and means that I might deliver it to him, rarely, if ever, did either of us mention Warder Braddle by name. We talked, instead, of our lives before and beyond Reading Gaol: principally we talked of Luck's adventures in the service of Richard Burton, in Trieste, Damascus, and Brazil.

Luck diverted me with recitations from Burton's notorious translation of the Kama Sutra and with tales of his former master's researches in the farther-flung fields of human sexuality. With much giggling, my Indian neighbour told me that it had been his particular duty to measure the reproductive organs of the male inhabitants in the regions of West Africa and South America they had explored. He told me, too, of Burton's discovery of what he termed the Sotadic zone, named in honour of the Greek poet Sotades. This zone is a vast region of the earth, encompassing pockets of southern Europe, Morocco and Egypt, swaths of Asia Minor, Mesopotamia, the Punjab and Kashmir, the South Sea Islands, and much of the New World, where men mate with men and it is considered neither vice nor taboo.

When I told Private Luck that he should follow his late master's example and write a travel book of his own and that it would make him a fortune to rival Conan Doyle's, he answered quite seriously, "Writing takes time and is very difficult. Killing is much simpler and more profitable, I have found."

On the morning of Luck's confession, when in chapel, as usual, Luck and I sat side by side, as the governor addressed the assembled company and announced the untimely death of Warder Braddle, Luck pushed his right foot beyond the confines of his stall and pressed his boot against the edge of mine. While the governor spoke, a curious hissing sound emanated from Luck's stall, as though the Indian was trying to suppress a fit of hysterical giggling.

Colonel Isaacson's statement was brief and received in silence and without emotion—as though what he had to say were already old news:

"Yesterday afternoon one of our senior warders was killed in a tragic accident on C Ward. Warder Braddle had served Her Majesty and this prison faithfully for thirty years, as his father and grandfather had done before him. His funeral will take place on Monday next but will not disrupt the business of the gaol, which will be as usual. Warder Braddle will be buried, as was his wish, in the remembrance garden within the prison walls. May his soul rest in peace."

I said, "Amen."

The weeks passed in Reading Gaol and the very existence of Warder Braddle seemed soon forgotten.

In the days immediately following the announcement

of his death, the prison's customary silence seemed to me particularly profound and our gaolers more than usually officious in the imposition of the "separate system." No one spoke out of turn; no one stepped out of line. On the evening of the day appointed for Braddle's obsequies, when Warder Stokes came to my cell to collect my day's oakum pickings, I asked him if he had attended the warder's funeral. He answered that he had, but had I not pressed him I know that he would have added nothing more.

"How was it?" I asked.

"Didn't last long," he said.

"Who was there?"

"The governor, the chaplain, some warders, that's all."

"Did Warder Braddle have any family?"

"I don't think so. I don't know."

"Did you attend the burial, too?" I enquired.

"The funeral was at the graveside," he said, adding, with a hint of pride, his awkward smile revealing his crooked teeth, "I dug the grave."

I looked up at the young man. "Was Warder Braddle your friend?"

"No, not specially, but it's an honour to dig a man's grave for him, isn't it?"

"Yes," I answered, "it must be." He picked up my small sack of oakum and carried it to the cell door. "Last week, when Warder Braddle fell to his death," I asked, "do you know what happened?"

"He'd been drinking, hadn't he?"

"Had he?"

"We're not supposed to talk about it."

"Who says so?"

"The governor. He says idle talk is bad for discipline."

"He is quite right, though in my experience, it can do wonders for morale."

What was most strange to me in the aftermath of Warder Braddle's death was that I had no communication of any kind with the prison surgeon. Twice, at close quarters, albeit wearing my prison cap and veil, I passed Dr. Maurice as I filed into chapel. On each occasion I nodded to him, conspicuously, but, as I did so, he turned away. Once I heard his voice immediately outside my cell, but he was on the gantry, I realised, to visit the sick prisoner in cell C.3.1., not me.

Nor, following our interview on the day of Braddle's death, did I have any further meeting with Colonel Isaacson. Some few weeks later, however, I did receive a most welcome message from him, brought to me one morning by Warder Stokes.

"The governor presents his compliments," he began.

The phrase rang so oddly in my ears that I looked at the youthful warder, half expecting him to touch his russet forelock as he spoke.

"Presents his compliments?" I echoed.

"The governor presents his compliments," Warder Stokes repeated. "The governor has spoken with the surgeon. From today's date you are to be spared the picking of oakum out of consideration for your health."

"The Lord be praised," I cried. "For this relief, much thanks. What am I to do instead?"

"You will work in the prison garden."

"Do you know what is today's date, Warder Stokes?"

"The twenty-first of March."

"It is an auspicious day, Warder Stokes."

"It is my birthday."

"I thought it must be."

"You will start work in the garden this morning."

"On the bank, I hope, where the wild thyme blows, where oxlips and the nodding violet grows, quite over-canopied with luscious woodbine, with sweet musk roses and with eglantine?" I got to my feet. "I am ready to begin my duties," I declared. "Happy birthday, Warder Stokes."

The young warder looked at me suspiciously. "How did you know it was my birthday?"

"On the day we first met, Warder Stokes," I murmured mysteriously, "you asked if I had been a detective in my time. Perhaps I still am. What do you think?"

"I don't know what to think," he said. "The governor said you would be pleased with the news and I see that you are."

"Yes, I am," I said, gratefully. "Please convey my sincere thanks to him."

"And he said that if you were pleased I was to give you this copy of the prison regulations." He took a folded sheet of foolscap from his trouser pocket and held it out towards me.

"I have them already. They are there." I pointed to the sheet of prison regulations pasted to the wall above my bed.

"The governor said I should give you this." I took the folded paper from him and opened it. I glanced down and saw that Rule 11 had been circled in black ink:

> Silence must be observed on all occasions by day and night.

"Thank you," I said. "Please present my compliments to the governor and tell him that I understand."

It was in the garden of Reading Gaol that I discovered that life is not complex. We are complex. Life is simple and in life the simple thing is the right thing.

My duties as a garden labourer were not onerous. There were few flowers for me to tend in the garden at Reading Gaol: none that Shakespeare wrote of and only a modest host of Mr. Wordsworth's daffodils. There was gravel to rake and grass to cut; there were hedges to trim and weeds to pull from pathways. The worst of it was digging and turning the heavy soil in the vegetable garden. The best of it was simply pushing a wheelbarrow from here to there.

It was in that garden, pushing that wheelbarrow, that I began to realise that I must make everything that had happened to me good for me. All the horrors of prison—the plank bed, the loathsome food, the hard ropes shredded into oakum till one's fingertips grew dull with pain, the menial offices with which each day began and ended, the harsh orders that routine seems to necessitate, the dreadful dress that makes sorrow grotesque to look at, the silence, the solitude, the shame—each and all of these things I knew I must transform somehow into a spiritual experience. There was not a single degradation of the body that I could not take and use to help cleanse the soul.

It was while walking with my wheelbarrow in the garden

of Reading Gaol that I came to see that I must reach the point where I might say quite simply, and without affectation, that the two great turning points of my life were when my father sent me to Oxford and when society sent me to prison. I would not say that prison was the best thing that could have happened to me: I would sooner say—or hear it said of me— that I was so typical a child of my age, that in my perversity, and for that perversity's sake, I turned the good things of my life to evil, and the evil things of my life to good.

In the spring and early summer of 1896, amid the spring showers and in the early-summer sunshine, in the wake of my mother's death and of the murder of Warder Braddle, I knew that I must make good from evil—and that I could.

At the east side of Reading Gaol, behind the boiler house, along the prison perimeter wall, is a strip of ground where those who have been hanged at the prison lie buried. On the west side, close to the vegetable garden and beyond the potting sheds, is the prison's formal garden of remembrance where Warder Braddle had been laid to rest. As, in desultory fashion, I swept the path that passed his grave—and the graves of a dozen other of the gaol's "good and faithful servants"—I thought of Braddle and of how he, and his father and his grandfather, and Warder Stokes, and Colonel Isaacson and all the rest, were as much imprisoned by Reading Gaol as were we, the convicts. In this life we are all of us confined in different ways. As I stood at Braddle's graveside, I thought, too, of my mother and of how, curiously, all her life, in Dublin and in London, she had chosen to dwell in curtained rooms, out of the light. I thought of my dear Constance, without a home to call her own, residing now in Genoa, imprisoned by her exile. I thought of my two sons, playing innocently in the Italian sunshine, but living lives of deception, under assumed names, forever locked in the shadow of my shame.

I thought especially of my sons whenever I caught sight of the boy prisoner, E.1.1., in the garden. Tom was several years older than my elder son, but he was evidently still a child. He was fourteen years of age, but no larger than a ten-year-old. He was thin and pale, with slender arms and sloping shoulders, and a narrow, fox-like face. His hair was the colour of burnt straw and grew down to his collar—he wore no prison cap. His cheeks were lightly freckled, his eyes were small and his nose was pointed, but he was beautiful because he was young. Youth is the one thing worth having!

One day I found him standing alone by Braddle's grave. He was holding a bundle of grasses and wildflowers in his hand. I looked along the path and back towards the vegetable garden: there was no sign of a watching turnkey.

"Do you miss him?" I asked.

"Who are you?" He looked at me suspiciously and answered roughly, though his skin was soft and his voice was that of a child's.

"My name is Oscar," I said.

"Is it?" he said, shrugging his shoulders to affect indifference.

"You're Tom, aren't you?" I persisted.

"I might be," he said.

"I know you are." I laughed. "You are everywhere, Tom, and everyone knows you."

He softened somewhat, evidently flattered. "Do they? Everyone knows the monkey, but the monkey knows no one."

"That's a fine phrase, Tom," I said. "Who taught you that?"

He said nothing. He gazed steadily down at the mound of earth before him. I pointed to his posy. "Are those flowers for Warder Braddle?" I asked.

This time he laughed. "They're weeds," he said. "They're for the bonfire."

"Was Warder Braddle your friend?"

He hesitated. "I don't know," he said.

"Did he look after you?"

"I've got others," he replied, and walked away.

On the following morning, when, through the cracks around the hatches in our cell doors, we were having what he now termed "our daily chinwag," Private Luck said to me, playfully, "I hear that you have been talking to our little monkey?"

"Do you mean Tom? Yes, I saw him in the garden. How do you know?"

"He is a pretty boy, isn't he?"

"He is young."

"You like young boys, Mr. Wilde, I know that." He lowered his voice. "Do you want him?" he whispered.

"What?" I answered, confused. "What do you mean?"

"Do you want the boy?"

"He is a child!" I hissed, outraged.

"It will not be easy, Mr. Wilde. It will cost money."

15

Execution

*B*etween me and life there has always been a mist of words. Since my boyhood, language has enveloped me. When I was young I liked to do all the talking myself, of course—it saved time and prevented arguments. It was the sound of my own voice that thrilled me. *Je parle donc je suis.* I would throw probability out of the window for the sake of a phrase, and for the sake of an epigram I would willingly desert truth. In time, I learnt to listen as well as to speak and discovered the beauty of reciprocity and the consolation of the give-and-take of conversation. Discourse, I know now, is everything.

But in Reading Gaol, apart from my daily "chinwag" with Private Luck—which lasted between three and eight minutes, never more—I had no sustained conversations of any kind during the spring and early summer of 1896. I spoke that one time with the boy prisoner, Tom, at Warder Braddle's graveside. With Warder Stokes, now and then, when he came to my cell, I attempted inconsequential small talk, but the poor fellow was so guarded in his responses, so desperately watchful of all he said, that I quickly understood that my well-intended pleasantries were a burden to him. With the other turnkeys my exchanges were rarely more than monosyllabic.

Late one afternoon in May, by the potting sheds, I saw a prisoner standing alone leaning against a wall, his head thrown back and his jaw thrust upwards towards the setting sun. There were no warders in sight, so, hungry for a friend to speak to, I went over to him. I saw from the badge on his uniform that it was C.3.5.—the poisoner, Atitis-Snake. His cap was pushed back a little on his head, so for the first time I saw his mouth and chin. In his hand he held a lighted cigarette. "By all that's wonderful," I cried, "where did you get that?"

He turned his shrouded head towards the potting sheds and nodded. There, sitting on the step by an open door, also with a lighted cigarette in hand, was the boy, Tom. I laughed and set down my wheelbarrow. The pair of them, man and boy, convicts at Reading Gaol, looked for all the world like a farmer and his lad enjoying an evening smoke at the end of a hard day's labour in the fields. "What must I do to beg a cigarette?" I asked.

As I spoke, in the distance I heard a woman's voice calling. "E.1.1., where are you? Come here now." I looked along the pathway that led back to the main prison buildings. I could see no one. The voice, louder and more urgent than before, repeated its call—not angrily, but as a clear command. The boy got lightly to his feet and ran off towards it.

"It was the wardress," I said. I smiled. "Her face has an unexpected grace that her voice most surely lacks." I turned back to Sebastian Atitis-Snake, but he was gone.

By the wall where he had been standing and on the step where the boy had sat, I foraged for the remains of their cigarettes, but there was nothing to be found.

Not long after this, on a day when I had learnt from Warder Stokes that my neighbour the dwarf had once been a circus tumbler and assistant to the Great Voltare, celebrated mesmerist, I attempted to speak to him as we trudged around the exercise yard, one after the other, five paces apart.

"You worked in the circus, my friend," I whispered when we were at the farthest point from the watching turnkey. "Have you ever thought that we are like elephants pacing around the ring?" I was excited to fill the air with sound.

The dwarf made no reply, but I sensed from a slight motion of his head that he had heard me. "In America," I continued, "I met P. T. Barnum and he did me the honour of presenting me to the mighty Jumbo."

I spoke absurdly, but not simply for the sake of speaking. I spoke to make contact with a fellow soul in torment.

"He won't answer," hissed another voice in the ring. It was the prisoner who paced ahead of him, Atitis-Snake. "He won't speak. He is silent as the grave. We are buried here. This is our grave. There is no escape for us—except death."

Before my incarceration, I used to live entirely for pleasure. I shunned suffering and sorrow of every kind. I hated both. I resolved to ignore them as far as possible. They were not part of my scheme of life. They had no place in my philosophy.

My mother, amid the troubles of her later life, used to quote to me Goethe's famous lines:

Who never ate his bread in sorrow,
Who never spent the midnight hours
Weeping and waiting for the morrow,
—He knows you not, ye heavenly powers

I heard the lines from my mother's lips—time and again— and absolutely declined to accept or admit the enormous truth hidden in them. I could not understand it. I remember how I used to tell her that I did not want to eat my bread in sorrow, or to pass any night weeping and watching for a more bitter dawn. I had no idea that it was one of the special things that the Fates had in store for me: that for a whole year of my life, indeed, I was to do little else.

On the anniversary of my imprisonment—Monday, 25 May 1896—the Reverend Friend, chaplain of Reading Gaol, came to call on me in my cell. Warder Stokes had forewarned me of the visit and I was resolved to receive the reverend gentleman courteously, and not as I had done previously, with rancour and ill-disguised hostility. He, too, it seemed, had come to call in a spirit of conciliation.

"Good morning, my friend," he said, smiling as he entered my cell. "May I sit with you a while?"

"By all means," I replied, getting to my feet and offering him my wooden chair to sit upon. "Warder Stokes told me that you might come to see me today. I am glad. I am grateful. I have not spoken at any length with another human being since the day in February when my wife came to tell me of my mother's death. That was three months ago. It was the day that Warder Braddle died."

"I remember," said the Reverend Friend, settling into the chair and laying his prayer book carefully on the table before him. I noticed his fingernails, clean and neatly cut: a novelty at Reading Gaol. "You will sit, also?" he said, pursing his lips and waving a delicate hand towards my bed. I perched on the edge of it and looked steadily into his pale-blue eyes. They told me nothing.

"Did Warder Braddle's death surprise you?" I asked.

"Your question does, my friend," he answered. "Why do you think of Warder Braddle?"

"Because he died outside my door," I said, "and now I tend his grave."

"Ah yes," said the chaplain, half closing his eyes, as if to picture it. "In the garden of remembrance."

"Is it unconsecrated ground?" I asked.

The chaplain looked at me, surprised. "Yes, it is—but it was a Christian burial. Suicide is a mortal sin in the eyes of God and a punishable offence in the eyes of the Law, but the soul of the man who takes his own life is not necessarily doomed to damnation."

"You believe Warder Braddle took his own life?" I asked.

"It is possible," he answered quietly, running his fingers around the rim of his prayer book. "I saw him at the last, leaning over the balustrade. I know the governor is certain it was an accident—and I trust the governor's judgement—but Braddle did not seem drunk to me."

"Did he have cause to kill himself?"

The Reverend Friend looked directly at me and smiled. "We are all sinners, C.3.3."

"You were his priest?"

"Yes."

"Were you also his confessor? Did you know the nature of his sins?"

The chaplain pursed his lips and narrowed his eyes. "I have not come here to speak ill of the dead. I have come to bring comfort to the living." He held out his hand, as if offering a benediction. "How are you?" he asked.

I smiled. "As today you are my confessor, I will tell you. I am in pain," I answered.

The chaplain adopted a look of concern. "Is it your ear?" he asked. "I know you've had trouble with your ear."

"My ear does bleed at night sometimes. My heart bleeds, also. The pain is overwhelming."

The chaplain sighed. "Suffering is a mystery, is it not?"

"A mystery and a revelation," I answered. "I have discovered lately that we can learn more from pain than we can from pleasure."

"I am moved to hear you say so," said the Reverend Friend, furrowing his brow. His face was featureless; his age difficult to determine. "Perhaps your year has not been wasted."

"When I was at Oxford," I said, holding the clergyman's gaze, "I remember telling one of my friends as we were strolling round Magdalen's narrow, bird-haunted walks one morning in the year before I took my degree, that I wanted to eat of the fruit of all the trees in the garden of the world, and that I was going out into the world with that passion in my soul."

"And so, indeed, you went out, and so you lived," said the prison chaplain, nodding his head sagaciously. "I have read much about you, my friend. There has been much to read."

"My only mistake," I continued, "was that I confined myself so exclusively to the trees of what seemed to me the sunlit side of the garden, and shunned the other side for its shadow and its gloom."

"Ah yes," murmured the chaplain.

"Failure, disgrace, poverty, sorrow, despair, suffering, tears, even, the broken words that come from lips in pain, remorse that makes one walk on thorns, conscience that condemns, self-abasement that punishes, the misery that puts ashes on its head, the anguish that chooses sackcloth for its raiment and into its own drink puts gall . . ."

"All these were things of which you were afraid?" he asked.

"Yes, and as I had determined to know nothing of them, in due course I was forced to taste each of them in turn, to feed on them, to have for a season, indeed, no other food at all."

The chaplain sat back, folded his arms across his chest and considered me carefully. "Do you regret having lived for pleasure?" he asked.

"Not for a single moment," I cried, leaning towards him eagerly. "I did it to the full, as one should do everything that one does. There was no pleasure I did not experience. I threw the pearl of my soul into a cup of wine. I went down the primrose path to the sound of flutes. I lived on honey-comb."

"But to have continued the same life would have been wrong—"

"Yes," I interrupted, "because it would have been limiting. I had to pass on. And now I find that the other half of the garden has its secrets for me, also."

The Reverend Friend patted his prayer book gently, as he might have patted my head had I been a child. "You have done well. You should be happy with what you have learnt. I am happy for you."

"I must learn how to be happy," I said. "Once I knew it, or thought I knew it, by instinct. It was always springtime once in my heart. My temperament was akin to joy. I filled my life to the very brim with pleasure, as one might fill a cup to the very brim with wine. Now I am approaching life from a completely new standpoint, and even to conceive happiness is often extremely difficult for me." I looked about my cell and spread out my fingers on either side of me on the hard board that was my bed. "Despair is my bedfellow here."

"Despair is a sin," said the chaplain.

"I know. I must not wilfully live in melancholy. But there are times when I think I will go mad here."

"Are the warders cruel to you?"

"No, some are harsh, but none is cruel."

"Is it your fellow prisoners?"

"My neighbour torments me," I said. "I will go mad."

"The dwarf? You surprise me."

"No," I said, laughing, "not the dwarf. C.3.2.—Private Luck."

"The Indian? The half Indian or whatever he is. I rarely see him. He will not see me. He is a Hindu or a Buddhist or some such. He is not a Christian."

"I am petitioning the Home Secretary. It is my right. I have been here long enough, among murderers and blackmailers. I must get out or I will go mad."

"Be patient," urged the chaplain, breathing heavily. "Think of all that you have been telling me just now; think of all that you have learnt thus far. A year from today you will be released—a better and a wiser man. It is not long."

"It is too long," I said, closing my eyes, suddenly exhausted. "I will petition the Home Secretary for my release. My mind is set on that. Pray for me, Padre, and wish me well with my petition."

"I wish you well with your petition," said the chaplain slowly. "It may even be granted," he added, "who knows? We have another prisoner here who is petitioning the Home Secretary and is hopeful of success. I have just come from him."

I opened my eyes. "Who is that? The poisoner, Atitis-Snake? He, too, is desperate, I know."

"No—a new prisoner, by the name of Wooldridge. He arrived two days ago. He is in the condemned cell. He is destined for the gallows. He murdered his wife in a jealous rage. He slit her throat from ear to ear—with a cut-throat razor. Ugly business. He gave himself up to the police and now he's here. It's three years since we last had a hanging."

"And this man is seeking a reprieve?"

"No," answered the chaplain, smiling. "Quite the reverse. He wants to be hanged. At his trial, the jury, when they brought in the guilty verdict, put in a plea for clemency. The judge ignored the jury and all sorts of committees have sprung up demanding that Wooldridge's life be spared. But he wants none of it. He told me when I saw him just now that he wants to die to pay for the crime he has committed. A life for a life. He is petitioning the Home Secretary to ignore those who are pleading for him to be spared. I think the Home Secretary will grant his wish. I am not so sure, C.3.3., that he will grant yours."

"Will you pray for me, Padre?" I asked, earnestly.

"I will pray for you. We are all of us in need of God's mercy."

On Thursday, 2 July 1896, I had a brief interview with Colonel Henry Isaacson, governor of Reading Gaol, at the conclusion of which he agreed to forward to the Home Secretary the petition I had drafted:

H M Prison, Reading
Prisoner C.3.3.—Oscar Wilde

2 July 1896.

To the Right Honourable Her Majesty's Principal Secretary of State for the Home Department.
The petition of the above-named prisoner humbly sheweth that he does not desire to attempt to palliate in any way the terrible offences of which he was rightly found guilty, but to point out that such offences are forms of sexual

madness and are recognised as such not merely by modern pathological science but by much modern legislation, notably in France, Austria, and Italy, where the laws affecting these misdemeanours have been repealed, on the ground that they are diseases to be cured by a physician, rather than crimes to be punished by a judge . . .

The petitioner is now keenly conscious of the fact that while the three years preceding his arrest were from the intellectual point of view the most brilliant years of his life (four plays from his pen having been produced on the stage with immense success, and played not merely in England, America, and Australia, but in almost every European capital, and many books that excited much interest at home and abroad having been published), still that during the entire time he was suffering from the most horrible form of erotomania, which made him forget his wife and children, his high social position in London and Paris, his European distinction as an artist, the honour of his name and family, his very humanity itself, and left him the helpless prey of the most revolting passions, and of a gang of people who for their own profit ministered to them, and then drove him to hideous ruin.

It is under the ceaseless apprehension lest this insanity, that displayed itself in monstrous sexual perversion before, may now extend to the entire nature and intellect, that the petitioner writes this appeal which he earnestly entreats may be at once considered. Horrible as all actual madness is, the terror of madness is no less appalling, and no less ruinous to the soul.

For more than thirteen dreadful months now, the

*petitioner has been subject to the fearful system of solitary
cellular confinement: without human intercourse of any
kind; without writing materials whose use might help
distract the mind: without suitable or sufficient books, so es-
sential to any literary man, so vital for the preservation of
mental balance: condemned to absolute silence: cut off from
all knowledge of the external world and the movements of
life: leading an existence composed of bitter degradations
and terrible hardships, hideous in its recurring monotony of
dreary task and sickening privation: the despair and misery
of this lonely and wretched life having been intensified
beyond words by the death of his mother, Lady Wilde, to
whom he was deeply attached, as well as by the contempla-
tion of the ruin he has brought on to his young wife and his
two children . . .*

*For more than a year the petitioner's mind has borne
this. It can bear it no longer. He is quite conscious of the approach of an insanity that will not be confined to one por-
tion of the nature merely, but will extend over all alike, and
his desire, his prayer, is that his sentence may be remitted
now, so that he may be taken abroad by his friends and may
put himself under medical care so that the sexual insanity
from which he suffers may be cured. He knows only too well
that his career as a dramatist and writer is ended, and his
name blotted from the scroll of English Literature never to
be replaced: that his children cannot bear that name again,
and that an obscure life in some remote country is in store
for him: he knows that, bankruptcy having come upon him,
poverty of a most bitter kind awaits him, and that all the
joy and beauty of existence is taken from him for ever; but*

at least in all his hopelessness he still clings to the hope that he will not have to pass directly from the common gaol to the common lunatic asylum . . .

There are other apprehensions of danger that the limitation of space does not allow the petitioner to enter on; his chief danger is that of madness, his chief terror that of madness, and his prayer that his long imprisonment may be considered with its attendant ruin a sufficient punishment, that the imprisonment may be ended now, and not uselessly or vindictively prolonged till insanity has claimed soul as well as body as its prey, and brought it to the same degradation and the same shame.

Oscar Wilde

Five days after I had submitted my petition, on Tuesday, 7 July 1896, Charles Wooldridge was hanged in Reading Gaol. His petition was considered before mine and, in Wooldridge's case, the Home Secretary was "pleased to accede to the prisoner's request that there should be no reprieve in this instance and no delay to his execution." The hanging took place, as was the custom, at 8:00 a.m., as the clock outside the prison walls struck the hour. According to Dr. Maurice, who witnessed it, alongside the governor, the chaplain, the undersheriff, and two warders on "special duty" for the occasion, it was a "clean execution": Wooldridge died instantly, his death caused by dislocation of the vertebrae. But a rumour ran round the prison that as the condemned man swung from the rope, his neck stretched by eleven inches and his face was distorted beyond recognition.

At 8:00 p.m. on the same day, Sebastian Atitis-Snake, at his own request, was taken from his cell to the governor's office and there, after making a full confession, was charged with the murder of Warder Braddle.

Interlude

Dieppe, France, 24 and 25 June 1897

In the small back dining room at the Café Suisse, Dr. Quilp raised his glass of green chartreuse to his companion. "Bravo, Monsieur Melmoth, that's quite a curtain line."

As he spoke, in the dark far corner of the empty room, the cuckoo clock on the wall above the dresser juddered into life and, with a hideous whirring and callooing, struck the midnight hour. Lizard-like, Monsieur Melmoth slowly closed his eyes. "And timed to perfection, too, if I may say so," he murmured.

Dr. Quilp put down his glass and closed the little notebook that lay on the table before him. He removed his spectacles, picked up his table napkin, and, with it, carefully wiped his thin moustache and tiny beard. "Yes," he said, contentedly, "we can continue tomorrow. You have told me enough to tantalise our readers."

"I have told you enough—*tout court*," declared Melmoth, opening his oyster eyes and smiling balefully. "I have given you my all, Dr. Quilp. I have earned my Perrier-Jouët 'ninety-two." He gazed at the litter of half-empty plates and glasses on the table. He reached for his cigarettes. With a trembling hand he put one to his lips and leant towards a guttering candle to light it. The stubble on his chin was grey as slate, but his face was flushed with drink.

"Oh, yes," said Quilp, smoothly, "and your yellow wines and your reds. You have earned your entertainment tonight, Monsieur Melmoth—and left us wanting more."

"There is no more," declared Melmoth, breathing deeply on his cigarette. "You have all you require."

"I don't think so," said Quilp, contemplating his liqueur rather than his guest. "You have just told me that Sebastian Atitis-Snake, the poisoner, confessed to the murder of Warder Braddle."

"He did."

"But earlier you told me that Private Achindra Acala Luck had claimed to be the murderer."

"Indeed, he had."

"Well, which was it?"

"One? T'other? Both? Neither? Did the doctor do it? Or the priest? Or perhaps it was the beautiful wardress disguised as the dwarf?" Melmoth laughed so that tears trickled from the corners of his eyes. He looked about the table for a half-filled glass and found one. "It won't have been Warder Stokes. He was a decent fellow. He gave the murderer Wooldridge a pipe to smoke on the day before he died."

Melmoth fell silent. Dr. Quilp smiled at him indulgently. "If we are to make our fortune from your story, Monsieur Melmoth, we must tell it in its entirety—from start to finish."

Melmoth drew on his cigarette. "I believe I have given you enough to work on, Dr. Quilp. Remember, when you have eliminated the impossible, whatever remains, however improbable, must be the truth."

Quilp pushed back his chair. "Shall we make for our beds, Monsieur Melmoth? We've worked enough for one night."

Melmoth dropped the remains of his cigarette into his wine-glass. "I will need a pony-and-trap to get me back to my lodgings, I'm afraid."

"There's no need for that," said Quilp agreeably. "I have booked us both rooms here for tonight."

Melmoth sat back in his chair. "Here? Upstairs? That's very generous."

"And to mark the Queen's jubilee, by way of celebration," said Quilp, getting to his feet, "I've ordered us a couple of tarts—for dessert."

Melmoth looked up at him, wide-eyed. "You don't mean *tartes aux fraises,* do you?"

"No, monsieur," chuckled Quilp, rubbing his heavy hands together, "I mean *women*—girls, I hope—from the brothel next door." He looked towards the cuckoo clock. "It's midnight. They should be waiting for us."

Melmoth did not move. "You are very kind, Dr. Quilp, but I have taken wine and I am not sure . . ."

"Nonsense. This is just what the doctor ordered. Isn't this the kind of Continental cure you promised the Home Secretary you'd be taking?"

Melmoth laughed. "I was a desperate man when I petitioned the Home Secretary—and it was a year ago . . . I am not sure now that I could rise to the occasion."

"I am an apothecary, Monsieur Melmoth. Remember?" Dr. Quilp pulled back his jacket and reached into his waist-coat pocket. He pulled from it a small twist of tissue paper. "I have a powder for you—a touch of Spanish fly."

Melmoth raised his eyebrows and smiled. "As recom-mended by the Marquis de Sade."

"Exactly so." Quilp handed the twist of paper to Mel-moth. "And Casanova," he added encouragingly.

Melmoth accepted the gift and carefully put the paper inside his coat pocket. "When do I take it?" he asked.

"For the best results, about twenty minutes before the act. Take it all. Half measures will go for nothing."

"I understand," said Melmoth, raising his glass to his companion. "Thank you for your thoughtfulness." He picked up his wine-glass and contemplated the dregs. "What time is it?" he asked.

Quilp peered through the gloom at the cuckoo clock. "A quarter past twelve."

"That's late," said Melmoth.

"Don't worry, there's no rush. We have the girls for the night. All paid for."

Melmoth pushed back his chair and, with a flourish, drained his glass. He took a deep breath and, a touch un-steadily, got to his feet. "To get back one's youth one has to repeat one's follies, I believe," he said, smiling. *"En avant."*

The following day the sun shone brightly in the street out-side the Café Suisse. Sebastian Melmoth and Dr. Quilp met, as they had arranged, at 2:00 p.m. for a late breakfast of eggs and ham and cheese, and coffee and Perrier-Jouët

'92, at a table in the shade beneath the café's blue- and white-striped awning. Melmoth was dressed in the clothes he had worn the night before, but he had shaved carefully and washed his hair and looked, he had felt as he considered himself in the looking-glass on the landing outside his bedroom, like an ageing Botticelli cherub. Quilp, also newly shaved, and freshly powdered, wore new linen and looked, to Melmoth, vulpine, and (for such a lovely day) oddly tense, on the qui vive, like a Prussian officer readying himself for a duel.

As Melmoth took his place at table, Quilp, adjusting his spectacles and peering down at his open notebook, asked: "Were you surprised?"

Melmoth settled himself. "By my prowess, do you mean?"

"No, that's not what I mean, but since you mention it . . ."

"Your aphrodisiac was efficacious," announced Melmoth, pouring himself a cup of coffee. "You clearly know your business, Doctor."

"And the girl?" enquired Quilp.

Melmoth smiled ruefully: "The first these ten years, and it shall be the last. It was like chewing cold mutton."

"I am sorry," said the apothecary, running a thumb and forefinger lightly over his moustache.

"But tell it in England," continued Melmoth, happily, sipping his coffee. "There it will entirely restore my reputation."

Quilp laughed. "Yes—and that may help in securing the right price for your prison memoir."

"I do need money," said Melmoth, earnestly. "Like Saint Francis of Assisi, I find I am wedded to Poverty: but in my case the marriage is not a success. I hate the bride that has been given to me. I see no beauty in her hunger and her rags; my thirst is for the beauty of life: my desire for the joy. I appreciate a proper breakfast." He gazed about the table before taking up a fork and skewering a slice of ham. "Money I must have. At the moment, for bread, for board, for everything, I am entirely dependent on the munificence of friends and the generosity of my dear Constance."

"Will you and your wife be reconciled?" asked Quilp.

"Perhaps," said Melmoth, laying down his fork. "If it were not for my friends and her family, I think certainly." He looked at Dr. Quilp. "My friends appear determined to indulge my weakness. I must resist them or I shall be lost. If I return to a certain individual, and it becomes known, my wife's family will cut off my allowance—completely. They will be within their rights. My agreement with my wife's lawyer clearly states that I must not be 'guilty of any moral misconduct' or 'notoriously consort with evil or disreputable companions.'"

"I hope last night's adventure will not compromise you."

Melmoth laughed. "Oh no, I think the word 'notoriously' protects me there. I imagine I could take as many women as I liked. It's boys they are frightened of."

"And it was because Private Luck taunted you with the boy, Tom, that you thought you would go mad? Is that it?"

"Yes, Dr. Quilp. You are a psychologist as well as an author and an apothecary, it seems." Melmoth scooped a spoonful of scrambled eggs onto his plate. "I knew that if I returned to the sexual perversity that had brought about my downfall I would be left without a penny to my name. And I would never see my wife or sons again."

"So—were you surprised?"

"Surprised?" Melmoth raised his eyebrows and began to eat.

"Surprised that Atitis-Snake confessed to the murder when—to you, at least—Luck had already done so?"

"I did not then know all that I would come to know about Private Achindra Acala Luck. And I did not know whether or not Atitis-Snake had murdered Warder Braddle, either alone or in harness with others, but I could see that he might claim to have done so."

"In heaven's name, why? Why confess to a murder you've not even been accused of? A murder, in fact, that you may not even have committed? You'd have to be mad to do such a thing. Atitis-Snake was not suspected of Braddle's murder, was he? No one was pointing an accusing finger at him? And the governor was clearly content for Braddle's death to be taken for an accident. That's what he wanted."

Melmoth grinned. "Oh, yes, Colonel Isaacson was all for the quiet life. But Atitis-Snake was a desperate man— and an instinctive risk-taker. He was desperate—frantic— to escape the hell of his life sentence. After a year at Reading Gaol, the prospect of a *lifetime* of incarceration— ten, twenty, thirty years—had dawned on him. And over- whelmed him. I can understand that." Melmoth reached for the iced champagne and poured his companion a glass. "He had to get out. There was no other way."

"But he put his life on the line."

"When you put your head above the parapet, you do.

Remember the famous last words of General Sedgwick at the Battle of Spotsylvania? 'They couldn't hit an elephant at this dist—'"

Quilp did not laugh. Slowly he raised his glass to his lips. "I am still puzzled," he said. "By confessing to a murder—and the murder of a prison warder, no less—Atitis-Snake was putting his head directly into the hangman's noose."

"Not if he managed to skip the country between his arrest and his trial."

"An unlikely prospect."

"Agreed, but not impossible. There's much coming and going between court-room and prison cell. And not if, at his trial, he were to be found 'guilty but insane.' To do as he did, after all, you'd have to be mad—you said so yourself. Perhaps the jury would be made up of men like you." Melmoth took a draught of champagne: his pale face was gaining some colour: he was warming to his theme. "'To be detained in safe custody until Her Majesty's pleasure be known'—there are worse things that can happen to a man. They dine quite well at Bedlam, I believe. And they are given canvases to paint on and any number of books to read. And according to my friend Dr. Conan Doyle, who knows about these matters, it is five times easier for a lunatic to escape from an asylum than for a convict to escape from gaol."

"Atitis-Snake took a calculated risk?"

"Exactly so."

"And was he mad?"

"He did not seem it to me. I hardly knew him, of course,

but what I saw I rather liked. I liked his name very much. And the boy, Tom, liked him—that was clear. When I found them smoking together by the potting shed I saw that at once. And a boy is like a dog—he can sniff out whom to trust."

"And what about you, Monsieur Melmoth—were you mad? How did the Home Secretary receive your petition?" Dr. Quilp had his pencil hovering over his notebook.

"Ah, yes, was I mad? That is the question. Mammon must be served. We must go on with the story."

"We must finish it," said Dr. Quilp pleasantly. He looked towards the café door and waved to the waiter. "And we shall have another bottle of the Perrier-Jouët while we're about it."

10 July 1896

Inquiry, held at HM Prison Reading, by direction of the Prison Commissioners, on Prisoner Oscar Wilde, in regard to a Petition made by him to the Home Secretary dated 2 July 1896

1. The Committee do not consider from the inquiry that there is danger of the Prisoner becoming insane, but as this Prisoner's petition is based upon the fear of insanity, always a difficult subject, the Committee think an expert Medical Inquiry may well be held upon his case, in which an examination of his hearing and eyesight could be added.

2. The Committee consider that the Prisoner has been well treated. He himself states that his treatment has been good and the diet sufficient. He has been relieved of oakum picking, has been allowed more books, and more exercise than the other prisoners. He has increased eight pounds in weight since he entered the prison. Prison life must of course be more internally severe to a prisoner of his educational achievement than it would be to an ordinary one.

A. W. Cobham

C. Hay

H. Hunter

H. Thursby

G. W. Palmer

16

The Reichenbach Falls

*W*as I mad?

One morning, during the first week in July 1896, in the room adjacent to the governor's office in Reading Gaol—the room in which I had had my last meeting with my wife—I was interviewed by a committee of middle-aged men of nondescript appearance who left no impression on me whatsoever. I answered their questions as honestly as I was able, and because I sensed that they were dull men leading dreary lives I did what I could to cheer them up. When one of them enquired whether I had ever found myself talking to myself in the solitude of my cell, I answered, foolishly, "I like talking to a brick wall: it's the only thing in the world that never contradicts me."

There are things that are right to say, but that may be said at the wrong time to the wrong people. The committee all laughed at my little joke and concluded that I clearly had my wits about me. I was not mad, in their opinion. When I protested that it was the *prospect* of madness that was driving me towards insanity, they told me that the future was beyond their remit and promised that a medical examination would be conducted to assess the likelihood of my becoming lunatic with the passage of time.

They were as good as their word.

In due course, the prison surgeon came to see me in my cell. It was at the end of one of my wheelbarrow days in the prison garden. "Good afternoon, C.3.3.," he said affably. "I have come to look at your eyes and your ears and to tell you that you are not mad, nor likely to become so."

I stood to greet my visitor. "Good afternoon, Dr. Maurice," I said. "I had hoped to see you before this. Where have you been?"

He made no reply, but came into the cell and placed his medical bag on my table. He stepped back and stood, with his arms akimbo, looking at me. I looked at him. He was tall and angular, with long legs and arms, and he struck me as more handsome than I had remembered and less diffident. Beneath his fine moustaches, his skin was tanned—he had caught the sun—and his walnut-coloured eyes alive and knowing.

"You are no longer wearing spectacles, Doctor," I remarked.

"Well observed," he said. "I am exercising my eyes to make them stronger. Spectacles, I have decided, are a mistake. They make our eyes lazy—and laziness will not do."

"And yet I see that you have been sitting in the sun, Doctor, taking your ease."

He smiled and unlocked his bag. "I have been out and about, certainly. I don't know about sitting in the sun, taking my ease."

"I do," I said. I was in a teasing mood. "The right-hand side of your face is darker than the left, which suggests to me that, on a regular basis, you have been sitting in the same place in the same corner of your garden at the same time of day, catching the sun on the same part of your face—no doubt while reading a good book in your favourite striped canvas deck chair."

The doctor let his stethoscope fall back into his bag. "How on earth do you know that the deck chair is striped?"

"They mostly are."

He laughed. His eyes shone even in the gloom of my cell. "I salute your genius."

"Thank you," I said, affecting a modest bow. "But I think 'genius' may be taking it too far."

"No, no," he insisted, smiling. "'Mediocrity knows nothing higher than itself, but talent instantly recognises genius.' The book I am reading is one of yours. Please take a seat and let me examine your ears. Move here nearer to the light."

I moved my chair and held my head to one side. "The book of mine?" I enquired. "Another gift from Conan Doyle?"

The doctor placed his otoscope inside my right ear. I flinched at the coldness of the steel.

"Indeed," he said, peering into his instrument. "Conan Doyle is a considerable admirer of your work."

"And I of his."

The doctor transferred his attention to my left ear. "I know," he said. "You told me." I flinched once more as the otoscope probed farther. "I assume it was you who introduced Atitis-Snake to the plot of 'The Final Problem'?"

"Atitis-Snake?" I said. "I do not follow you."

The doctor completed his examination and stepped back to look me in the eye. "Atitis-Snake claims that it was Conan Doyle's account of the struggle between Sherlock Holmes and Professor Moriarty at the Reichenbach Falls that inspired him to fling Warder Braddle to his death over the balustrade outside your cell. You did not know that?"

"I did not," I exclaimed, dumbfounded. "It's absurd. It's lunatic."

The doctor chuckled. "I imagine that's exactly what Atitis-Snake hopes the jury will think."

I shook my head in disbelief. "At his last trial, as I recall, Atitis-Snake claimed that he was Napoleon avenging himself on an unfaithful wife. This time he is claiming to be Sherlock Holmes casting Moriarty to his doom—is that it? The notion is preposterous. Will he be wearing a deerstalker and smoking a meerschaum pipe in the dock?"

"Atitis-Snake is not so deluded as to present himself as Sherlock Holmes. He claims to be Professor Moriarty— 'the Napoleon of crime.'"

I laughed. "So there is a method to his madness . . ."

Dr. Maurice fetched an ophthalmoscope from his bag and, with the thumb and forefinger of his left hand, held my right eyelid open. "Atitis-Snake is no more mad than you are, but perhaps better at playing the game. Your letter to the Home Secretary was a model of sanity. You will have to reconcile yourself to completing your sentence here." He peered into my other eye. "It is not so long now. Ten months and then you will be a free man."

He returned his instruments to his bag and stood back once more, looking down at me indulgently. "There is no obvious damage to your eyes. There's the deterioration that age brings, but no signs of incipient disease."

"The poet Milton went blind in prison," I said.

Maurice smiled. "That might have been the line to take with the visiting committee. 'Milton, thou shouldst be living at this hour!' 'I am locked in cell C.3.3. Release me!' It's too late now. You missed your opportunity. You are not going blind and you're no more John Milton than Atitis-Snake is Professor Moriarty." He snapped closed his bag. "But your right ear is more of a problem. There's blood and pus: inflammation of the middle ear—otitis media."

"Otitis media!" I exclaimed. "That is a name to rival Atitis-Snake! I collect extraordinary names, Doctor. Yours is curiously disappointing. At Trinity College, Dublin, I knew a surgeon who gloried in the name of Bent Ball."

"Professor Bent Ball?" said Dr. Maurice. "He is famous. I have his magnum opus—*Rectum and Anus: Their Diseases and Treatment.*"

"A gift from Conan Doyle?" I asked.

"No. Believe it or not, a birthday present from my mother. I was consulting it only the other day."

We both laughed.

The prison surgeon put a hand on my shoulder. "Beyond your ear, which should mend with time, there is nothing wrong with you. Look at you. You are laughing."

"I am laughing because here and now I am happy—in the civilised company of a civilised man. I feel alive."

The doctor clenched his bony fist and gently punched my shoulder blade. "That's more like it," he said.

"One can live for years sometimes without living at all, and then all life comes crowding into one single hour."

Dr. Maurice stepped back and took his bag from the table. "Command the moment to remain. Sustain the hour."

"I cannot, Doctor," I said. "I do not know how. At this moment, in your company, I can be happy, but tonight, when the moon shines and I cannot see her, and the clock strikes midnight beyond the prison walls, I shall lie on this wretched plank, incapable of sleep, picturing my wife and children, thinking of those I have betrayed and those who have betrayed me, and I will not be happy. I will be a soul in torment." I laughed. "My moods are somewhat volatile."

"I understand."

I looked into the prison surgeon's charm-filled walnut-coloured eyes. "You are a married man, aren't you, Doctor?" I asked.

"I am," he said, tilting his head to one side and tugging at his beard a little nervously.

"And when you married your wife, did you promise to love and to cherish her always—for better for worse, for richer for poorer, in sickness and in health . . ."

". . . From this day forward, till death us do part . . . Yes," he said. "Yes, I did."

"And will you keep your promise, Doctor?"

"I hope so."

"I hope so, too," I said. "A man should keep his promises. I see that now."

Dr. Maurice took out his pocket-watch. "I must be on my way. Duty calls. C.3.1. has been moved to the infirmary. He is not long for this world, alas." The surgeon stepped towards my cell door.

"I am sorry to hear it," I said. "Death is all around us."

"'Twas ever thus," replied the doctor cheerily. "I will look in on you again soon . . . If your ear does not clear itself, I will need to drain it."

"Thank you, Doctor," I said, standing to bid my visitor good-bye. "Why did you not come to see me before?" I asked.

He hesitated. "It was the governor's orders," he said simply. "The governor—doubtless with the interests of the prison at heart—had convinced himself that Warder Braddle's death was an accident. That's what he wanted it to be. My suggestion of somehow involving you in an 'investigation' of the matter he considered wholly ill advised. He was not happy that he allowed that initial conference we attended in his office. He was angry with me for proposing it."

"So why are you here now? Why are you able to visit me again?"

"Because Colonel Isaacson has gone."

I was bemused.

"Had you not heard?" asked the surgeon, looking at me in surprise. "He has left us—this week. He has been sent to Lewes by way of 'promotion.' In the wake of Warder Braddle's death and in anticipation of what the trial of Atitis-Snake may show the world about life at Reading Gaol, the Prison Commissioners thought it time for a change. Colonel Isaacson is no more."

"And the new man?" I asked.

"I've not met him yet," said Dr. Maurice. "His name is Major Nelson."

"Ah," I said. "A lower rank, but a better name. It has a ring to it."

The prison surgeon smiled. "Good day, C.3.3." He pulled open the heavy cell door.

"And did you take a second look at Braddle's body?" I asked, as he began to depart.

He stood still for a moment and turned back to look at me. "I did," he said.

"And what did you find?" I asked. "Anything you had not noticed before? The little things are infinitely the most important."

"Yes, I found something I had not noticed before," replied the doctor, smiling. "What were you expecting me to find?"

"Small blisters . . ."

"That is what I found."

". . . Around the nose and mouth?"

"That is exactly what I found."

17

The Nelson Touch

*M*ajor J. O. Nelson was a good man. I sensed that
the moment that I first saw him, at a distance,
standing at the front of the prison chapel reading the lesson
at our morning worship. He had a voice that was easy on
the ear, clear but not declamatory. He read the lesson as if it
meant something, as if he wanted us to hear it and understand it. And when he looked up and out over his congrega-
tion of convicts, his eyes suggested neither contempt nor
insecurity, neither rat nor weasel. He seemed to see us as
individual men and women—which, of course, he could not.
Our faces were hidden beneath masks and behind veils. His
face was open, wide and weather-beaten, lined by life's adventures, I surmised, rather than her sorrows. He had thick
black hair, which he wore *en brosse;* heavy, arched eyebrows;
and a walrus moustache. His moustache reminded me of
my friend Arthur Conan Doyle. Indeed, much about Major
Nelson reminded me of Conan Doyle.

I knew for sure that he was a good man the moment

that he first spoke to me. A week or so after his arrival at Reading, towards the end of July 1896, I was summoned to his presence.

"The governor wants to see you," said Warder Stokes.

"What's he like?" I asked, as we marched across the inner yard towards the governor's office.

"Silence," ordered Stokes. "You know the rule."

"What's he like?" I asked again, lowering my voice.

"I don't rightly know," said Stokes. "He seems decent enough."

When we reached the governor's office, I stood to attention as the warder announced me: "Prisoner C.3.3., sir."

Major Nelson looked up from his desk. He was holding a slim, blue-bound volume in his right hand. He held it out towards me and said: "The Prison Commission is allowing you some books, C.3.3. Perhaps you would like to read this one. I have just been reading it myself."

These were the very first words that Major Nelson spoke to me. What a beginning! I stood silent, bereft of speech, tears pricking at my eyes.

"You must let me have a list of other books that you might like," he continued easily. "We'll see what can be done." He pushed back his chair and got to his feet. He was not a tall man, but sturdy and brisk in his movements. He came around his desk and stood before me. "The Home Secretary is not inclined to grant you an early release, C.3.3." He paused and looked directly into my eyes. "That does not surprise you, does it?" I said nothing. "You will be with us for another ten months," he continued. "Let us make the best of it." He walked on past me to address Warder Stokes.

"Does the prisoner have any writing materials in his cell, Warder?"

"No, sir."

"Is the cell adequately lit?"

"Yes, sir."

Major Nelson turned back towards me. "Are you inclined to write, C.3.3.?"

"Write, sir?" I stumbled with the words as I spoke them.

"Write," he said, "other than to the Home Secretary and to your wife's solicitors. Write something original, something creative?"

"I hope to write about prison life one day, sir, and try to change it for others, but it is too terrible and ugly to make a work of art of. And I have suffered too much to write plays about it."

"A poem, perhaps?" suggested the governor, moving behind his desk once more and resuming his seat.

"I have an idea for a poem," I said.

"'The Ballad of Reading Gaol'?"

I looked at the prison governor. In that moment he seemed to me to be the most Christ-like man I had ever met. "Or 'The Nelson Touch'?" I suggested.

He gave a short, barking laugh. "I am not sure the Prison Commission would approve of that." He looked up at me ruefully. "And do not be deceived by my surname. I come from different stock. There will be no blind eye turned on my watch. You are to be allowed some books, subject to my approval, to keep your mind active—and free from vicious thoughts. If we let you have pen and ink, it will be to a purpose. Your outdoor work is to continue. You have been sentenced to hard labour and there is to be no reprieve. You understand that?"

"I understand, sir."

"Very good. You may go. And watch how you go. No malingering now—and stay away from the boy."

"The boy?"

He glanced down at a paper on his desk. "There is a boy in E Ward who works in the gardens and as a cleaner on your ward."

"Tom?" I said. "E.1.1.?"

"You know his name and number? How do you know his name?"

"Everyone knows his name."

"You should not use his Christian name. Wipe it from your mind. Keep clear of him."

"He is an innocent child."

Major Nelson looked down again at the paper on his desk. "He is fifteen years of age and far from innocent." The governor looked up at me. "You would do well to remember that you were found guilty of gross indecency and sentenced to two years' imprisonment with hard labour on the evidence of boys who were no older than him when you first knew them. You have been observed with this boy." He picked up the paper he had before him. "You have been seen 'consorting' with him on more than one occasion."

"Who says so?" I cried. "This is untrue."

"Keep away from him. He is a bad lot. Here, under the very noses of the warders, he has been dealing in illicit tobacco, opiates, alcohol—God knows what. He is to be punished—and you must have no dealings with him of any kind. I am moving him to the stone-breaking yard."

"But the boy is sick," I protested.

"No, he is not."

"In the infirmary, I heard . . ." I faltered.

Major Nelson let fall the paper he was holding. "I have read Dr. Maurice's report. The boy is quite well now—fit enough to break stones for a day or two, I can assure you." The governor picked up the slim blue-bound volume from his desk and held it out towards me. "Go—and take the book."

That night, alone once more in my wretched cell, I felt the refusal to commute my sentence like a blow from a leaden sword. I lay awake, dazed with a dull sense of pain. I had fed on hope and now anguish grown hungry fed her fill on me as though she had been starved of her proper appetite. From that day's first, brief encounter with Major Nelson, and from his kindness towards me with the book, I recognised, with gratitude, that there were gentler elements in the evil prison air than before, but nonetheless I was where I was, and as I was, immured, broken, and disgraced. Prison life makes one see people and things as they really are and that is why it turns one to stone.

The next morning, when breakfast had been cleared and before chapel had been called, I stood crouching by the hatch in my cell door waiting to hear the girlish voice of Private Luck. At the very moment I expected him to speak, he spoke. "Good morning, my friend. Today I am planning to tell you of Vikram and the Vampire—it was a favourite tale of Sir Richard Burton in the good old days."

"Stop!" I hissed through the iron door. "Stop, Private Luck. Are you my friend? Are you?"

"Of course I am your friend," he answered indignantly. "I may be your only friend here, Mr. Oscar Wilde. I have killed another man for you—does that not show friendship?"

"Atitis-Snake, the poisoner, is to be tried for Warder Braddle's murder," I said.

"That is his story, Mr. Wilde, but we know the truth. It is our secret—and you will pay me my one hundred pounds. I know you will because you are a man of honour. You will give me an I-owe-you."

"This is madness," I cried. "Did you speak to the governor about me and the boy? Did you? Did you, Private Luck? Answer me."

It was a moment before Luck spoke—and then I had to strain to hear his whisper. "I know you want the boy, Mr. Wilde. I will do what I can for you, but it will not be easy. Things are not as they were once upon a time. It will be very expensive."

"I do not want the boy," I cried aloud, in desperation. "*I do not want the boy!* Do you hear me?"

"Everyone will hear you, Mr. Wilde. Take care."

"What have you told the governor? What have you said?"

"I have told him nothing, Mr. Wilde. I have said nothing. I have not seen the governor. I will keep your secret. You will pay me, Mr. Wilde, and I will stay silent as the grave."

18

Punishment

*T*he weeks passed.

In Reading Gaol, where the seasons run their course unnoticed, and in whose garden no bird is ever heard to sing, summer turned to autumn, slowly. Each morning, between breakfast and chapel, without fail, like grotesque parodies of Flute and Bottom playing Thisbe and Pyramus in a prisoners' production of *A Midsummer Night's Dream*, Private Luck and I whispered and called to one another through the wall between our cells. (Our conversations were a habit I could not break; Luck was a personality I could not fathom.) Each night, I lay awake on the wooden plank that was my bed, thinking of all that I had had and lost and knew that I would never have again.

In November I wrote again to the Home Secretary, pleading once more for my release. Even as I wrote I knew it was a futile exercise. Pity seems to beat in vain at the doors of officialdom. Power, no less than punishment, kills what else were good and gentle in a man: the man without knowing it loses his natural kindliness, or grows afraid of its exercise. I looked forward with horror to the prospect of another winter in prison: there is something terrible in it: one has to get up before daybreak and in the dark-cold cell begin one's work by the flaring gas-jet; through the small barred window only gloom seems to find an entrance; and days often go over without one's being once even in the open air: days on which one stifles: days that are endless in their dull monotony of apathy or despair.

That said, I must acknowledge that with the arrival of Major Nelson the atmosphere within the prison gradually changed—almost entirely for the better. Beyond my fear of Luck, and of what he might say and do, in every other respect, my lot improved. I was allowed more books—and spectacles with which to read them. I was permitted writing materials at all times in my cell. What I wrote would be removed each night before "lights out," but that did not trouble me. I could read Dante at my leisure and make excerpts and notes for the sheer pleasure of using pen and ink. (I read Dante every day, in Italian, and all through. It was his *Inferno* above all that I read. How could I help liking it? Hell, we were in it. Hell—even with Nelson at the helm—that was Reading Gaol.) I decided to take up the study of German. (Indeed, prison seems to me the proper place for such a study.)

I was invited to inspect the "prison library"—a single shelf containing an assortment of prayer books and religious texts, half a dozen sentimental novels, *The Pilgrim's Progress,* and an expurgated edition of the complete works of Shakespeare—and propose suitable additions. With assistance from the chaplain (now a regular visitor to my cell), I selected Milman's *The History of the Jews,* Farrar's *The Life and Work of St. Paul,* and Renan's *Life of Jesus* and *The Apostles.* The chaplain saw no objection to these last two, so long as they were in the original French. "Is French much spoken in the prison?" I asked. "Not at all," said the chaplain. I suggested the poems of Chaucer, Spenser, Keats, and Tennyson—and the governor agreed. I told Major Nelson that the existing library contained none of the novels of Thackeray or Dickens and suggested that a complete set of their works would be as great a boon to many among the other prisoners as it would be to myself. "Yes," he agreed, with a glint in his eye, "I think we can run to a cheap edition of the works of Dickens. Ten pounds is what the Prison Commission allows us to spend on recreational materials in a year. You may spend it all."

I spoke with the governor infrequently, but when I did, invariably he enquired about my reading—and my writing. I think the good man had hopes that I would prove a Victorian John Bunyan and that my "Ballad of Reading Gaol" would be the *Pilgrim's Progress de nos jours.*

I knew that I must write again—or try to do so—but I could not settle on a theme. From the window of my cell, on the eve of the execution of Charles Wooldridge, I had watched the executioner, just arrived at the prison, crossing the yard at a steady pace, wearing a pair of gardener's gloves and carrying a little bag. The picture of one man on his way to prepare for the death of another haunted me. I thought that might be the starting point for my prison ballad.

My hours of recreation were now spent profitably, reading poetry, writing notes, learning German. My hours of labour were spent in the garden at Reading Gaol, pushing my wheelbarrow, pulling up weeds, turning the earth, raking the gravel, brushing away leaves.

The tools of my gardener's trade—my barrow, broom, trowel, rake, and spade—were all stored in a small, square lean-to hut affixed to the side of one of the potting sheds. My supervising turnkey would unlock and lock the hut for me at the start and finish of each day's endeavour. Close by the hut, surrounded by a ridge of bricks, two feet high, was the garden's compost heap. Standing on the ridge, I could see across the garden wall to the adjacent yard where the prisoners assigned to the punishments of shot-drill and stone-breaking spent their days. My life was one of bucolic ease. Theirs was one of torture.

Shot-drill required the prisoner to lift a twenty-five-pound cannonball from the ground to his chest height, move it three paces to the left or right, and then set it down again. This task was performed repeatedly, continuously, for hours on end, with occasional minute-long breaks at the watching turnkey's discretion. Its only purpose was punitive. Stone-breaking, which took place alongside shot-drill, was an equally punishing exercise, but offered more variety: you could swing your pick from left or right. And a least there was some useful outcome to the stone-breaking: the broken stone was sold on to local builders.

On one occasion, out of idle curiosity, I stood balancing precariously on the brickwork ridge around the compost heap, and saw the boy, Tom, now capped and hooded like the adult prisoners, wielding his pick at the centre of the group of stone-breakers. As I watched him in dismay, I realised that, beyond him, the warder on the far side of the stone-breakers was standing, hands on hips, watching me. He blew his whistle. "Get down. Get down now," he shouted to me. As I obeyed on the instant, I noted, with relief, that he had not called me by my number or my name.

On another occasion, unobserved, I went over to the hut mid-afternoon. My supervising turnkey had seen me by the vegetable garden pushing my wheelbarrow and had ordered me to "stop malingering" and start pulling weeds. I had gone to fetch gloves and a trug for the purpose. As I pulled open the hut door, there was a sudden movement within—and a furtive, scrabbling sound. For a moment, forgetting where I was, I thought it might have been a dog or fox and started, startled. Almost at once, I realised it was not an animal at all, but the crouching figure of a child.

"For Christ's sake, Tom," I cried, "what are you doing huddled here?"

He made no answer, but shrank back into the darkness of the hut. "You can't stay here," I whispered. "They'll find you. You'll be whipped."

He could retreat no farther. He was squatting on all fours, squeezed between bags of peat, backed up against a wall of filthy sacking, his head jutting towards me. I reached out to touch his shoulder. "Tom," I said. His terror was palpable. He flinched as my hand reached towards him and threw up his arm to ward me off. As he did so, he tumbled forward and his cap fell to the ground. It was not Tom. It was the dwarf.

"It's you," I gasped.

Still he said nothing.

"Joseph Smith." I pulled off my cap. "We occupy adjacent cells. I am Oscar Wilde."

He looked up at me with terror in his eyes, cowering like a cornered animal.

"I will not harm you, but it's not safe here. A warder comes to lock the hut at night. They'll find you. You'll be beaten."

"I have been beaten before," he said. He spoke in a husky whisper. His eyes did not leave mine.

"That was in Warder Braddle's time," I said.

"He's dead," he rasped.

"Yes, you are safe from him now."

"I would not pleasure him," he whispered. "I would rather die."

"He is dead now," I said.

He held me with his haunting, haunted eyes. "I know."

"Are you on shot-drill?" I asked. "Are you in the next yard breaking stones? You've been excused to use the latrines—is that it? Is it?" He would not answer. "You can't escape," I counselled him. "You'd best go back." He said nothing more, but stared at me, fixedly, silently. I recognised fury as much as fear in his fierce gaze.

I picked up my gloves and trug and left him there. As I reached the corner of the vegetable garden, by the archway leading towards the main exercise yard, I turned back and saw him running along the path away from me, like a goblin in a fairy tale.

• • •

A week later he was taken to the landing on Ward B, strapped to the punishment block, and given a dozen strokes of the cat-o'-nine-tails. It was on the same day that we were told at chapel of the death of Prisoner C.3.1.

The flogging of the dwarf took place before supper, at the end of the working day. From my cell on C Ward I could not hear the crack of the flail, but I did hear the distant sounds of the little man shrieking in agony.

I sat at my table, gazing at my book without taking in a word. I listened out for my neighbour's return. He did not come. Instead, about half an hour after the beating, I heard brisk footsteps striding along the gantry. My cell door was thrown open—there was a new turnkey on duty determined to do nothing by halves. "Stand up, prisoner. Surgeon to see you."

Dr. Maurice stepped into my cell. "I have come to syringe your ears," he said.

I stood looking at him. His face was flushed. His temples shone with sweat. "Are you familiar with Dante's *Inferno?*" I asked, turning to him, my book in hand. *"Considerate la vostra semenza: fatti non foste a viver come bruti, ma per seguir virtute e canoscenza."*

"Italian is not my forte," he said, offering me a smile. He put down his bag on my table.

"'Consider the seed you spring from: you were not born to live as a brute, but to be a follower of virtue and knowledge.'"

"What's this about?" he asked, widening his eyes.

"You have just come from the flogging of that wretched dwarf," I cried.

"I attended the punishment, yes. With the governor. I did my duty."

"You are a *physician*, Doctor, a *healer*. How can you do your duty here?"

"You forget yourself, C.3.3.," he said quietly.

"Perhaps I do," I said. "The present prison system seems almost to have for its aim the wrecking and destruction of the mental faculties. Deprived of human intercourse, isolated from every humane and humanising influence, condemned to eternal silence, robbed of all contact with the outside world, treated like an unintelligent animal, brutalised below the level of any of the brute creation, the man confined in an English prison can hardly escape becoming insane."

"If you have finished your tirade, take a seat and let me examine your ear." The doctor spoke coolly, but without rancour. "You should not say these things. You should remember where you are—and with whom."

I sat in silence and let my head fall towards my left shoulder. The surgeon produced a small metal dish from his bag. "Hold this under your ear," he instructed. "The tip of the syringe will be cold, I warn you, and you will feel a strange sensation in your middle ear—like rushing water. And there will be some pain, I fear. But to a purpose."

"Thank you, Doctor," I murmured, doing as I was told. "Was the dwarf's punishment to a purpose, I wonder?"

"Yes," said Dr. Maurice, simply. "The prisoner had attempted to escape. He had done so before."

"To escape from Warder Braddle," I said, flinching as the doctor pressed the cold syringe into my ear.

"Warder Braddle is dead. That's no excuse. There is no excuse. Last time this happened, C.3.4. was given three days in the dark cell on bread and water."

"To what effect?"

"To no effect. So the beating was incvitable. He is a recalcitrant."

"He is a dwarf, Doctor."

"Indeed. And that is why I brought the beating to a halt. After eight strokes."

"What happened?"

"He became unconscious. They had used the wrong cat-o'-nine-tails on him. They had prepared a four-footer. Strictly correct according to the regulations—the prisoner is over sixteen—but wrong in this instance. C.3.4. is no bigger than a child. He's in the infirmary now. I trust he will have learned his lesson."

"If he lives." I flinched again as the steel point of the syringe penetrated deeper.

"He'll live," said the surgeon, looking over me.

"Who administered the punishment?" I asked.

"Warder Stokes. It was his first time with the cat."

"And he wanted to impress the new governor, no doubt."

"No doubt." A Niagara of sound suddenly engulfed my head. I cried out more in surprise than pain.

"Nearly done," said the doctor, lightly, "and clearly necessary. There may be some bleeding after this, but it will be superficial."

I closed my eyes, not inclined to see what horrors the surgeon was extracting from my middle ear. "Poor Warder Stokes," I went on, talking to distract myself. "He seems to be losing his charges one by one. C.3.5. is gone, C.3.1. is dead, C.3.4. has been beaten to a pulp. Shall I be next, do you think, Doctor? Or will it be Private Luck, next door?"

"C.3.4. has not been beaten to a pulp," said the surgeon sternly, removing the syringe and emptying its vile contents into the metal tray. "He will recover in a day or two."

"What killed C.3.1.?" I asked, my eyes still closed.

"He died of old age and emphysema. There is no mystery there."

"And what killed Warder Braddle?"

"A broken neck and a broken back. The fall killed him. That's not in doubt."

The surgeon took the metal tray from me and went to the corner of the cell to empty its contents into my slop bucket. I opened my eyes. "And the blisters on his face?" I enquired. "What do the blisters tell us?"

"I am not sure," he answered. He returned to the table and wrapped his syringe in a flannel cloth. "Do you have something with which to mop your ear?" he asked.

I smiled. "We are in Reading Gaol, doctor. We get our meals served to us in our cells, with a certain style, but we get no linen napkins, alas." He took the handkerchief from his breast pocket and gave it to me. "Thank you," I said. I held the handkerchief to my ear. The surgeon closed his bag. "When you are called to give evidence in the trial of Sebastian Atitis-Snake," I asked, "what will you say, Doctor?"

"Say?"

"Say about how Warder Braddle died."

"I shall say that it was the fall from the gantry that killed him. That's the truth, pure and simple."

"The truth . . . ," I began, but my ear ached and I had not the spirit to continue.

"I am done," said Dr. Maurice.

19

Secrets

*F*or the last several months of my time in Reading Gaol, I knew myself to be in contact with a new spirit working in the prison—a spirit that helped me beyond any possibility of expression in words. For the first year of my imprisonment I did nothing but wring my hands in impotent despair, and say, "What an ending, what an appalling ending!" Now, with the death of Warder Braddle and the arrival of Major Nelson, I would try to say to myself and (when not torturing myself! or not being tortured by the taunts of Private Luck) would really and sincerely say, "What a beginning, what a wonderful beginning! It may really be so . . . It may become so . . . If it does I shall owe much to this new personality that has altered every man's life in this place."

If I had been released when I had first petitioned the Home Secretary, I would have left Reading Gaol loathing it and every official in it with a bitterness of hatred that would have poisoned my life. But I had a year longer of imprisonment to endure and in that year I discovered a new humanity inside the prison alongside us all.

The English prison style is absolutely and entirely wrong. I would give anything to be able to alter it. But there is nothing in the world so wrong but that the spirit of humanity, which is the spirit of love, the spirit of the Christ who is not in churches, may make it, if not right, at least possible to be borne without too much bitterness of heart.

I recall how once, many years ago, as an undergraduate at university, I was required to fill in a census paper. I gave my age as nineteen, my profession as genius, and my infirmity as talent. I thought myself vastly amusing. And, no doubt, in my way, I was. But then, at Oxford, so free and young, I knew nothing. It took imprisonment in middle age for me to learn the simple truth that kindness is all.

I shall always remember the individual acts of kindness done to me in Reading Gaol. The afternoon when the prison surgeon gave me his own handkerchief to hold against my ear. The morning when the wardress with the lovely face (whose name I never knew) passed by me in the garden and smiled and went on her way, only to return a moment later to say, simply, "My mother has your book of fairy stories. It is her favourite book." The evening (it was the night before Christmas) when Warder Stokes brought a bag of toffees to my cell and told me I could have as many of them as I desired! He insisted that I take at least three. These tokens of tenderness were to me like minor miracles. And it was the presence in the prison of Major Nelson that made them possible.

In January 1897, in anticipation of my release in five

months' time, the governor gave me permission to let my hair grow long again. He encouraged me to write every day and gave me writing paper and a manuscript book for the purpose. He allowed me to order more books for the prison library and to be bolder in my choices. When I suggested that some of my fellow prisoners might enjoy *Treasure Island* by Robert Louis Stevenson, he said, "A good choice, C.3.3. And I am grateful to you for not proposing *Dr. Jekyll and Mr. Hyde* by the same author. There I would have had to draw the line."

He was a man of humanity and humour and imagination. As an experiment, he appointed me "book orderly" and told me that, at a set time each week, under supervision, I might visit certain convicts in their cells to provide them with books from the library and to encourage them to read. I undertook this new duty with enthusiasm, although on the whole, it must be said, my fellow prisoners (even those that could read) were not much interested in what the library or I had to offer.

As "book orderly," I went on my rounds with Warder Stokes, accompanying him as the prisoners' evening dish of skilly was being served. On my first outing, the first cells I visited were those of my immediate neighbours. It was an inauspicious start. Holding a small clutch of assorted volumes, I made to enter the first cell. The dwarf, squatting like a toad upon his bed, turned his angry mesmeriser's eyes upon me, and shouted, "Get out. Leave me be. Get out!"

"I have brought you books to read," I said. "*Oliver Twist, Treasure Island . . .*"

"Get out!" he cried, beating his tiny fists on the bed. "Let me die in peace."

I retreated at once, pulling the cell door to after me. Warder Stokes, working his way along the gantry with the skilly, laughed. "He's a little devil at times, isn't he? We've not managed to beat it out of him. You'll get a warmer welcome from the Indian princess. She seems to be expecting you."

I pushed open the door to cell C.3.2. Except for the few nights that I had spent in the prison infirmary and in the darkness of the punishment cells, I had spoken with Private A. A. Luck on each and every morning of my incarceration. I knew his curious voice so well. I also knew his particular way of walking. Every day we trudged, one before the other, five paces apart, in single file, on our way to morning chapel and to afternoon exercise. Luck was not tall—he was of average height—but, unlike so many of the inmates of Reading Gaol, he did not shuffle as he moved along: he walked with an easy step, without stooping, and always held his head up high. I knew the grace of his gait and the quaintness of his way of speaking, but I had not seen his face before. The moment that I did, I understood everything.

He stood at the far end of his cell, beneath his window—as if he were posing there, awaiting my arrival. There was no light from the window, of course (it was early evening at the end of January), but in the flickering glow of the gas-jets on the wall I could see well enough. Private Luck turned his face towards me as I entered: his cheeks were daubed with rouge; his lips were painted scarlet; his eyelids were coloured green as emeralds.

"We will draw the curtain and show you the picture," he said, throwing the cap that he was holding onto the bed and tossing his head coquettishly. "Look you, sir," he giggled, "such a one as I was this present. Is't not well done?"

"Excellently done, if God did all," I answered.

"'Tis in grain, sir; 'twill endure wind and weather . . ." He turned his head to one side to show off his profile. He giggled some more. "I played Olivia when Sir Richard Burton produced *Twelfth Night* at the embassy in Trieste," he explained in his fluting voice. "He played the Count Orsino. He was far too old for the part, but he was still handsome. He was a swordsman to the last. In every sense." He stifled more laughter, holding his hands up to his face.

I stepped towards him. "Your hands are brown," I said, "but your neck is white, your *skin* is white . . ."

"All our hands are brown here," he replied, looking at them in disgust. "It is the wind and the rain. And the work they make us do." He turned his gaze on me and fluttered his emerald eyelids. "But, yes, my skin is white and smooth as alabaster." He pulled up the sleeve of his shirt to reveal a slim wrist and a pale forearm. "I am only half Indian."

"Your mother was Indian?" I asked.

"Yes, my lovely mother was Indian. My father was British. Very much so. And a bugger, like you, Mr. Oscar Wilde." He laughed. I said nothing. What could I say? "Warder Stokes told me that you were coming to see me today."

"Good," I answered.

"Have you brought me my I-owe-you? It is one hundred pounds that you owe me—and more if I am to keep all your secrets."

"I cannot pay you one hundred pounds," I said. "You must know that."

"Not now, I know, but in five months—when we are released. We are released at the same time, you know. You will pay me then, Mr. Wilde."

"I cannot."

"If I am to keep your secrets, then you must. The boy may not talk, but I will. I would have my bond. Have you brought the I-owe-you?"

"I have brought you some books," I said, showing him the handful of volumes that I was holding.

"I cannot read," he said, petulantly.

"But you told me that you read the *Daily Chronicle*."

"Warder Braddle brought me the *Daily Chronicle*. He read to me from it." Luck twisted his head away from me sharply. "I cannot read," he repeated.

"But you know Shakespeare," I protested. "And you know the Kama Sutra!"

He turned back and looked into my eyes. "By heart. I learnt what I know by heart. Sir Richard taught me the words. I repeated them for him."

I put down my books on his table. "I see what you are," I said. "I should have guessed at once—when you told me your names."

"What do you mean?" He narrowed his eyes, but kept them turned towards me.

"Achindra Acala—they are Sanskrit names, are they not?"

"Yes."

"And they are unusual because they are names that can be given to girls as well as to boys."

"Yes."

I smiled at Private A. A. Luck, late of the Bombay Grenadiers. "You are a *hijra,* are you not?"

He returned my smile and brought his hands together in front of his chin. "Yes, Mr. Wilde, I am a eunuch." He bobbed a curtsy.

"I should have guessed before," I said.

"My mother had me castrated when I was just a baby. She thought it best."

I looked at this absurd figure, with his crudely painted face, posturing before me in his prison garb stamped with black arrows. "Was she right?" I asked.

"She knew what you British men really like." He giggled again and clapped his hands together coyly. "She gave me a way of life. She gave me a means to earn my living. It was a happy way of life. It was a good living."

"While it lasted," I said.

"It would have lasted longer, much longer. Sir Richard Burton loved me very much."

"But Lady Burton did not?"

"She did not understand. She was stupid—and vile. When Sir Richard died, she found a Catholic priest to give him the last rites. But Sir Richard was already dead! He died in my arms. And he was not a Catholic. Sir Richard Burton was very much not a Catholic, I promise you."

"But he was Lady Burton's husband and she loved him."

"That woman is the devil. She does not know what love means. She burnt all his papers—his journal, his beautiful book all about me, his new translation of *The Perfumed Garden* . . . She was offered six thousand guineas for his manuscripts—six thousand guineas! And she burnt them all. She said it was his spirit that had instructed her. She was a madwoman. I am glad she is dead."

"She is dead? When did she die?"

"A year ago. Warder Braddle brought me the good news. It was in all the papers." Private Luck suddenly raised his arms above his head as if adopting the pose of Ellen Terry as Lady Macbeth in Sargent's celebrated portrait. "If she had not died, I vow I would have killed her."

I did not laugh: the man seemed so much in earnest. "It is because of Lady Burton that you are here?" I asked.

He lowered his arms and looked at me intently. "Yes, Mr. Oscar Wilde. I am like you—in prison for what I am. I helped Lady Burton bring Sir Richard's body back to England from Trieste. I organised it—coffin and all. Very complicated. And then, as soon as we had arrived in London, she threw me out of the house and betrayed me to the police."

"Why? What provoked her?"

"She did not want me at his funeral."

"But why did she go to the police?"

"Revenge!" he cried dramatically, adopting his Lady Macbeth pose once more.

"I understand," I said gently. "But what was the precise nature of your alleged offence?"

"I loved her husband and he loved me."

"Is that what Lady Burton told the police?"

Private Luck put his hands on his hips and laughed. "No, no. Of course not. She never mentioned her husband to the police. She did not need to. She simply told the police that I am *hijra*."

"And that is a crime?"

"Yes, according to the Criminal Tribes Act of 1871. Did you not know?"

"I fear that the Criminal Tribes Act is a piece of legislation that passed me by. I was only seventeen in 1871 and politics was never my forte."

"This is no laughing matter, Mr. Oscar Wilde," said Luck reprovingly. "According to this Act of Parliament, we are outlaws."

"I did not know that."

"Oh, yes, because we *hijra* dress as ladies, it is a breach of public decency. The Governor-General of India wanted to stop the rot. He called us 'the third sex' and accused us of corrupting every Englishman in India with our filthy habits. He insisted on this law."

"Ah." I smiled. "You were bringing the British Empire to its knees."

Private Luck clapped his hands delightedly. "That is exactly Sir Richard Burton's joke. That is exactly the words he used. You are very like him, Mr. Wilde. And you have a wife, too."

"Yes," I said, "I have a wife."

"And she will pay me to keep your secrets. I know she will."

"Did you ask Lady Burton for money?"

"Of course," he said defiantly, "I must be paid. When Sir Richard was alive, he paid me. He looked after me. He protected me. He would have wanted Lady Burton to look after me when he died, but she would not do so. I asked her for a proper pension. She said no. She threw me out and she sent all my beautiful saris to the police—and photographs."

"Photographs?"

"Lovely photographs of me that Sir Richard had taken with his camera."

"And the police arrested you?"

"Of course."

"And you were sent for trial—accused of a breach of public decency under this Criminal Tribes Act?"

"Yes."

"And blackmail? Were you also charged with attempted blackmail?"

Private Luck waved his hands about in the air. "They said all sorts of things—I do not remember." He paused and looked directly at me. His eyelids were green and gay, yet his eyes were brown and mournful. "But is it a crime to give pleasure, Mr. Wilde? Is it a crime, if you are poor, to want to be paid for it?"

"Is that what you told the court?" I asked.

"I told the court the truth."

I smiled. "They must have found that quite disconcerting."

"They did not want to hear it. My barrister told me to plead guilty. He said that is what Sir Richard would have wanted. He said it would save everybody a lot of time."

"Given my own experience," I said, "I think perhaps your barrister was right. When the world is against you, it is sometimes best not to argue."

"That is true, Mr. Wilde—and all's well that ends well, as our good friend Shakespeare tells us. Lady Burton threw me out of the house, but a better lady took me in. Now it is Her Majesty the Queen who gives me my board and lodging."

He looked around his bare cell with what seemed like unfeigned satisfaction. I glanced down at the cold dish of skilly that sat upon his table. "You are content here?" I asked.

"I have found friends in Reading Gaol," he said, lowering his eyelids demurely.

"Warder Braddle was your special friend," I suggested.

"Yes," he said simply.

"You pleased him—in your way. And he looked after you—in his."

"Until I had to kill him for you, Mr. Wilde."

I sighed and shook my head. He pushed his painted face towards me and hissed: "You must give me my I-owe-you. I will have my money. Or I will tell everybody about you and the boy."

"I will deny it," I protested.

He stood back and laughed. "And who will they believe, Mr. Oscar Wilde—you or me?"

20

Warder Martin

*E*very morning, between breakfast and chapel muster, through the cracks around the hatches in the doors to our cells, I continued to have my daily "chinwag" with Private Achindra Acala Luck, late of the Bombay Grenadiers. I could not break myself of the habit.

My feelings regarding Private Luck were mixed—decidedly so. He alarmed me: he made his demands for his wretched I-owe-you on an almost daily basis and his accompanying threats became ever less charming and more lurid. I went on speaking with him in the belief that so long as we were in direct contact I could in some way contain him. He intrigued me: his stories of growing up among the *hijra* of Kakamuchee were fascinating. He had been given to the *hijra* community by his mother when he was a baby. The other boys had either been stolen from their families or abandoned by them. Luck insisted that his childhood had been a wholly happy one. "We were a band of brothers, who became sisters," he said. "I have always loved the eunuch's life. I am a man who dresses as a lady, but is neither one nor the other. I like to be different. I like to be special. When I joined the Bombay Grenadiers, I was one of a kind, believe you me." He amused me: he gave wonderful accounts of the *hijra* mastery of the mysteries of the arts of love. He told tales deliberately to arouse me. And, in Reading Gaol in the hard spring of 1897, I was grateful for that.

I did not see him face-to-face again, but I learned from our conversations that, beneath his cap, he wore his elaborate ladies' make-up every day. "The cap is like the veil of a sari," he explained. "Whenever we are outside our cells our faces are hidden, so I can paint mine as I please. I do it from memory because I have no looking-glass." The make-up sticks he used had been supplied to him by Warder Braddle—as a thank-you present for services rendered. They were sticks of theatrical greasepaint bought by Braddle, specially, from Herr Ludwig Leichner's shop in Covent Garden. Luck kept them secreted between the plank that was the base of his bed and the metal frame of his bedstead. The other warders knew of his painted face, of course, and mocked it, but so long as Luck did not attempt to flaunt his femininity outside his cell, they let him be. They called him the Indian princess.

The presence of the painted Private Luck in the cell adjacent to my own brought me moments of distraction and hours of anxiety. I feared what he might say, however unfounded, and to whom he might say it and when. I had nothing left in the world but one thing. Through my own folly and indulgence I had lost my name, my position, my happiness, my freedom, my wealth. I was a prisoner and a pauper. But I still had my children left. I was a good father to my children. I love them dearly and was dearly loved by them. I knew that one further whiff of scandal—let alone a direct charge of unnatural vice—and I should never be permitted to see either of my boys again.

In February 1897 my wife's solicitor came to see me in Reading Gaol. He brought with him legal papers that I had no option but to sign. In return for the promise of a modest allowance after my release, I agreed to the handing over of the custody of my children to my wife and a male member of her family. The documents I signed contained a clause to the effect that the promised allowance would be cut off completely should I, after my release, make any attempt to visit my children without their guardians' permission or should I live in any way "notoriously." That the law could decide that I was one unfit to be with my own children was something quite horrible to me. The disgrace of prison was nothing compared with it. I envied the men who trod the prison yard with me. I was sure that their children waited for them beyond the prison walls. I knew that Private Luck had it within his power to keep my children from me for ever.

In the end, I believe, I bore up against everything by learning to accept everything. I lived in the shadow of Luck's threats: I had no choice. My ear ached: I endured the discomfort. The Home Secretary ignored my petitions: it was his prerogative to do so.

And with acceptance came reward. Towards the end of February, I made a wonderful new friend in Reading Gaol. His name was Warder Martin and the kindnesses he showed to me, and to other poor, sad creatures in the prison, mark him out as one of the unsung saints of this world. He was young and rough, ill favoured and ill spoken, but he had a heart of gold. Warder Stokes was friendly enough (and his crooked teeth and freckled face were endearing), but he was always careful to keep a proper distance from the prisoners in his charge and he never broke the rules. Warder Martin was less handsome, but, bless him, he broke the rules on my behalf almost every day. When I was hungry he brought me ginger biscuits. When I was poorly he brought me boiling beef tea—hiding the bottle in which he was carrying it to my cell inside his jacket and scalding his chest in the process. Best of all, whenever he was able, he brought me a copy of the *Daily Chronicle.*

As we all know, the public have an insatiable curiosity to know everything, except what is worth knowing, and journalism, conscious of this, and having tradesman-like habits, supplies their demands. In centuries before ours, the public nailed the ears of journalists to the pump. In this century, journalists have nailed their own ears to the keyhole. As a consequence, the newspapers today chronicle with degrading avidity the sins of the second-rate, and with the conscientiousness of the illiterate, give us accurate and prosaic details of the doings of people of absolutely no interest whatever. I despise journalists: they always apologise to one in private for what they have written against one in public. And I am not much more enamoured of leader writers. (After all, what is behind the leading article but prejudice, stupidity, cant, and twaddle?) Nevertheless, after twenty months without seeing a newspaper of any kind, whenever Warder Martin brought it to me, I *devoured* the *Daily Chronicle*.

I was relieved to find that Victoria was still Queen and not surprised to discover that Lord Salisbury was still Prime Minister. I was interested to read that there was a new Archbishop of Canterbury (a churchman who gloried in the name of Temple) and happy to learn that my friend Arthur Conan Doyle had published a new novel—featuring, not Sherlock Holmes, but the Prince Regent and Beau Brummell. I also consumed (with a glee bordering on the shaming) accounts of death and divorce and disaster. In London, the dear Duchess of Bolton had succumbed to a fever; in Paris, Marcel Proust was rumoured to have taken part in a duel; in the United States of America, a meteorite had fallen on West Virginia. And at Reading Assizes, I read, one Sebastian Atitis-Snake, thirty-nine, was on trial for his life, charged with the murder of a long-serving and much-respected prison warder at Reading Gaol, "where the accused had been serving as a prisoner alongside the disgraced poet and playwright Oscar Wilde."

According to the newspaper, between his arrest at Reading Gaol and his trial at Reading Assizes, Atitis-Snake had been held at the Broadmoor Criminal Lunatic Asylum in Crowthorne, Berkshire, where his "condition was closely observed over a period of many weeks" in order to assess both his "fitness for trial" and "the state of his mind."

Atitis-Snake admitted that he had been responsible for the death of the warder at Reading Gaol, but pleaded "not guilty by reason of insanity." He told the court that as a young man he had developed a fascination with the life and achievements of the Emperor Napoleon of France and that, at certain periods of his life, he had become convinced that he was the reincarnation of the late Emperor. At Reading Gaol, however, associating with criminals for the first time in his life, his fixation with Bonaparte had mutated into a belief that he was not, in fact, the Napoleon of France, but the so-called Napoleon of crime, Professor Moriarty, the character created by Arthur Conan Doyle as the nemesis of his most celebrated creation, Sherlock Holmes. Atitis-Snake maintained that he had flung the unfortunate prison warder from the gantry outside his cell in a "moment of madness" in which he believed himself to be Moriarty locked in a life-or-death struggle with Holmes at the Reichenbach Falls at Meiringen in Switzerland. Atitis-Snake bore no malice towards the warder. He claimed that he barely knew the man. He had merely been enacting the scene depicted by Dr. Conan Doyle in his story "The Final Problem," which Atitis-Snake had first read in the *Strand Magazine* on its publication in December 1893.

Only four witnesses were called to give evidence at the trial. Two were medical men of some standing who had examined the accused during his sojourn at the Broadmoor asylum and had detected "no signs whatsoever" of "any recognised mental illness or condition." Dr. O. C. Maurice, the surgeon at Reading Gaol, who had examined the victim's body immediately after his fall and signed the death certificate, confirmed that it was the impact of the fall that was the cause of death. Colonel Henry Isaacson, the governor of Reading Gaol at the time of the incident, reported that there had been no witnesses to the attack and that Warder

Braddle was an officer of good character and long service. There was no reason to suppose that the warder's fall had been anything other than a tragic accident until the accused had come forward to admit that he had been the warder's assassin.

The death of Warder Braddle at Reading Gaol had occurred on Wednesday, 19 February 1896. Sebastian Atitis-Snake had owned up to the killing on Tuesday, 7 July, more than four months later. The judge, Mr. Justice Crawford, seventy-one, asked Colonel Isaacson if he had any idea why the accused had waited so long to make his confession. Colonel Isaacson said that he had asked the accused that very question and received no very satisfactory answer. Colonel Isaacson noted, however, that Atitis-Snake had applied for his interview with the governor just an hour after the execution had taken place at Reading Gaol of another murderer, one Charles Wooldridge, a private soldier who had been sentenced to death for the murder of his wife. "In my experience," said Colonel Isaacson, "an execution concentrates the mind of each and every individual in a prison on the day that it takes place. Trooper Wooldridge, consumed with guilt at the murder that he had committed, had given himself up to the police voluntarily and confessed his crime. It is possible that Wooldridge's execution prompted Atitis-Snake to do the same."

"When you interviewed the accused on the seventh of July," asked the judge, "did he tell you that he believed that he had killed Warder Braddle in 'a moment of madness'?"

"I think the phrase that he used was 'a fit of madness.' As I recall, he said that Warder Braddle had come to his cell in the normal way, as any warder might going about his duties, and that he had seized him on the spur of the moment and 'in a fit of madness' had manhandled him out of the cell and onto the gantry, where he had pushed him over the gantry balustrade. He said little more than that."

"Did he say what prompted this 'fit of madness'?"

"No."

"Did he mention this story of the Reichenbach Falls and the struggle between Sherlock Holmes and Professor Moriarty?"

"No."

"Did Atitis-Snake then, or at any time when he was a prisoner in your charge at Reading Gaol, give the impression that he was a man prone to suffering from delusions or from any other form of mental instability or insanity?"

"None whatsoever."

"Was he prone to violence?"

"Inside the prison?"

"Yes—inside the prison."

"Most prisoners are liable to display occasional bursts of anger or frustration. Atitis-Snake was no exception, but he was not notably violent and, so far as I can recollect, had not infringed any of the prison regulations to the extent that would have warranted punishment."

The trial of Sebastian Atitis-Snake for the murder of Warder Braddle lasted two days. During it no mention was made of the accused's earlier conviction for the attempted murder of his wife. At the end of it, the jury took no more than a matter of minutes to find the prisoner guilty.

According to the *Daily Chronicle,* "gasps were heard

throughout the courtroom" when the judge, in passing sentence, revealed that Atitis-Snake had appeared before him on a previous occasion on a charge of attempted murder and that this earlier conviction was, in fact, the reason that he had been a prisoner at Reading Gaol. Mr. Justice Crawford, placing the traditional black cap upon his head, said: "A crime such as murder is denounced both by God and man. Prisoner at the bar, you have been convicted of a brutal murder carried out in cold blood. It has been established beyond doubt that you are a ruthless killer in full possession of his wits. Your fanciful story of being possessed by the spirit of the fictional character of Professor Moriarty was all too cunningly thought through. You are entirely sane and wholly responsible for your own actions. It is my responsibility to ensure that you commit no further acts of murder and I do so now. The court doth order you, Sebastian Atitis-Snake, to be taken from hence to the place from whence you came, and thence to the place of execution, and that you then be hanged by the neck until you are dead, and that your body be afterwards buried within the precincts of the prison in which you shall be confined after your conviction. And may the Lord in his infinite mercy have compassion on your immortal soul."

As the sentence was passed, Sebastian Atitis-Snake inclined his head towards the judge in courteous acknowledgement. In the words of the reporter from the *Daily Chronicle:* "The guilty man appeared to smile at the prospect of the gallows."

21

The Condemned Man

I learnt of Atitis-Snake's return to Reading Gaol from the Reverend M. T. Friend. The chaplain was now all too frequent a visitor to my little cell. Since the day when he had urged me not to let my mind "dwell upon the clouds, but on Him who is above the clouds" and I had bundled him unceremoniously out onto the gantry, I had done my best to show the insistent clergyman some civility. I realised that he was not a bad man, merely a dull one—which, of course, is far worse. He visited me each week, usually on a Wednesday, and invariably brought with him a text that he hoped might form the basis of what he termed "a spiritually renewing conversation." I tried to explain to him that, while I was ready to admire Christ above all other men, it was with Christ's church that I had a problem. "I understand," he said earnestly, but I knew that he did not.

On this particular Wednesday—14 April 1897—I had steeled myself for his visitation. I expected the priest to be at his most platitudinous: it was the Wednesday before Easter. In the event, the Reverend Friend took me by surprise. When he appeared at my cell door, he looked different: he looked *interesting*. He was a lightly built man of about sixty, with thinning grey hair and a featureless face, smoother than you would expect in a man of his years. Customarily, his skin was pale and putty-like. Today, his face was flushed and animated. He appeared oddly alive—and excited.

"It is Holy Wednesday," he announced as he came into the cell. He carried a small case in one hand and a prayer book in the other.

"It is Spy Wednesday," I replied, "the day on which Judas Iscariot betrayed Our Lord for thirty pieces of silver."

"Do you know where Our Lord was that Wednesday?" he asked. "At the moment of His betrayal?" He bustled towards me, holding up his prayer book as he approached.

"Yes," I answered, "at Bethany, at the house of Simon the Leper." I stood and offered the chaplain my chair. "Welcome to my house, Padre," I said, smiling.

He took the seat, gratefully, and, as he did so, he looked up at me with unexpectedly gleaming eyes. "Thank you, C.3.3.," he said. "You have been meditating on Judas's cowardly betrayal of Our Lord?" he asked.

"Yes," I answered truthfully, "and on the death of Trooper Wooldridge."

"Ah yes . . . Wooldridge." The chaplain sighed and shook his head sorrowfully. He placed his case on the ground beside my table. "A hanging in the prison touches every one of us." He studied me enquiringly. "And why were you thinking of Judas and Wooldridge at one and the same time?"

"Judas betrayed Jesus, though he loved him. Wooldridge murdered his wife, though he loved her. Each man kills the thing he loves . . . It is curious, is it not, Father?"

"The coward does it with a kiss," said the clergyman.

"And the soldier with a cut-throat razor."

The Reverend Friend ran his tongue over his lips to moisten them. "You have been expecting me?" he asked.

"Yes," I answered.

"I am glad. I have been looking forward to our time together." He began to leaf through the prayer book. "I have prepared our reading." He found the page he was seeking. "I was delayed unexpectedly," he added, apologetically.

"You have your duties, I know," I said ingratiatingly.

"Yes, indeed." He nodded. "I am interested that you have been reflecting on the hanging of the prisoner Wooldridge. I have just now come from giving communion to another condemned man."

"Here?"

"In the condemned cell. He will be kept in close confinement until his time comes. He cannot attend chapel, of course, so I must go to him." He indicated the small case he had placed beside the table. "I have a portable communion set for the purpose. It was given me by my parents on the day of my ordination."

"This is Sebastian Atitis-Snake?" I asked. "He has returned?" (It was the first that I had heard of it.)

"Yes, he arrived last night. The poor man has been sent back to us for his execution. A bitter business." The chaplain threw back his head and briefly closed his eyes.

"You do not approve of hanging?" I enquired, somewhat surprised.

"It is barbaric," said the clergyman, looking at me sharply. His eyes were bulbous and rimmed with tears. "'An eye for an eye' is the philosophy of the Old Testament. Christ died on Good Friday to redeem us from our sins."

"Yes," I said, "you are right, Father." I sat on the edge of my bed and looked at him. I was startled to find myself suddenly in sympathy with this pedestrian clergyman with the whining voice. "When is the hanging due to take place?"

"Within the month—unless there is an appeal or a plea for clemency, which I doubt there will be. Atitis-Snake has killed before."

"I know," I said.

The chaplain looked at me. "You know his story?"

"His first trial took place at the same time as my own," I explained. "I read about it in the newspapers. 'The Napoleon Poisoner.'"

"His life was spared on that occasion—though the unfortunate wife he sought to kill was entirely blameless." The chaplain sighed. "On this occasion the judge showed no mercy."

"Though Warder Braddle was far from blameless?"

The chaplain gripped the sides of the prayer book. "'If a man also lie with mankind, as he lieth with a woman, both of them have committed an abomination: they shall surely be put to death; their blood shall be upon them.' Leviticus, chapter twenty, verse thirteen."

"Is that to be our text for today, Father?" I asked, raising an eyebrow.

"No," muttered the hapless cleric, his face turning scarlet. He looked at me in a state of confusion. "I was not thinking of you, C.3.3.," he stammered.

"I understand, Father," I said. "Warder Braddle was a wicked man—and not only in your eyes."

"He was an abomination," murmured the chaplain. Suddenly, he sat up and took a deep breath, and smiled at me, as if to indicate that he was himself again. He reached into his coat pocket and found a handkerchief. He wiped his brow and blew his nose. "Let us not speak ill of the dead," he said sonorously. "And let us not forget the Sixth Commandment: 'Thou shalt do no murder.' Mr. Braddle was a prison warder of many years' standing. Atitis-Snake admitted the unlawful killing and the defence he offered was risible. I fear the sentence the judge passed was inevitable."

"You have just come from Atitis-Snake's cell?"

"Yes."

"And how does he seem in the face of death?" I asked.

The chaplain breathed deeply. "It is a terrible prospect, but he appears resigned. Calm. Almost serene."

"Is he remorseful?" I asked.

"I believe so," answered the chaplain eagerly. "He requested the blessed sacrament. I felt his need was urgent. He is seeking absolution."

I smiled. "As are we all, Father," I said.

"Are we?" demanded the clergyman, his eyes shining, his skin glistening. He turned his head to heaven and gazed up at the ceiling of my cell. It was peppered with drops of condensation.

"The walls weep in this prison," I said.

"'Out of the depths have I cried unto Thee, O Lord; Lord, hear my voice: let Thine ears be attentive to the voice of my supplications.' Our redeemer waiteth, C.3.3. Let us pray together now."

I had not the heart not to indulge him. I sat at his side while, in his plaintive, monotonous voice, he intoned psalms and responses, and offered up loud prayers to the Almighty. When he was done, he appeared utterly exhausted by the experience.

"I trust you are refreshed, my son," he rasped, his voice drained of life. He took a deep breath and closed his prayer book. "I must be about my duties. C.3.4. is in the depths of despair, I fear."

"Do you have a text ready for him?" I asked.

"'Despair is the damp of hell, as joy is the serenity of heaven.'"

"John Donne," I said, smiling. "I know it—though how the dwarf will receive it I cannot say. He certainly is singularly miserable for a man who worked in a circus."

The chaplain, now obviously exhausted, got to his feet slowly. "At least C.3.4. will admit me. C.3.2. will not let me beyond his door. He is a Hindu or a Buddhist or some such."

"Yes, Father, you told me. I remember."

When the chaplain reached the door of my cell he stood for a moment, gathering his strength and gazing at me with tear-filled eyes. "Good-bye, C.3.3.," he said, making the sign of the cross.

"I think you will go over to Rome at the last, Padre," I

said. "As I think I may myself. The Catholic Church is for saints and sinners alone. For respectable people the Anglican Church will do."

"You are amusing, C.3.3.," answered the Reverend Friend, smiling beneficently, "and that is a gift of God."

They were kind parting words and, as it turned out, they were the last words he spoke to me. When he left my cell, I heard him enter the cell next door. I heard him say something to the dwarf as he entered and then—though I stood close to my door listening—for a minute or so I heard nothing, until, suddenly, through the wall came the noise of a fight: bodies tussling violently, the voice of a man calling frantically for assistance, then shrieking in desperation. The cries were accompanied by the dreadful sounds of violence—furniture crashing to the ground followed by the insistent thud of pounding fists and kicking boots.

It lasted only moments, but by the time that Warder Stokes and Warder Martin had reached the dwarf's cell, the chaplain was already dead.

22

Aftermath

I can only picture what happened next. I did not see it. I only heard it as I stood with my ear pressed to the cold iron of my cell door.

The assault was over by the time the warders reached the dwarf's cell. I heard Warder Stokes cry, "My God, he's dead," and then I heard what sounded like the crack of a whip, followed by the screeching and squealing of a stuck pig. I heard a third warder arrive and then a fourth, and perhaps one more. The voices were now subdued, but I caught stray words and phrases, enough to understand that the chaplain's body was to be moved by stretcher to the morgue—the surgeon would see it there—while the dwarf would be left in his cell.

The whole episode—from the moment when the Reverend Friend left my cell to the moment when his broken body was taken from the cell next to mine and borne by stretcher to the prison morgue—lasted no more than twenty minutes. When it was over, when the hubbub had subsided and I sensed there were no turnkeys left lurking on the gantry, I stood at the left side of my door and called out to the dwarf. "C.3.4. . . . C.3.4.—Joseph Smith, are you there?" But answer came there none.

Two and a half hours later, as the clock beyond the prison walls was striking eight, I was marched along the silent corridors and passageways of Reading Gaol towards the governor's office. Warder Martin was my guard. "Governor wants to see you," was all he had said as he unlocked my cell door. I waited until we were away from the cells and beyond the range of other warders before I spoke.

"Why am I being taken to the governor?" I whispered from beneath my mask.

"You're a witness. You was the last to see the reverend alive."

"He's dead, then?" I said softly, properly registering the reality of what had occurred for the first time.

"Oh, yes," muttered Martin, with a grim chuckle. "There's no doubt about that. You should 'ave seen the poor old boy. That little man kicked 'im to death. 'E was as lifeless as a rag doll."

"Did you beat him?" I asked, turning my capped head towards the warder. "I thought I heard the crack of a whip."

"Warder Stokes struck 'im with a towel—across the face. That's what you've got to do with 'ysterics."

"Is it? I did not know."

"Oh yes."

Warder Martin seemed strangely unperturbed by the evening's events. The awful alchemy of prison life transforms sheer horror into something commonplace. "And then we put on the 'andcuffs," he continued cheerfully. "The surgeon'll put 'im in a jacket later, I don't doubt—before they sends 'im off to Bedlam. 'E's a wild thing, that little man."

"Where are we going?" I asked. We had taken an unexpected turning. Instead of going along the corridor towards the stairs leading to the governor's office and the visiting magistrates' room, Warder Martin had marched us beneath the stone archway that leads to the prison's outer courtyard.

"You're going to the governor's 'ouse. You're honoured, C.3.3."

As we crossed the courtyard, on the far side of it, by the opening that leads towards D Ward, I saw a trio of boys walking past, accompanied by the comely wardress. It was dark now; I only saw their silhouettes; but the boy, Tom, seemed to be among them. I had not seen him for several weeks. He looked taller than I remembered. As I stared at him, he turned and looked at me.

"They're out late," I said.

"Punishment," answered Warder Martin. "They've been sluicing out the latrines. The governor won't 'ave 'em beaten 'cos of their age, so they gets these little extra duties. Latrines before lights out."

In the gloom I could see Warder Martin smiling. It was not a vicious smile, nor even a cruel smirk. It was a simple acknowledgement of the way of the world at Reading Gaol.

We reached the steps of the castellated turret that is the home of the prison governor. Warder Martin, with a touch of braggadocio, pulled on the bell. "I've not been 'ere before," he said.

"Nor I," I said. "I forgot to pack my evening clothes, so I hope the governor's not expecting us to dine."

The heavy door—made of black oak panels studded with iron nails—swung slowly open. I sensed that both Martin and I anticipated an old retainer plucked from the pages of a Gothic novel. If so, we were disappointed. Dr. Maurice, in waistcoat and shirtsleeves, stood on the threshold. The prison surgeon was wearing his spectacles once more, I noticed, and smoking a cigarette.

"It is the butler's night off," I murmured.

"Remember where you are, C.3.3.," rebuked the doctor. He beckoned me into the hallway and nodded to Martin. "Thank you, Warder. Wait here while the governor sees the prisoner. He'll not be long."

With a bony knuckle the doctor knocked lightly on the door immediately to the right of the front door and, without waiting for an answer, took me into a small gas-lit parlour where the governor stood by the fireplace with his back to us.

"Take off your cap," ordered the doctor. "Remember where you are," he repeated.

I did as I was commanded and glanced around the room. It was small, bare, and comfortless. It was a front parlour, evidently, but beyond a rough Turkish rug on the grey stone floor and a plain wooden mantelpiece above an empty grate, it was bereft of both furniture and decoration.

The governor swung round on his heels. He was dressed for dinner, in regimental mess kit, sporting his decorations and smoking a small cigar. His black hair stood to attention, shiny like a bearskin. In the gloom of the ill-lit chamber, his lined face looked wan and weary. He smiled at me grimly.

"They are dying all around you, C.3.3.," he said. "What's going on?"

"What do you mean, sir?"

"The surgeon tells me you'll know all about it."

I looked round towards Dr. Maurice. He was standing behind me, resting his long back against the parlour door. He nodded, as though encouraging me to speak, and drew on his cigarette.

"I do not understand, sir," I said.

"The doctor tells me that you and he have a mutual acquaintance—'the great Arthur Conan Doyle,' the celebrated creator of the 'gentleman detective,' Sherlock Holmes."

"I knew Dr. Conan Doyle," I said, "in younger and happier days."

"According to Dr. Maurice, you more than knew him—*you* were the Holmes to his Watson! You unravelled mysteries together—real ones. You solved crimes, side by side—and all by means of keen observation and careful consideration. You saw, you pondered, you cracked the nut." He puffed on his little cigar and looked at me beadily. "Well, what do you say?"

I said nothing. I was uncertain what to say.

"I have read your story, 'Lord Arthur Savile's Crime,'" he went on, lifting himself up onto his toes as he spoke. "You clearly have a feeling for this kind of thing. Detection is your *métier manqué*, it seems." He pulled a half-hunter out of his waistcoat pocket and checked the time. He shook his head and looked at me again, raising his eyebrows enquiringly. "So, what's been going on?"

"I really know nothing, sir," I protested.

"We'll be the judges of that," said Major Nelson, turning to the fireplace and throwing the remains of his cigar into the grate. "I am dining with Mr. Palmer tonight—or I hope to be. His bakery is next to the prison, you know."

"Mr. Palmer of Huntley and Palmers?"

"The same. He tells me that you and he were involved in unravelling a mystery a year or two ago. The police got nowhere, but you solved it—according to Palmer."

"I recall the adventure," I said, half smiling. "It afforded me my first visit to Reading." As I spoke I looked down and caught sight of the grotesque black arrows printed on my prison uniform. "My wife and Mr. Palmer's family are friends. If you think it will not embarrass him, please remember me to Mr. Palmer when you see him."

"At this rate, I shall not be seeing him tonight, alas. Once I have heard what you have to say, if anything, I shall have to summon the police."

"They have not been called already?" I asked.

"No. The prison is my jurisdiction. I wanted to gather the facts myself first. I shall call them very shortly. The Prison Commissioners have recently endowed us with a telephone. I am told Colonel Isaacson never used it, but I shall."

"There may be no need."

"No need to use the telephone?"

"No need to call the police."

The governor rocked back gently on his heels and tucked his thumbs into his waistcoat pockets. "The chaplain is dead, C.3.3. You do know that?"

"I do, sir. And I know that the dwarf attacked him. And did so mercilessly. I heard it happen."

"He'll be for the gallows—unless he can prove he's mad."

"He is mad, no doubt, sir—or has been driven mad here by the cruelty meted out to him. He attacked the chaplain—brutally—but he did not murder him."

"The Reverend Friend is dead—beaten and kicked to death by the prisoner Joseph Smith. Five warders were at the scene within moments of the occurrence."

I looked at the governor steadily. His face was open: not free of care, but free of guile. He was my gaoler-in-chief, but I liked the man and knew how much I owed to him. "The dwarf contributed to the chaplain's death, no doubt, sir," I said, "but I do not believe he should be held responsible for it."

"We'll let the courts decide whether or not he should be held responsible for his actions. If he is found guilty of murdering a prison chaplain, and he's not judged insane, he'll hang for it. Justice must be done."

"But if someone else is the murderer, sir," I persisted, "someone quite else—and the dwarf merely compounded the felony, what then?"

"What do you mean?" Major Nelson stopped rocking to and fro and considered me carefully.

I spoke slowly now. I was unaccustomed to standing in a room before a fireplace having a rational conversation with a gentleman dressed for dinner. I was unaccustomed to speaking with my head unbowed. "If the dwarf had merely attacked the chaplain, in however brutal a fashion, and the chaplain had survived that attack, would it then have been a matter for the police?"

Major Nelson hesitated. "No. No, not necessarily." He tugged on his walrus moustache. "An affray within the prison, an assault on a member of the prison staff—that would be a matter of prison discipline."

"For you to decide—as governor?"

"Yes—in consultation with the prison surgeon and, possibly, the visiting committee, depending on what punishment was considered to be appropriate in the circumstances."

I turned to Dr. Maurice. "You have examined the chaplain's body, doctor?"

"Yes."

"What killed him?" I asked.

"What killed him, I would say—and will say when I sign his death certificate—is cardiac arrest. He had a heart attack."

"Provoked, you assume," I said, "by the pounding he received?"

The doctor drew on the remains of his cigarette. "Possibly provoked by the attack itself. Mr. Friend may have suffered his seizure at the moment that the prisoner leapt upon him."

I nodded. "I think that very likely, Doctor. It sounded to me as if the dwarf was kicking and punching a lifeless corpse."

"Are you saying it was not the beating that killed the chaplain?" asked the governor.

"The assault provoked the heart attack," I replied. "The heart attack is what killed him."

"And what provoked the assault, I wonder?" pondered the governor, his hands in his pockets, jangling coins and keys.

"A line of John Donne's, I believe." I smiled. "Donne's poetry was ever contentious."

The governor looked at me askance.

"Pardon me, sir," I said. "I fear that the chaplain will have riled C.3.4. with a well-intentioned but ill-timed exhortation. It was his way."

Major Nelson looked over to the prison doctor. Although the doctor was of lower rank, he was of higher social standing, and I sensed the governor deferring to him. "Did Mr. Friend have a weak heart?" he asked.

"He was sixty years of age," replied the doctor.

"Were you his physician?" I asked.

"Yes."

"Did he have a weak heart?" I asked.

"Not that I had noticed previously."

Major Nelson, chewing the fringe of his moustache, looked once more at his half-hunter. "Where is this taking us, C.3.3.?"

"I hope it is taking you to dinner, sir," I answered, looking at him directly. "You need not trouble the telephone exchange tonight. This is not a matter for the police. Nothing need be done in haste. If you go now, even if you have missed the bisque, you'll catch the turbot. The chaplain is dead. God rest his soul. The poor dwarf is in his cell. You can decide his fate when you are ready to do so. He has infringed the prison regulations and whether he should be beaten once again or sent to a secure hospital is a matter for

you to decide—and probably better decided on a full stomach than an empty one."

The governor returned my gaze. "That is all very well,
and I thank you for your consideration for my digestion, but
I know my duty. Justice must be done."

"Oh, justice will be done, sir," I said quickly. "The chaplain's murderer will hang. You can be certain of that."

23

Sebastian Atitis-Snake

$\mathcal{M}$ajor Nelson left the parlour to make his telephone call.

I stood where I was, facing the empty fireplace. Dr. Maurice stood behind me. I heard him lighting a second cigarette.

"What killed the chaplain," I said, "killed Warder Braddle. And what killed Warder Braddle killed Warder Braddle's brother, also. I am convinced of that."

"And what was it?" asked the doctor.

"Cantharides," I said. "I recognised the symptoms. When we have finished here, go back to the morgue and look at the chaplain's face. You will see what I mean."

"The bulging eyes, the darkened skin, the blisters . . . I have seen them already." I listened as he drew slowly on his cigarette. (Oh, how I longed for one!) "What will you tell the governor?" he asked.

"What I know. At least, what I think I know. I owe him that. This is a cruel place and he has made it less so."

"You will tell him everything?"

"It is remarkable how one good action always breeds another."

"You will tell him about the boy?" he asked.

"I used to make jokes about the truth," I answered. "I do not find them so amusing now. I will tell him everything that I can."

"You will tell him about the boy?" The doctor repeated his question.

I turned to look at him. "For the governor to understand, I think that I must. You have not done so, Doctor?"

The prison surgeon contemplated the plume of white smoke rising from the tip of his cigarette. "I saw no need," he said. Still he considered his cigarette. "What was to be gained? Who needs the pain—and the shame—of what is past? It is all over now. The boy is safe—and getting better. He'll be released before the month is out. And he has a home to go to. I have made enquiries. He can start afresh."

"I am glad to hear it," I said. "That is good news."

"And your news is good news, too, C.3.3. You are due to be released in six weeks, are you not? Your ordeal is nearly over." The prison surgeon stood upright, bracing his shoulders and looking me directly in the eyes. "Yes, tell the governor what you know. Tell him everything. You have nothing to lose."

"Except my sons," I said. "Thus far I have lost everything—except my boys."

"You are fortunate to have sons. You will see them soon, I am sure."

I looked down at my hands. My fingers were fat, swollen, and rough. My nails were torn and grubby from my labours in the prison yard. The doctor's fingers, holding his cigarette, were long and slender. His fingernails gleamed. "Perhaps," I said. "Perhaps not." I smiled. "I have lost my reputation, Doctor. Any lie can be told about me now and it will be believed. That is the price I must pay for my folly."

"You can rebuild your reputation."

"No. When I leave here, there is nothing for me but the life of a pariah, a life of disgrace and penury and contempt. I know that. I say it not out of self-pity only, but as a matter of fact."

"You still have your way with words. You are Oscar Wilde. You can write. You can build your reputation anew."

"I wrote when I did not know life, Doctor. Now that I do know the meaning of life, I have no more to write. Life cannot be written; life can only be lived."

Major Nelson broke the elegiac moment as he bustled back into the room. He was humming "The Band Played On." He had lit a fresh cigar. He held it between his teeth because in his hands he carried a laden tray. He glanced around the room and then, with a sharp intake of breath, crouched down and placed the tray on the floor in front of the grate. "You may have a cheese sandwich, and some water. Help yourself." He rose to his feet holding a pair of crystal tumblers and handed one to Dr. Maurice. The liquid it contained was pale gold.

"Might I have a cigarette, sir?" I asked.

The governor clicked his tongue. "No," he said emphatically, "absolutely not. You forget yourself." He sipped his whisky and looked at me, raising an eyebrow. "You were sentenced at the Old Bailey to two years' hard labour, C.3.3. I don't need to remind you. According to the prison regulations, 'hard labour' means 'hard labour, hard fare and a hard bed.' You have more than a month of your sentence still to serve. I am only allowing you the sandwich because the Cheddar is peculiarly hard." He smiled. "Don't push your luck . . . And explain yourself." He took a second sip of whisky and sucked on his moustache. "You can take your time. I have spoken with Mr. Palmer. His custard creams have afforded him the luxury of a telephone, also. He knows I will be late. He asks to be remembered to you."

I stood with my head bowed, concentrating on the shaming black arrows on my trouser legs. "That is most gracious of him."

"He is a decent man," said the major. He stood before the fireplace, his arms loosely held out before him, his glass in one hand, his cigar in the other. "Look at me, C.3.3.," he instructed. "A prison is a necessary evil. I want to run this one as well as I can. When I arrived here, I smelt something rotten in the air, but the source of the stench I could not find. And others here—out of loyalty to the past, no doubt—gave me no clues." He threw a look towards Dr. Maurice and half raised his glass to him. He looked back at me and suddenly his eyes blazed. "I am exhilarated, C.3.3., because I sense that at last, tonight, here, in this room, with you, of all people, I am going to get to the root of the matter." He nodded towards the tray on the floor at my feet. "Now, take a bite of your sandwich, man, and explain yourself."

"I am not hungry, sir," I lied. Pride is a curious thing. "But thank you."

He shrugged his shoulders. "Very well. To business." He glanced once more towards Dr. Maurice. "Whatever is said in this room tonight need go no farther—so long as the law is not broken and justice is done." The prison doctor had moved to the far side of the parlour, away from the flickering gas-jets. He stood in the shadows, erect, his long arms behind his back, his tumbler of whisky held from view. The prison governor turned back to me. Major Nelson's appearance brought Conan Doyle to mind, but his avuncular, gently chiding manner reminded me more of my defending counsel at the Old Bailey. "So," he began, "you say that the chaplain's murderer 'will hang—we can be certain of that' . . . You mean, I take it, that . . ."

"Yes, sir. I mean that Sebastian Atitis-Snake is the chaplain's murderer."

"Is it *possible?*"

"Quite possible, sir."

"But *how?* The wretched man is locked in the condemned cell. He is guarded night and day. And *why?*"

"Why?" I repeated the governor's question because I was not certain that I knew the answer—or all of it. "I am not entirely sure why, sir, but I think it could be that Atitis-Snake murdered poor Mr. Friend simply to show that he could. He rose to the challenge!"

The major rose onto his toes. "The challenge? Whose challenge?"

"The judge's challenge," I said.

The prison governor sank back onto his heels. "No riddles now. A man lies dead in the morgue tonight—a good man. This is not a game we're playing."

"Were you in court, sir, at the recent trial of Sebastian Atitis-Snake?" I asked.

"No, but I read the reports, of course."

"Then you will recall that in passing sentence, Mr. Justice Crawford—who had tried Atitis-Snake once before—stated that he saw it as his 'responsibility' to ensure that the guilty man would never commit murder again. I understand that Atitis-Snake listened to the judgement and smiled. I imagine that it was at that very moment that the condemned man conceived the notion of proving his lordship wrong . . ."

"You mean he stood in the dock contemplating another murder?"

"Exactly. And given the frequency with which Mr. Justice Crawford invoked the name of the Almighty as he passed sentence, I reckon that Atitis-Snake decided that the Reverend Friend, God's man in Reading Gaol, was as apt a victim for a final murder as any."

"Extraordinary," murmured Major Nelson. He looked at me with narrowed eyes and a furrowed brow. "And how do you happen to know what the judge said in the court?"

"I read it in the *Daily Chronicle,* sir."

"And how did you come to be reading the *Daily Chronicle,* C.3.3.?"

"I do not recollect, Major Nelson."

The prison governor chewed on his whiskers. "Very well," he grumbled. He held his head back and exhaled a slate-coloured cloud of cigar smoke. "So . . . Atitis-Snake murders the chaplain to prove to the judge that he can . . ."

"I think, sir," I interrupted, "to prove to himself that he can."

"That's a nice distinction."

"But an important one. These murderers in my experience are all disciples of Narcissus. It is all about how they see themselves . . . It is all about them, never about anyone else."

"So Atitis-Snake murders Mr. Friend to prove to himself that he can."

"Yes."

"But *how?*"

"Very simply. He poisons him."

The governor laughed. "What? He *poisons* him?"

"This is 'Atitis-Snake, the poisoner.' This is his modus operandi. This is what he does."

The governor looked unconvinced. "So how does he carry through this poisoning? He slips a few belladonna leaves into the chaplain's cheese sandwich, does he?"

I smiled. "More or less. In fact, I believe it was a powder of cantharides slipped into the chaplain's communion wine."

"A single grain of cantharides can kill a man," said the doctor from the shadows.

The governor drew slowly on his cigar and regarded me closely. "What precisely do you think happened?"

"Well, sir . . . ," I began. It was strange for me to find myself speaking at length after so many months of silence. It was testing for me to be speaking at all without a cigarette in hand. "According to the prison regulations, any prisoner at any time can ask to see the prison governor or the prison chaplain and cannot be refused."

"Correct."

"On his return to Reading Gaol, the prisoner Atitis-Snake asked to see the prison chaplain. Mr. Friend found the condemned man full of remorse, desirous of absolution, and in need—in urgent need, so the chaplain told me—of the comfort of Holy Communion. The Reverend Friend celebrated Mass with Atitis-Snake in the condemned man's cell. For the purpose, he took with him his portable communion set—a small leather case containing pyx and paten for the host and a glass cruet and silver chalice for the wine. In the course of the ritual the chaplain served the condemned man the blessed sacraments of bread and wine—in the usual way. But when Atitis-Snake took the wine, he did not drink it. He held the chalice to his mouth, he let the wine touch his lips, and as it did so he spewed the powder of cantharides from his mouth, where it was hidden between his lower teeth and his gum, into the wine. The unfortunate priest, having served communion, did as priests are required to do—he consumed the remainder of the consecrated wine himself before cleaning the chalice."

"How do you know this?" asked Major Nelson. "This was not reported in the *Daily Chronicle*."

"No, but it was as good as told to me by the Reverend Friend. He came to my cell just after quitting Atitis-Snake. He told me how he had given Atitis-Snake communion and even as he told the story—with pride and hope—I could see the first symptoms of the poisoning appearing on his face. Atitis-Snake poisoned the Reverend Friend in the same way that he poisoned Warder Braddle."

Major Nelson held up a hand, fingers splayed, palm outward, as a road-sweeper might to hold up the traffic. "Atitis-Snake threw Braddle over the gantry balustrade. That much we know. Atitis-Snake admitted it in court—boasted of it, in fact, with his tomfool story of Sherlock Holmes and Professor Moriarty struggling to the death at the Reichenbach Falls."

"Yes, Atitis-Snake threw Braddle to his death, but first he poisoned him—to weaken him, I suppose. Braddle was a heavy man."

"I examined Braddle's body," said the surgeon. "I recognised the symptoms—blistered skin, swollen membranes, bulging eyes. Cantharidin is an irritant—it irritates as it takes its hold on a body."

"It is a stimulant, too, in its way," I added, smiling.

"How do you know so much about this 'cantharides,' C.3.3.?" enquired the governor.

"My father was a physician, sir. He prescribed it for certain patients—in moderation. It causes the blood vessels to widen."

"It must be used with great care," said Dr. Maurice. "It's all in the measure of the dose."

"My father used it on occasion himself, I believe," I continued, amused at the recollection, "to enhance his prowess."

Major Nelson widened his eyes and pursed his lips.

"To sustain his performance," I explained. "To give vigour to his member—"

The governor raised his road-sweeper's hand to silence me. "I follow you entirely, C.3.3. I served in the British army, remember."

I stood reproached.

"Where on earth did he get the powder?" asked the governor.

"It is not hard to come by," answered the doctor.

"Do you have any?" demanded Major Nelson, turning abruptly towards the prison surgeon.

"No, sir," said Dr. Maurice quickly. He stepped forward into the light. "It is a quack remedy in the main, used to stimulate the senses." He smiled grimly. "And to counter baldness, I believe. I would not touch it."

"But others do?" reflected Major Nelson, sucking on his cigar.

"Oh, yes. You can get it almost anywhere that's disreputable. It is frequently used by abortionists, alas—with deadly results." The governor raised an eyebrow. "It helps propel the foetus from the womb," explained the doctor, "and all too frequently kills the mother as well as the child."

Major Nelson tugged solemnly on his moustache.

I filled the silence. "A little goes a long way," I said. "And because it is a powder, it is easily hidden."

"And simply administered?" asked Major Nelson.

"Yes." I nodded. "I imagine that Atitis-Snake gave it to Warder Braddle in a cup of Braddle's illicit grog. Braddle was a drinker."

The governor of Reading Gaol lifted himself onto his toes. "That I knew. That much I'd heard. He had his 'favourites' and favoured them with nips from his hip flask, I suppose."

"Atitis-Snake was one such favourite," I said.

"Exactly," retorted the governor. "So I've been told.

Atitis-Snake was a 'favourite' of Warder Braddle. So why did Atitis-Snake murder Warder Braddle? Why? Was it another whim? Was he rising to another challenge?"

"He might have been, sir," I answered. "The narcissist as murderer will often kill simply to feed his own vanity."

"Is that so?" said the governor, without conviction.

"But in this instance," I went on, "I think we will find a traditional motive for the murder—betrayal. Sebastian Atitis-Snake murdered Warder Braddle because Warder Braddle betrayed him. I believe, sir, that you will find that Warder Braddle is the source of your stench."

"I did not know this Warder Braddle," said Major Nelson, falling back on his heels and gently rolling the remains of his whisky around in his glass, "but I have read his record. It is virtually blemish free. When I arrived I heard the stories of his drinking and his 'favourites,' but they did not seem to add up to much. On paper, at least, it would appear that Warder Braddle served the prison faithfully—and well—for many years."

"He was a monster," said the surgeon quietly.

"A monster?" The governor looked at the doctor with narrowed eyes. The doctor held his gaze, but said nothing further. Major Nelson turned to me. "A monster?" he repeated.

"He drank," I said. "On duty. I wondered why. Was it to drown his sorrows—or his shame? He vilified me—more than most and not so casually. There was anger in his spite. He despised me with such zeal that I began to wonder: Did he protest too much? Was there something in me that he recognised in himself—something that he feared, something in his own nature that he despised?"

"You are speaking in riddles," said the governor reprovingly.

"Warder Braddle had a secret," I said.

The governor laughed bleakly. "That's clear. What was it?"

"He was perverse," said Dr. Maurice. "He was an invert."

Major Nelson lowered his eyes and contemplated the tray that lay on the floor between us. "That's not unknown," he said.

"He was perverse," I said, "and corrupt. He pleasured himself with a boy called Tom."

"Prisoner E.1.1., sir," said the surgeon.

"I know the boy," said Major Nelson. "He's on the cleaning party. A wilful lad."

"The boy was Braddle's creature," I said, "his plaything. Braddle used the boy not lovingly, but brutishly."

"He abused him as though he were a man," said the doctor.

"You know this for a certainty?"

"The boy was sick. Eventually, when I examined him fully, I discovered why."

I looked at the doctor and smiled. "I thought that might be the case when you mentioned to me that you had been studying the work of my old college acquaintance, Professor Bent Ball."

"Braddle abused E.1.1. brutally—with unnatural force. He ruptured his anus. He put the boy in mortal danger."

Major Nelson sucked on his moustache and shook his head in dismay. "If that is why Atitis-Snake killed Braddle, I think we could be excused for forgiving the man. He surely did rid us of a monster."

"No, no," I cried. "Atitis-Snake was complicit in Braddle's perversity. He was part of the corruption. When Braddle wanted the boy, he would use Atitis-Snake to provide his alibi, to cover his tracks. Braddle the turnkey could accompany Atitis-Snake the prisoner to any part of the prison he chose and no one would suspect a thing. Braddle would escort Atitis-Snake to a discreet corner of the gaol where the boy would be found about his cleaning duties, and there—while Atitis-Snake stood sentinel—Braddle would have his way with the lad."

"You know this to be true?"

"I chanced upon the tail-end of one of these encounters when I was locked one night in the punishment cells. I heard the boy's voice. At the time I thought it was a woman's. I assumed it was one of the wardresses."

"Why was Atitis-Snake complicit in this bestiality?"

"He had nothing to lose—he did not care for the boy one way or the other. Atitis-Snake was always Atitis-Snake's only concern. He had nothing to lose—and much to gain. I imagine that Braddle implied to Atitis-Snake that he might one day be able to assist him either to escape or at least to make a case for early release from his incarceration. I believe that Atitis-Snake murdered Braddle because Braddle had promised him a path to freedom and Atitis-Snake eventually realised that he could not—or would not—deliver on his promise. Outside Colonel Isaacson's office, on the day my wife came to tell me of my mother's death, I overheard an exchange of words between the two men that told me so much."

"Colonel Isaacson was fearful of Warder Braddle—I know that," said Major Nelson. "It's not unheard of in the army—the commanding officer who allows himself to become the victim of a bullying NCO."

"On C Ward, Braddle was cock of the walk," I observed. "He ruled the roost—and he had done for many years. He drank, yes, but he did his job. He maintained discipline. And none but a few—his handful of favourites—knew his secret."

"And those beyond the few that knew his secret, kept it," said Major Nelson, looking towards Dr. Maurice.

"When I discovered the extent of the boy's injuries, I did not know what to do," said the surgeon, lowering his eyes. "Colonel Isaacson was a man who sought to avoid trouble rather than confront it. I did not think that he would prove an ally." He looked up, but did not catch the governor's eye. "I hesitated to act when I should have done. I am ashamed of that. It cannot be excused. But as I hesitated, Warder Braddle died, and with his death the matter appeared to resolve itself." The doctor drained his glass and a heavy silence filled the room.

I broke it. "No one called Warder Braddle to account," I said. "No one had the courage to do so—other than his brother, the other Warder Braddle." As I spoke I saw the gas-jets above the mantelpiece flicker. I thought suddenly of Conan Doyle and of how he would have appreciated the moment. "Our Warder Braddle could well have continued as he was had it not been for his censorious older brother."

"This is the fellow who was a turnkey at Wandsworth?" asked the governor.

"Yes," I said, "that is where I met him. That is where he died—on the night that he had come back from visiting his brother here. Thomas Braddle was vicious, but not, I think, perverse. He was cruel, but not, I suspect, corrupt. Thomas Braddle had a horror of inverts. He made that clear enough to me during our brief acquaintance. I imagine that he learned his brother's secret and was revolted by it. I imagine he threatened to expose his brother unless his brother mended his ways. And our Warder Braddle did what a cornered animal will sometimes do—he struck first. He rid himself of the threat to his perverted way of life. He killed his elder brother by poisoning him."

"With cantharides supplied to him by Sebastian Atitis-Snake?" suggested Major Nelson, on his toes once more.

"With cantharides *suggested* by Atitis-Snake, but I would imagine purchased and brought into the prison by Warder Braddle. Braddle supplied Atitis-Snake with the poisonous powder. Atitis-Snake then advised Braddle on the dose required—gave him what he needed and secreted the rest about his cell. When Thomas Braddle came to see his brother here, Warder Braddle simply laced his drink with poison. Thomas Braddle returned to Wandsworth, a doomed man—the worse for wear for drink and an overdose of cantharides."

"How do you know the detail of this, C.3.3.?"

"Because I saw Thomas Braddle on the night that he died. He died before my very eyes—in my cell in the infirmary at Wandsworth Gaol. I saw the symptoms of the poisoning on his arms and in his face. It was a ghastly sight."

"So," said the governor, who had been levering himself up and down with increasing rapidity as the story reached its climax, "Atitis-Snake gave Warder Braddle the means by which to murder his brother—and expected a proper reward for services rendered?"

"Correct."

"And when Atitis-Snake learnt that his wife—the unfortunate woman for whose attempted murder he was imprisoned in the first place—had died, he realised that he would spend the rest of his life in Reading Gaol unless he could find a means of escape—and Warder Braddle was to be his means of escape?"

"Exactly so, sir," I said. "But when Atitis-Snake realised that Warder Braddle would not—could not—deliver him from a lifetime's incarceration, Atitis-Snake felt betrayed. 'Keep your word,' I heard him tell Braddle. 'That's all I ask.' But Atitis-Snake knew that Braddle would fail him and he sought revenge. It was easily achieved. Braddle visited Atitis-Snake in his cell—as he often did. And there, as the two men shared a drink, Atitis-Snake spewed his poison into Braddle's hip flask. As Braddle left the prisoner's cell and stepped out onto the gantry, Atitis-Snake followed him. He saw the coast was clear and seized his moment. Quickly, quietly, all unobserved, he tipped his weakened victim over the iron balustrade to a certain death."

Major Nelson gave a grunt of agreement and settled back on his heels. "Why did Atitis-Snake not admit to the poisoning at his trial?" asked Dr. Maurice. "He confessed to the killing, after all."

"I do not know," I said. "Perhaps because the poisoning would have made him appear too sane. He poisoned his wife—and he was found guilty of her attempted murder and not deemed insane. A poisoner poisons—that's what he does. It seems quite rational. But only a true madman would be under the delusion that he is Professor Moriarty engaged in hurling Sherlock Holmes to his doom in the Reichenbach Falls. Atitis-Snake confessed to the murder of Warder Braddle in order to be able to stand trial—not to be found guilty, but to prove his madness. Only by proving himself insane could he escape Reading Gaol—or the gallows."

"Well, he failed," said the governor, "on both counts." He swilled the remains of whisky around his glass and drained it with a single swig. He mopped his moustache with the back of his hand. "You tell a convincing tale." He took his half-hunter from his waistcoat pocket and peered down at it. "It's hard not to feel that Warder Braddle as good as deserved his fate. And Atitis-Snake is set to hang within the month." He smacked his lips and looked at Dr. Maurice. "Justice has been done to the one and will be done to the other. We cannot excuse the prisoner Smith's attack on the chaplain, of course, but plainly it was not murder." The prison surgeon nodded his acquiescence. "I will leave C.3.4.'s fate in your hands, Doctor," said the governor. "You can keep him in a strait-jacket until he has calmed himself and then decide what's best for the future."

The prison surgeon loosely stood to attention and murmured, "Yes, sir."

Major Nelson turned his gaze back to me. "You are quite right, C.3.3., we need not trouble the police tonight." He dropped the stub of his cigar into his empty whisky glass and put out a hand to take the doctor's glass from him. He bent down to place the glasses on the tray. He stood again and looked at me. "You are a brilliant man, Oscar Wilde.

I trust that when you leave this place, you will be able to use your remarkable talents to the benefit of others. Thank you for what you have told us tonight. Thank you for what you have taught us." He glanced towards the prison surgeon. "Dr. Maurice will see you conveyed back to your cell. I shall go to Mr. Palmer's now. I am sorry you did not want the sandwich."

24

The Stink of Fear

*I*n prison, there may be occasional moments of high
drama, but they are few and far between. There is a pre-
dictability—an inevitability—a suffocating monotony—a
paralysing immobility—about a place where every cir-
cumstance of life is regulated after an unchangeable pattern. We labour, we exercise, we eat, we drink, we line up
to empty our slops, we lie down to sleep, we pray (or kneel
at least for prayer), according to the inflexible laws of an
iron formula that makes each dreadful day in the very mi-
nutest detail like its brother. Outside, in the living world,
ceaseless change is the very essence of existence. Not so
within the dead walls of Reading Gaol. Even out-of-doors
in the prison garden, where as I pushed my wheelbarrow
to and fro, high above me I could spy the sky and clouds,
I saw no birds fly past and, whatever the season, there
were no butterflies. Of seed-time or harvest, of the reapers
bending over the corn, or the grape gatherers threading
through the vines, of the grass in the orchard made white

with broken blossoms or strewn with fallen fruit, I knew nothing.

Nothing changes in Reading Gaol: that is one of the prison's unwritten rules. Except, towards the very end of my incarceration, for the first time in almost two years, something did. Just weeks before my release, the Prison Commissioners introduced a new class of inmate: "star prisoners," so called, convicts who had been sent to gaol for the first time. The idea was a simple one, and laudable in its way: it was to keep the first offenders wholly apart from the recidivists, to prevent the "new boys" from becoming contaminated by the "old lags." Why this new category was considered necessary I am not sure. Under the "separate system" all prisoners were already kept apart and the rules of "no communication between prisoners" and "absolute silence on all occasions" were, for the most part, strictly enforced. Perhaps it was with a view to making assurance doubly sure that the new star-class prisoner was created and marked out from the rest of us by a red star on his cap and another on his uniform? I do not know. What I do know is that whenever such a being came into view, we established prisoners—the starless ones—were required immediately to turn away and face the wall.

I was, of course, a first offender, but I was no longer new to Reading Gaol and it was only the prison's latest recruits who were admitted to the new star class. One day, after he had caught sight of me on the landing, returning from the latrines, standing with my nose to the wall, waiting until a new inmate had filed past, Warder Martin remarked to me, "It's not right, C.3.3. You're a poet and a gentleman. Standing with your face to the wall whilst a villainous-looking ruffian passes by—I don't like it."

I did not like it, either, but I accepted it and took it for what I judged the gods meant it to be: a final humiliation.

As the days passed and the moment of my release grew closer, I began to tremble with pleasure at the thought that on the very day of my leaving prison, both the laburnum and the lilac would be blooming—and that, somehow, I might find them together in a garden and see the wind stir into restless beauty the swaying gold of the one and make the other toss the pale purple of its plumes. I dreamed that the air that day would be Arabia for me. In Reading Gaol, meanwhile, through those last weeks locked in the pit of shame, all I could smell was the acrid odour of apprehension.

"It's sweat," said Warder Stokes. "It's the stink of fear." He told me, as though it were a proud tradition, "A prison always smells different when there's a hanging coming."

I looked at his young, freckled face, at his shining, unknowing eyes. "Was it like this last year," I asked, "when Trooper Wooldridge was hanged?"

"It was," he said, nodding his carrot head with satisfaction at the recollection. "Don't you remember? Everyone was nervy—inmates, turnkeys, even the governor. Especially the governor. The day of the hanging was the day Atitis-Snake gave himself up, wasn't it? A hanging 'concentrates the mind'—that's what my granddad says. He was here when they had public hangings, my granddad."

"Ah," I murmured softly, "the good old days . . ."

"That's what he says. He was one of the turnkeys on special duty on the day of the last public hanging. He was

there, up on the gallows, above the gate-house. It was a famous day. The whole county came."

"Did the condemned man's legs twitch?" I asked. "I believe they do."

"Yes, they did," answered Stokes eagerly. "You've heard
the story?"

"No, Warder Stokes," I cried. "I have not heard the story.
But I can imagine it."

"My granddad loves to tell it."

"I have no doubt that he does."

"You are planning to tell the story of Wooldridge's
hanging in one of your poems, aren't you?" He presented
the question as a challenge. "You told me you was," he said
defiantly.

"I have thought of it," I replied, my eyes averted. "I have
written nothing yet."

"A hanging makes a good story," confided Warder
Stokes. "I don't know if I'll be on special duty for this one,
but if I am, I can bring you the details."

I could not think what to answer, so I smiled at the young
warder with the crooked teeth and said simply, "Thank you."

From Warder Martin I learned that on the morning that
followed my interview with Major Nelson in his parlour,
Sebastian Atitis-Snake was taken from the condemned cell
and escorted to the prison bath-house. There, in the presence of both the governor and the prison surgeon, he was
stripped naked, washed, and searched. Atitis-Snake demanded an explanation: none was given.

The body-search, according to Martin, was carried out by Dr. Maurice and included examination of the prisoner's hair, ears, nose, mouth, fingers, nails, toes, and private parts. "What they was looking for, they didn't say. Whatever it was, they didn't find it." Before he was locked up again, the condemned man's cell was searched by four warders, including Martin—nothing untoward was discovered—and swabbed out, from floor to ceiling, by the lads from the cleaning party.

On that same morning—the morning following the death of the prison chaplain—the dwarf was moved to the punishment block and chapel was cancelled.

"It is like execution day," whispered Private Luck, calling to me from his cell at the accustomed time. "They always have chapel except when there is a hanging. Always, always. Every day. Always. It is very strange not to have chapel. Like the lady in the song, I am all dressed up with nowhere to go."

"You know that the chaplain is dead," I said.

"Yes, yes, Warder Martin told me. C.3.4. jumped up on him like a mad dog and the poor old man had a heart attack. And now C.3.4. is in a punishment cell in a strait-jacket and the chaplain is in a coffin on his way to heaven."

"The chaplain was a good man," I said.

"I believe you," said Private Luck. "I did not know him at all. He came to see me once, but I was busy." The Indian started to giggle as he spoke. "The poor chaplain was very shocked. He came into my cell and found me pleasuring Warder Braddle." Luck burst into a peal of high-pitched laughter. "I was on my knees, but not saying my prayers!"

"Hush, man," I hissed. "Take care what you say."

"We are quite safe," said my neighbour coolly. "There is no one near. I can always hear them coming."

Luck was due to be released from prison on 12 May—"That is a week before you, Mr. Oscar Wilde, is it not? I will be waiting for you outside," he said, "and together we will go to Mrs. Wilde and collect my one hundred pounds."

"You did not kill Warder Braddle," I protested. "I owe you nothing."

"You owe me one hundred pounds—and more," he cried gaily. "And I will have it or I will be telling everybody all your secrets. I will tell them about you and the boy, Mr. Wilde, and they will believe me."

25

A Hanging at Reading Gaol

*T*he execution of Sebastian Atitis-Snake was set to take place at 8:00 a.m. on the morning of Tuesday, 11 May 1897. As the date approached, the feeling of unease within Reading Gaol grew ever more unsettling. It was a nameless dread—acknowledged, but not understood. By night, men, customarily silent, called out wantonly from their cells, either in anger or madness or in fear. By day, scuffles broke out among inmates in the lines waiting to go to chapel or for exercise or to visit the latrines.

In the garden one morning, the wardress with the look of Joan of Arc walked close by me. She did not smile and in her large blue eyes I saw what seemed to me to be a look of unbounded sadness. I realised then why I had always found her appearance so striking. She looked as my Constance had looked when we first met—before time and motherhood had exacted their toll. On that same day, at lunchtime, I heard from Warder Martin that Dr. Maurice had been called away from Reading Gaol unexpectedly. The warder brought me a note from the prison surgeon in which the doctor expressed his regret that he would not see me before my release, but hoped that our paths might cross in happier circumstances in times to come. The note included an address in Whitechapel. That same afternoon, I chanced to see the boy, Tom, running towards the boiler house from the direction of the small memorial garden where Warder Braddle lay buried. As the lad crossed my path, I looked away—and at once I sensed the youth sensing my fear. I heard him stop abruptly in his tracks. Still I looked away. He stood for a moment quite close to me (I felt the heat of his breath) and then he laughed, mockingly, before running on.

One evening—it was the eve of the execution: I had seen the hangman and Major Nelson walking together across the outer prison yard—I witnessed a hauntingly unpleasant scene. A.2.11., a prisoner from another ward—a half-witted old soldier by the name of Prince—was returning from his day's labour in the stone-breaking yard. I recognised the man from his jerking arms and awkward, halting gait. His hands were torn and bloodied from his work and he could scarcely put one foot before the other. He was the first in line and his shambling progress delayed the half dozen men behind him. I watched as the poor wretch stumbled and fell forward on his knees onto the ground. I heard the two warders in command of the party curse the fellow and I saw them, without mercy, pull him roughly to his feet, one of them kicking him on the ankles as he did so. One of the warders barked at the old soldier, "Malingerer!" At this, the other prisoners in the line began to growl and grind their teeth like angry curs.

And this was not the only violence that night, Warder Stokes reported. He came with my dinner of bread and potatoes the evening of the day Atitis-Snake was hanged eager to share the news.

"There's always violence the night before a hanging," Stokes said, so the fracas in the corridor outside the condemned man's cell had not been altogether a surprise. Atitis-Snake, escorted by two turnkeys, was being brought back to his cell from a final strip-search and sluicing in the bathhouse. As he reached the door of his cell, a voice close by called out, "Hang well, Professor Moriarty!" Atitis-Snake, enraged, had turned to confront his abuser.

"Who was it?" I asked.

"You couldn't tell," said Stokes. "They was all wearing their caps. There was three of them coming down the corridor—star prisoners—and then there was the Indian princess—C.3.2.—standing just along from the condemned cell, on the other side of the corridor, with his face to the wall."

"What was he doing there?"

"He was coming the other way—back from working in the kitchen. He'd seen the star prisoners and stopped, like a good boy. He was obeying the new rules."

"Are you sure it wasn't Luck who shouted out?"

Warder Stokes chuckled. "No, it was a proper man's voice. I was up on the gantry. I didn't get down there till the fight had broken out—but I heard the voice what shouted and it wasn't the princess. I'm sure of that."

"What happened?"

Stokes was grinning. "All hell broke loose. Atitis-Snake—he was like a lunatic on the run. Just went berserk.

He rushed at the men, lashing out like a madman. The star prisoners—because there was three of them—pushed him away, no problem—and he fell back against the Indian princess and half knocked him to the ground." Warder Stokes ran his tongue along the line of his jagged teeth with relish. "And then, when Atitis-Snake saw it was C.3.2., he began hitting him, pummelling him, beating him with his fists like there was no tomorrow."

The warder's enthusiasm for the fight was infectious. I pushed my meal, untouched, across my table. "Well, for Atitis-Snake," I said, "I suppose, there really was no tomorrow."

Stokes punched the palm of his hand. "That's just what the governor said. The condemned man had nothing to lose. 'This was his last hurrah'—that's what the governor said. But you've got to hand it to the Indian princess. He gave as good as he got—if not better. He turned on Atitis-Snake like a bat out of hell—spitting, scratching, biting, hitting back hard."

"He served with the Bombay Grenadiers, you know." Warder Stokes laughed. "Didn't the turnkeys try to part them?" I asked.

"Of course they did—and I was running down the gantry to the rescue and all. And Martin was on his way. It was all hands on deck. It had to be 'cos that's when around the corner, from the end of the ward, who should come marching home but the men from the stone-breaking yard?"

"Good gracious," I said. I had not known Warder Stokes so eloquent—or so exhilarated.

"And something was up with them 'cos as soon as they

saw the fight, they decided to join in. Oh, my God, it was a right messy business. Atitis-Snake was like a mad bull in the middle of it all."

"So this was a last-ditch attempt to prove his madness?" I suggested.

"That's exactly what the governor said. Those was his very words." Stokes looked at me, confounded, as if a mighty revelation had suddenly come upon him. "Perhaps you'll come back here one day—as governor." He grinned and revealed his absurdly crooked teeth once more. "Why not? *Why not?* You've got the hang of it here now, haven't you?"

"What happened next?" I asked.

"'The turnkeys guarding the condemned man showed great presence of mind.' Those was the governor's words. There was just two of them and they got hold of Atitis-Snake and the Indian princess—they grabbed hold of 'em, as well as they could. They couldn't part 'em, but they wasn't going to lose 'em. They pushed 'em together into the condemned man's cell and slammed shut the door."

"They left the pair of them to fight it out together?"

"Yes," roared Warder Stokes. He was swaying from side to side with the excitement of his story. "They had to do something 'cos by now the corridor was swarming. There was the seven men from the stone-breaking yard—well, six, because poor old A.2.11. wasn't up for the scrap—and the three star prisoners, all slugging it out with each other, with the turnkeys from the working party, with the two special turnkeys who was guarding Atitis-Snake . . . It was a bear-pit."

I looked at the warder, wreathed in smiles, and suddenly thought back to the horror of the morning: the hanging that had gone ahead, as planned, at eight o'clock.

"But the fighting stopped?" I said.

"Oh yes," chuckled Stokes.

"How? What stopped it?"

The warder's eyes brightened. "My whistle." From his pocket, Warder Stokes produced a small tin whistle, no more than three inches in length. He held it up proudly for me to inspect. "This was my dad's whistle. As I came chasing down the corridor, I remembered I had it and out it came and I blew it full blast . . ."

"And it worked?" I asked, incredulous.

"It worked a treat," said Warder Stokes, his freckled face flushed in triumph. "I blew the whistle and the fighting just stopped—like a train juddering into the station, it just ran out of steam. The governor says I'm due for a medal."

"Congratulations, Warder."

"And the inmates—all ten of them—they're due for the cat. It was an 'insurrection'—that's what the governor called it."

"I heard a whipping last night," I said, looking up at Stokes. "Have they started already?"

"Oh no, last night—that was the Indian princess. He was given six strokes of the birch—right away, governor's orders. He'd left Atitis-Snake as good as dead. He mashed him up right and proper—took his head and scraped it against the cell wall, half tore his face off. And when we opened the cell door there he was, kicking the poor bastard's throat in."

"C.3.2. was doing this?" I marvelled.

"He was. C.3.2. was kicking Atitis-Snake's head in. I saw him do it. Do you know what the governor called him? 'A thing possessed.'" Stokes's face glowed with the thrill of the drama. "And once the princess saw the cell door was open, he was through it like a scalded cat." Stokes laughed. "There was no holding him. He was along the corridor, like greased lightning—up the stairs, onto the gantry, back in his cell. You must have heard him?"

"Yes, I heard him," I said, now closing my eyes briefly and thinking back to the night before. "I heard the running footsteps, I heard the cell door slam. I didn't know what had happened."

"We locked him up and got the others back to their cells and called the doctor for Atitis-Snake and went to report to the governor. The governor ordered the beating for C.3.2. there and then."

I studied the young warder's freckled face. I knew him to be a good man at heart. "You told Major Nelson you didn't believe it was Luck that started the fight?"

"It wasn't C.3.2. that shouted that stuff about 'Hang well, Professor Moriarty.' I told the governor that, but he said that C.3.2. had to be punished 'cos he was part of the fight and 'cos of the damage he done Atitis-Snake. He half killed him."

"And Luck, I suppose, had to be punished last night because today he is due for release."

Stokes chuckled. "He's already gone. Went this morning—twelve o'clock, sharp. It'll be your turn next, C.3.3. You're off in a week's time, aren't you?"

"I did not know that Luck had gone already," I said. "I

did not hear him go. He did not call good-bye. How was he?"

"Quiet as a mouse. He hobbled out. Half doubled up, he was. He took quite a lashing last night. But he'd dressed for the occasion—put on his fancy woman's make-up and wrapped his head in a sari . . . He looked a proper Indian tart."

I looked up at Warder Stokes, suddenly perturbed. "Who carried out the beating last night?" I asked.

"I did," replied the young warder.

"You were administering rough justice," I said. "The beating hadn't been sanctioned by the visiting committee."

"The governor was acting within his rights. He had to restore order. He had to have calm before the hanging."

"Yes," I said. I looked down at my cold plate of hard bread and black potatoes. I looked about my empty, soulless cell. It was early evening and the month was May, but if there was still sunshine in the sky outside, it did not find its way through my barred window. I felt a darkness closing in. "I am surprised the hanging went ahead," I said.

"It had to," answered Warder Stokes emphatically. He folded his arms across his chest. "It had to. That's what the governor said. He said Atitis-Snake had 'tried it on'—fought like a lunatic to make us think he was one. 'He must not get away with it.' That's what the governor said."

"And perhaps Atitis-Snake half hoped that Luck might indeed half kill him because then he'd be in no fit state for his own hanging?" I suggested.

Stokes gazed down at me in wonderment. "That's exactly what the governor said, too. A man's got to be fit enough for the gallows—that's the rule."

"And, from all you say, Sebastian Atitis-Snake was far from fit enough . . ."

Warder Stokes shrugged his shoulders. "Well, he'd lost his voice and his face was turned to pulp, but he had a pulse. That's what the doctor said."

"Has Dr. Maurice returned?" I asked, surprised.

"No—another doctor. Dr. Roberts. He comes in when the surgeon's on leave. The governor asked him, straight out, 'Is the condemned man alive, Doctor?' 'He is,' said the doctor. 'Then he can hang at eight, as the court ordered.'"

"And that was that," I said.

"The hangman wasn't too happy—it was Mr. Billington—but the governor stood firm—and the hanging happened."

I nodded, looking down at my plate once more. "I assumed it had," I said. "There was no chapel and we were kept in our cells all morning. I remembered the routine from last time."

"It was done proper. It was dignified. As it ought to be."

"I listened out for the church bell at eight o'clock." I looked up at Stokes. There was no malice in his freckled face. "Does the hanging happen on the first stroke or the last?" I asked.

"The first," he said. It was apparent that he was eager to tell me more.

"Were you on special duty, Warder Stokes?" I asked. "I know you hoped to be."

The young turnkey shook his head. "I was not. I asked 'cos I know you wants the detail for your poem—"

"There may be no poem," I protested gently.

"But Major Nelson said it had to be done by the book. The condemned man has to have warders who don't know him at the last—so they don't show him any favour. I was with Wooldridge when he went 'cos I didn't know him. This time they had two lads from D Ward. They did their duty."

"It is a frightful enterprise," I said, "taking another man's life."

"Mr. Billington does a good, clean job."

"He wears gardener's gloves as he goes about his business," I said.

"He's the best there is," replied Warder Stokes, nodding sagely.

"Your father knew him?"

"And my granddad knew his dad. And I knows his sons. He's got three boys."

"All in the hanging trade, are they?"

"And proud of it," said Warder Stokes happily.

"And was Mr. Billington content with the way it went this morning? Did you speak to him after it was over?"

"I did," said Warder Stokes, now looking a little pleased with himself. "We had a beer together in the warders' mess. It went really well in the end, he said."

"I am glad," I said—not thinking what I said.

"It's all in the preparation," continued Stokes complacently. "That's why he has to come the night before—observe the condemned man, take a good look at his neck, make sure the gallows is in good working order."

"Where is the gallows kept?" I asked. "I have seen Mr. Billington crossing the yard, but not known where he was going."

"We erect the gallows in the photographic house, at the back of D Ward. It's where they make the photographs of the prisoners when they arrive. It was the potato store—you know the place."

"I don't think I do," I said.

"It's a bit cramped for the gallows, but it does the job."

"Did you help build the scaffold?" I asked.

"I did. Platform, trapdoor, gallows—all erected in an hour. Heavy work 'cos it's solid oak. Oak for the gallows, elm for the coffin. I done it with Warder Martin and a couple of the other, younger warders—and then Mr. Billington tests it. That's the other reason he has to be here the night before. He gets a bag of sand the exact weight of the condemned man and he hangs it from the rope—to test it, and to stretch the rope, and to make sure he's got enough room under the trapdoor for the drop."

"It's an art," I murmured.

"It's a science, according to Mr. Billington. It's all about attention to detail.* The sack of sand hangs from the rope all night and then, about six o'clock in the morning, Mr. Billington goes in and takes it down and checks the apparatus one last time."

"At six in the morning? But the execution isn't until eight?"

Stokes laughed. "Then he has his cup of tea and a slice of bread and dripping."

"Go on," I said, fascinated as much by the manner of Stokes's telling of his terrible tale as by the matter of it.

"At quarter to eight, on the dot, the dignitaries all meet at the governor's house—"

---

* See page 311.

"The dignitaries?"

"That's the governor and the undersheriff and the chaplain and the surgeon—all in their Sunday best. At ten to eight they march, all solemn, like, from the governor's house to the photographic house and they gets into position beside the gallows and they wait. At five to eight, the governor checks his time-piece and gives the hangman the nod. That's when Mr. Billington makes his way to the condemned man's cell. The two special-duty warders are waiting for him there. At three minutes to eight, the warders get the condemned man to his feet and they tie his hands with leather straps and the executioner puts a white sack over his head and they walk him from his cell to the photographic house."

"He doesn't see the gallows?"

"No."

"It is a hideous game of blind man's buff," I cried. "They walk him from his cell, you say . . ."

"It's only a matter of yards."

"Doesn't the man resist?"

"Not usually—but they had to drag Atitis-Snake. He'd been broken in that fight last night. He couldn't speak. He could barely stand. I don't think he knew what was happening to him."

"Was that right? Was that 'doing it by the book'?"

"Right or wrong, it's what happened. And it's all over in a moment. It's only thirty seconds from the condemned cell, along the passage and out into the photographic house."

"But if the wretched man is being dragged . . ."

"He gets there all the same—and at one minute to eight he's marched onto the platform under the rope."

"But he cannot see the rope? His head is hidden in a sack?"

"He can't see the rope, but he can feel it. Mr. Billington puts the rope around his neck. And it's a science, as he says, 'cos the rope is adjusted to the left side of the jaw so it forces the head to twist and turn backwards." Warder Stokes looked at me with gleaming eyes. "That's what helps break the neck," he declared.

"Of course," I murmured.

"At eight o'clock, as the clock beyond the wall *begins* to strike," he continued, "the special warders stands back, the governor nods, Mr. Billington pulls the lever, the trapdoor opens—"

"And the poor wretch tumbles to his doom."

"He does—and as he goes the chaplain says a prayer."

"Who was the chaplain?" I asked.

"The vicar from St. Jude's. He's an old man. I don't think he's really up to it any more."

"And for how long is the poor dead man left hanging there?"

"An hour."

"An hour?" I gasped, in horror.

"It's to give his soul time to leave his body—that's the idea."

"And does everybody stand about and watch?" I asked, appalled.

"No. The dignitaries goes back to the governor's house for breakfast. It's just the specials and the hangman who wait behind."

"And when the hour is up?"

"When the hour's up, the dignitaries come back and the body comes down. The doctor does a quick postmortem and signs the death certificate. And the undersheriff signs a bit of paper confirming the death was lawful. And then the warders put the body in the coffin." Stokes leant towards me knowingly. "I know you wants the detail, C.3.3. It is a special coffin."

"Made of elm, I know."

"It's got large holes on the sides and ends . . . Big ones."

"To hasten the decay?" I said, with a dry mouth.

"That's it. That's it exactly. And then they all escorts the coffin out into the garden and down to the bit of ground by the east wall, behind the boiler house, where the hanged ones get buried. That's where I was. I wasn't on special duty, but I did get to help dig the grave—and shovel in the lime. It's the lime what makes it decay all the quicker." The young warder looked at me with satisfaction. He folded his arms once more. It seemed his story was done.

"Well, you played your part, Warder Stokes," I said. "You did your duty."

"And I've told you all about it—as I said I would."

"You have indeed," I said. "Thank you." I looked up at him and smiled. "But there was one detail you forgot. Did the condemned man's legs twitch? You didn't say."

Warder Stokes laughed. "But I did ask Mr. Billington. And no, his legs didn't twitch."

Conclusion

Dieppe, France, 25 June 1897

"'Who can foretell what joys the day shall bring,
Or why before the dawn the linnets sing?'"

Sebastian Melmoth smiled as he spoke. And as he smiled he contemplated the bubbles that danced towards the brim of his newly filled glass of champagne. "I never lose count of the number of glasses I have drunk," he said, "because I never begin to count them in the first place." He laughed softly at his own joke and closed his eyes. The sun was less bright than before: the warmth of it was wonderful.

"Are those lines from the poem that you are writing?" enquired Dr. Quilp, putting down his pen and pulling his chair closer to the table.

"No, they are from a poem that I wrote a long time ago." Melmoth opened his eyes. "I am surprised you do not know it. You know so much about me."

It was gone half past four in the afternoon. The two men

had been sitting for more than two hours at the same corner table on the pavement outside the Café Suisse. They
were alone. The café always seemed dead at this time of
day. Where they sat was no longer in the shade, but the sun
was not so high now and Melmoth, at least, was revelling in
its rays. "When I was young," he murmured, "the moon was
everything to me. I knew her. I could reach out my hand to
touch her. She was my friend. Now I find her cold and distant. Now that I am old I need the comfort of the sun."

"You are not old," said Quilp. He shifted on his chair
and pulled a linen handkerchief from his trouser pocket.
He began to mop his brow.

"And you are not well, Doctor," answered Melmoth, sitting up and setting his glass down on the table. "The sun is
too much for you."

"I am quite well," said Quilp, smiling.

Melmoth took out his half-hunter to check the time.
He turned and looked down the empty street, towards the
docks. "The paddle-steamer will be here quite soon and the
foot passengers will all come trundling past. The English
will notice us sitting here, but if they recognise me they will
pretend that they don't. That is what happens when fame
turns to infamy."

A seagull screeched overhead. "Perhaps they will not
recognise you," said Dr. Quilp. "It is your name that gives
you your reputation, and your work, not your face."

"You are quite right, Doctor. Thank you. And it may
be for the best. I am no longer the Adonis I once was."
He grinned and showed off his ungainly yellow teeth. "I
caught sight of myself in the looking-glass this morning.

I look *exactly* like an overblown Botticelli cherub run to seed."

Quilp laughed. "And what do I look like?" he asked.

"An hour ago I would have said a vulpine Prussian officer on his way to fight a duel, but now I am not so sure. You are sweating, Doctor. You are *weeping*. You don't look well." Melmoth picked up his glass. "You need to rest, Doctor. You need to lie down." Melmoth looked about the table with its litter of empty glasses and overflowing ashtrays. "We are done here, aren't we? You must go to bed and I must go home." He pushed his chair a little from the table and nodded towards Quilp's pen and notebook. "I take it that you have heard all that you came to hear? I hope that I have earned my entertainment—and more?" He reached out his right hand and lightly touched Quilp's cheque-book, which was also lying on the table.

"Almost," answered Quilp. He returned his handkerchief to his pocket and sat forward. He pushed his spectacles up his nose and looked directly at Sebastian Melmoth. "A few moments more. We must round off the story. I feel that you have not told me everything."

"I have given you the tale of Atitis-Snake, the poisoner. Isn't that what you came for?"

"In part, of course—yes." Quilp glanced down at his cheque-book. "It is murder that excites the public. We both know that."

"And I have brought the tale to a fitting climax with the condemned man swinging from the rope."

"You have," said Quilp, "and I am grateful." He sat back and with his right hand lifted the last bottle of Perrier-Jouët from the ice-bucket beside the table. "There's a glass more here for each of us. Let us finish the bottle—and finish the story."

"Very well," said Melmoth, easing himself to his feet. "If you will excuse me a moment. I must go and powder my nose—as American women like to say. Do you know the expression? It is one of my favourite euphemisms." He took up his cigarette and his glass of champagne and looked down at Dr. Quilp. "I notice that you powder yours literally, Dr. Quilp."

Quilp laughed as Melmoth, lumbering like a sacred elephant, made his stately way into the darkness of the café.

He was not long gone and when he returned to the table he appeared lighter on his feet—less inebriate, more alert. Before he resumed his seat, he cleared some space on the table, moving the ashtrays and empty glasses to another table. *"Finite la comedia,"* he said, smiling at Dr. Quilp. "When you have eliminated the impossible, whatever remains, however improbable, must be the truth."

Quilp looked up, confused. "I do not quite follow you," he said.

Melmoth sat down. "You will, Doctor. You will." Melmoth's energy had returned to him. He laid his hands flat upon the table and spread out his fingers. He looked at Quilp. "Where were we?" he asked.

Quilp picked up his pen. "At the hanging of Atitis-Snake."

"Ah yes," murmured Melmoth, reaching into his pockets for another cigarette. "In my end is my beginning."

Quilp had moved his chair while Melmoth had been "powdering his nose." He was no longer in the direct sunlight. He opened his notebook and stared down at it. "You had just given me Warder Stokes's account of the execution," he said. "That was Tuesday, the eleventh of May."

"Yes," said Melmoth, holding a lighted match to his cigarette. "Tuesday, eleventh May. And a week later to the day, I was released."

"How was that final week at Reading Gaol?" asked Quilp.

"Horrible," answered Melmoth, his brow suddenly furrowing at the recollection. "Ghastly. The men who had been involved in the fracas outside the condemned man's cell on the eve of the execution—each one of them was given twelve strokes of the cat-o'-nine-tails, including the crippled half-witted soldier, Prince."

"A.2.11.?" said Quilp.

"You recall his number?" said Melmoth, drawing on his cigarette. "I am impressed."

"I have it written down," said Quilp, holding up his notebook.

"Prince was not a party to the so-called insurrection, but he was cruelly beaten all the same. I heard it happen and the next day I saw him as we took our daily exercise in the fool's parade. The lashing he had been given had made him mad." Tears now filled Melmoth's eyes. "Oh, the pity of it," he murmured. "But there was worse."

"Worse?"

"Yes. On the Friday before my release, as I was making my way across the outer courtyard towards the garden shed to collect my tools for my day's labour, I passed the wardress."

"The woman with the fine features whose name you never knew?"

Melmoth smiled. "You *have* been attentive, Dr. Quilp. Yes, the same." He drew slowly on his cigarette, studying Quilp carefully as he spoke. "And as I looked at those fine features I believe, for the first time, I understood them. I had been looking for a mystery where there was none. Her beauty reflected her nature. Her open face reflected her spirit. We must remember that there is outright good in the world as well as outright evil."

"Did you speak with her?"

"Only for a moment. She had three children with her."

"Her own children?"

"No—young prisoners. They were in prison uniform."

"And was the boy, Tom, one of them?" asked Quilp.

"Oh no. These were younger than Tom. These were ten or eleven years of age at most—at most. They looked no bigger than my boys. I said to the wardress, 'Why are they here?' She told me, 'They have been convicted of snaring rabbits and cannot pay their fine.'" With his right hand, Melmoth struck the café table angrily. Quilp steadied his glass of champagne. "Can you believe it? Children imprisoned for snaring rabbits! Later that day I told Warder Martin about the children. I asked him to seek them out. I asked him to find out their names and the amount of their fine. I told him I wanted to pay the fine to get them out. I could not bear the idea of those poor children in that vile place."

"And did Warder Martin do as you asked?"

"He did—and more. He found the children for me and, to the smallest of them, he gave a biscuit."

Quilp took a sip of his champagne. "That was an act of kindness," he said.

"It was an act of folly," cried Melmoth. "As ill-chance would have it, a senior warder saw Martin give the child the biscuit and reported what he had seen to the governor. Warder Martin was instantly dismissed. I did not see him again. And when I saw Major Nelson on the day of my departure, I was too cowed—too craven—too cowardly—to protest. I could not believe that the governor—so good a man—could have done so cruel a thing."

"He did it 'by the book,'" reflected Quilp, with a shrug. He drank more of his champagne. "Did you see the boy again before you left?" he asked.

"The boy, Tom? No."

"And the dwarf?"

"No, but Warder Stokes told me that he was certain that C.3.4. would be transferred to an asylum."

"That is something," said Quilp, taking out his handkerchief once more and mopping his brow. "And you?"

"I left Reading Gaol on the evening of the eighteenth of May," answered Melmoth. "I was to be released 'officially' from Pentonville, the prison in which my two-year sentence properly began. I was allowed to leave in my own clothes. I had my half-hunter and my cigarette case returned to me. I was not handcuffed. Major Nelson wanted to spare me what I had endured at Clapham Junction on my way to Reading, so two warders took me by cab from the prison gates to Twyford Station for the train journey to London. The sun was setting as we left and on the platform at Twyford, there were bushes in bud. I walked towards them with open arms. 'Oh beautiful world!' I cried. 'Oh *beautiful* world!'" Melmoth laughed at the recollection of it. "One of the warders begged me to stop. 'Now, Mr. Wilde, you mustn't give yourself away like that. You're the only man in England who would talk like that in a railway station.'"

Quilp smiled. Melmoth, still laughing, leant across the table towards him. "You do not look well, Dr. Quilp, but since you insist on hearing out my story, will you raise your glass and drink to my freedom?"

"I will, sir," said Quilp. The two men lifted their glasses and drank from them, deeply.

Melmoth lit up another cigarette. "On the nineteenth of May, early in the morning, I was released from Pentonville—a free man. By nightfall, I was here."

"You came to France at once?"

"First, I had breakfast—with old friends. Then I went shopping."

"Shopping?"

"I needed clothes. I bought a blue serge suit—and a fine brown hat, from Heath's. I bought shirts in assorted colours of the rainbow, eighteen collars, two dozen white handkerchiefs and a dozen with coloured borders, some dark-blue neckties with white spots on, eight pairs of socks—coloured summer things . . . and new gloves." Melmoth held up his hand and spread his fingers wide. "Size eight and three-quarters. My hand is notoriously broad."

Quilp looked at Melmoth. He was no longer making

notes. He had put down his pen. "This was extravagant," he said, smiling.

"This was necessary," answered Melmoth, earnestly. "My brother, Willie, had all my old clothes—and he had pawned them. My dear sweet wife had sent me money from Genoa for new clothes—and for food and travelling expenses. I bought some scent in her honour—Canterbury Wood Violet from Pritchard's in St. James's. It is her favourite—and mine. I wanted, for psychological reasons, to feel entirely physically cleansed of the stain and soil of prison life." He looked down at the backs of his hands and inspected his well-manicured fingernails. "I shopped during most of the day and then, in the evening, after I had run a particular errand, I took the train to Newhaven and caught the night boat to Dieppe."

"You came here—why here? Why Dieppe?"

"Why not? I had considered escaping to the other side of the world—to Brazil or Brisbane. But my Portuguese is poor and my Australian worse. I thought of Bruges or Brussels or Boulogne. I am proficient in French and alliterative in geography . . ." He smiled. "I had almost settled on Boulogne, but then I learnt that the young man with whom I was once infatuated—the young man whose presence in my life brought about my downfall—was living there, *is* living there . . . I did not wish to see him. I do not want to see him. If I see him I will never see my sons again, and my wife will take my allowance from me. I need my wife, in spite of everything. Life is a stormy sea. My wife is a harbour of refuge."

"Oh, yes," said Dr. Quilp, shifting in his seat, "your

wife—and your terror of losing your allowance. That had preyed upon you in prison, I know." He sat forward at the table and pressed the tips of his fingers against his temples for a moment. He closed his eyes and then opened them wide as if making a determined effort to concentrate. "That reminds me. What about Private A. A. Luck," he asked, "'late of the Bombay Grenadiers'? Was he not at the prison gates to greet you—and demand his hundred pounds?"

"There were two reporters at the prison gates to greet me. One asked me for my immediate plans. 'To breakfast on caviar and champagne,' I told him. He appeared shocked. 'A proper breakfast is the duty a writer owes to the dignity of letters,' I explained. He seemed none the wiser. The other reporter asked a more discerning question. He wanted to know what I hoped for in the future. I told him that I coveted neither notoriety nor oblivion. He appeared satisfied with that."

"But there was no sign of Private Luck?"

"No, Dr. Quilp, there was no sign of Private Luck."

"I am surprised."

Melmoth paused before responding. He set his cigarette down on the ashtray and moved his glass of champagne so that it stood immediately before him. He sat forward and rested his elbows on the table, placing his right hand across his left. "You are not surprised, Dr. Quilp. You cannot be."

"I am," insisted the other man.

Melmoth spoke softly. "I know what you are, 'Dr. Quilp,' and you are certainly not what you claim to be." Melmoth gazed steadily at the man facing him. "For a brief moment yesterday—fleetingly—I thought you might be Private Luck. I only saw Luck once without his prison cap—and then his face was hidden beneath a layer of rouge and eye-shadow. He was about your height and build—and age. When I saw the powder on your face and considered your newly grown moustache and beard, I realised straight away that you were a man in disguise. For a moment, as I watched you hiding behind your spectacles, I thought you might be Luck—but then I saw the roughness of your hands and knew you could not be."

The man said nothing. He did not move. He barely breathed.

"When you introduced yourself to me yesterday," Melmoth continued, "I was intrigued that, in passing, you quoted *The Importance of Being Earnest*. I was charmed, even. But I was baffled by your name. Where did you find it? There's a Quilp in Dickens, of course, in *The Old Curiosity Shop*—but why *Doctor* Quilp? Did you know about my father? In Dublin, when I was a boy, Dr. Wilde was accused of rape by a woman who had once been his patient and his mistress. She published a scurrilous pamphlet in which she called my parents 'Dr. and Mrs. Quilp.' I thought perhaps you knew the story—and chose the name to tease or wound me."

"No," said the man. He spoke softly, too. "I had not heard that story." He gazed steadily at Melmoth. "But my name is Quilp," he insisted.

"You are no more Dr. Quilp than I am Sebastian Melmoth! Indeed, when you showed me your visiting card, I saw that it had been printed by the same printer who printed mine—a little man called Pascaud who trades not three streets from where we are seated now. You had your cards printed a matter of days ago. You are an impostor."

The man raised a hand in protest.

Melmoth brooked no interruption. "A seasoned impostor at that!" He laughed. "For everything you had an answer. When you told me that you were an apothecary and I said you did not have an apothecary's hands, you said, at once, that your father was a blacksmith! The answer was absurd, but it came to you so readily that I knew that I was dealing with a man to whom the manufacture of instant untruths is second nature." Melmoth took a sip of wine. "I knew at once that you were not who you claimed to be, 'Dr. Quilp'—but who were you? And why had you come to see me? Who is that man? I wondered. And what does he want?"

The man touched his cheque-book. "I wanted to hear your story," he said. "I was ready to pay for it."

"No," insisted Melmoth. "You did not want my story. You wanted the story of the murderer Atitis-Snake. You made that clear. You wanted what I knew of Atitis-Snake—nothing more. And by midnight last night you'd heard enough."

"By midnight we were both exhausted," said "Dr. Quilp."

"By midnight, you knew that I knew more than was good for you. And I knew that you knew more than you pretended." Melmoth drew on his cigarette and sat back for a moment. "For example, I had only mentioned Private Luck's Sanskrit names once, in passing, and yet, hours later, you recalled them instantly."

"I wrote them down."

Melmoth waved a dismissive hand. "You knew them already. You knew the whole story already, 'Dr. Quilp.' What you sought to discover was what *I* knew—and when you found that I knew too much, you packed me off to bed with a prostitute and a twist of Spanish fly."

"It is an aphrodisiac," said the man.

"Indeed, famously so," said Melmoth, laughing derisively. "It is the most notorious aphrodisiac in history. It comes from the Spanish fly beetle, does it not? I believe *Cantharis* is the Latin name. The correct dose will rouse a man. The incorrect dose will kill him."

"But, Mr. Melmoth—Mr. Wilde—you are alive . . ."

"And well," added Melmoth, with an inclination of his head. "I thank you." With his thumb and forefinger he picked a stray leaf of cigarette tobacco from his lower lip. "I count my blessings. But Achindra Acala Luck is dead. The Reverend M. T. Friend is dead. The Braddle brothers are dead. Your wife is dead."

"What are you saying?" The man looked about the deserted café. "What do you mean?"

"You know what I mean."

"You are quite mad."

"No, I am not mad," said Melmoth. "I am as sane as you are—Sebastian Atitis-Snake."

The man pushed back his chair. Melmoth held up a hand. "Don't go. There is no point. I know everything."

"Do you?" The man spat out the words contemptuously, but he did not move.

"I believe so. You have a wonderful name, Sebastian Atitis-Snake. I think you love it. I think it has been the making of you—at least, the making of your personality. It has also been your undoing. Names do make—and un-make—a man. I know. Were I called John Smith, I would not be Oscar Wilde. And if I cannot be Oscar Wilde, I will be Sebastian Melmoth. My new name has a ring to it—as my old one did. I imagine that's why you chose the name of Quilp as your nom de guerre. It's a name to reckon with. Will you say it for me? Say it out loud. Say it with pride. Let it roll off your tongue, Sebastian Atitis-Snake."

The man looked about him. The street was all but empty. The café barman and the waiter were nowhere to be seen. "Yes," said the man, softly, "I am Sebastian Atitis-Snake. That is my name."

"I raise my glass to it," said Melmoth, suiting the action to the words. "It is a remarkable name—quite special. And I believe that it has made you believe all your life that you, too, are remarkable—quite special. You are one of those in this world who must have his way—who will not be crossed, who cannot be denied. Your belief in yourself is colossal. I know the type—all too well. Your name is unique—and so are you. You believe that you can achieve whatever you want and will stop at nothing to do so."

"Is that so very wrong?" asked the man. The anger in his voice had subsided.

"When you tired of your wife, you rid yourself of her. That *was* wrong."

"You wronged your wife," murmured Atitis-Snake.

"I did not kill her," said Melmoth calmly. "When you found yourself in prison, you murdered one man—the first Warder Braddle—in the expectation that another, his brother, the second Warder Braddle, would find a way to free you. When he failed you, you took your revenge—you killed him, also. That was wrong."

"I was not going to rot my life away in Reading Gaol," said the man angrily. He had removed his spectacles. Visibly his temples throbbed. "You were sentenced to two years' hard labour, Oscar Wilde. I was sentenced for life." The man hit the table with a clenched fist. "I would be free."

"Yes—you would have your way, Sebastian Atitis-Snake, always. And to achieve your end, you conceived a plan to free yourself that was as dangerous as it was daring."

"I did," breathed Atitis-Snake. "I most surely did." He raised his glass and drank from it greedily.

"When you did not need to do so, you confessed to the murder of the second Warder Braddle. That was extraordinary. You pleaded 'Guilty but insane'—when you must have known that such a plea would fail. It had failed before—at your first trial in front of the same judge. Why should it succeed now?"

Atitis-Snake shrugged. "The idea of posing as a lunatic appealed to me. The idea of claiming that I was 'Professor Moriarty, the Napoleon of Crime,' amused me."

"And appealed to your histrionic vanity," said Melmoth. "And your plea might prove successful. And if it did, so be it. You would go to an asylum—and escape from there. But if it did not, you would be condemned to death. You can have been in no doubt about that."

"I was in no doubt about that," said Atitis-Snake emphatically.

"I believe that is what you wanted."

"I had a plan."

"A brilliant plan—and it almost worked, Sebastian Atitis-Snake. Indeed it would have worked had you not encountered another uniquely named self-styled genius along the way." Melmoth laughed. "My name is Oscar Fingal O'Flahertie Wills Wilde," he declared, throwing up his hands towards heaven. As he made the gesture, a dog ran out from under the archway alongside the café and began to chase a sheet of newspaper that the breeze was blowing down the street. "Forgive me," murmured Melmoth. "I am a little drunk."

"And I am a free man," said Atitis-Snake.

Melmoth looked at him. "You are. And poor Private Luck, late of the Bombay Grenadiers, is dead. He was hanged when you should have been."

Atitis-Snake said nothing, but held Melmoth's gaze.

"I believe the idea of another man hanging in your stead first entered your head on the day that Trooper Wooldridge was hanged. That was the day of your confession. That was the day when word went round the prison that when Wooldridge swung from the rope, his neck stretched by eleven inches and his face was distorted beyond recognition. Postmortem, the hanged man was unrecognisable."

"I raise my glass to you, Oscar Wilde."

"I raise mine to you, Sebastian Atitis-Snake. Wooldridge was unrecognisable postmortem, but how could you ensure that if another went to the gallows in your place, he would not be recognised *before* he reached the scaffold? Who sees the condemned man at the last? Who is with him at the dreadful moment when the white sack is put over his head and his face is obscured for ever? Four people. Just four. Two special warders—chosen for the very reason that they do not know the prisoner well. The hangman himself—who has never seen the condemned man before. And the prison chaplain—who knows the condemned man very well indeed. Therefore, you eliminate the prison chaplain. You must. And it is easily done. You are a master poisoner. Cantharides is your special friend."

"It was not easily done," said Atitis-Snake. "I had to hold a lethal dose of Spanish fly behind my teeth until I could spew it into the chaplain's communion wine. I foully burned my tongue and gums."

"But you achieved your end."

"Yes," said Atitis-Snake, complacently. "I did the chaplain a favour, didn't I? I sent him to meet his maker."

"Eliminating a potential witness is relatively easy for the great Atitis-Snake. But how to find your substitute—the man who would hang instead of you?"

"Any man of about the right height and weight and age would do. The prison was full of them."

"Indeed, but you needed one who was about to be released. You had to choose your man—and choose your moment. You had to leave it to the very last. And you did. You left it until the eve of the execution. You left it until the last time you were taken from your cell. As the warders brought you back from the bath-house you seized your opportunity. *You* created the disturbance—the near insurrection—that brought about your freedom."

"And how did I do that, Mr. Sherlock Holmes?"

"Yes," said Melmoth, smiling. "Holmes is the clue. As

the star prisoners walked towards you along the corridor outside your cell, from beneath your cap *you* called out, 'Hang well, Professor Moriarty!' I knew it would not have been one of them—they were star prisoners, new to Reading Gaol. And Warder Stokes was clear it was not Private Luck. It was a man's voice that called out—not the shrill voice of an Indian eunuch."

"Bravo, Holmes. Bravo, Melmoth. Bravo, Wilde. Three cheers."

"You threw yourself into the fray—with nothing to lose and everything to gain. You cannot have been certain of the outcome, but you seized the moment—and you seized it well. When the warders flung you and Luck into the condemned cell, you knew at once what you had to do. You had to make your victim instantly unrecognisable. You took the poor eunuch by the head and scraped his face against the wall. You threw him to the ground and kicked in his windpipe. You robbed him of his features. You robbed him of his voice."

Atitis-Snake laughed. "He put up a good fight."

"He was Private A. A. Luck, late of the Bombay Grenadiers. He'd been a soldier—but, poor man, he was a girl at heart and he was not your match. You overwhelmed him and when you had the unhappy wretch upon the ground, you took his number from his uniform and substituted your own. You took his cap from his head and hid your own face beneath it—and the moment the cell door opened, you fled through it 'like a scalded cat' and sped, 'like greased lightning,' along the corridor and up the gantry to his cell."

Atitis-Snake chuckled. "I knew the way."

"You must have held your breath that night—wondering whether your plan would work. When they came to take you from Luck's cell to have you beaten for your part in the 'insurrection,' you knew that it had."

"I was ready for them."

"I imagine that you were. In your own cell, I assume that you hid your stash of poison in your bed—in the cracks between the wooden plank and the metal frame. That's where Luck hid his face paints and his powders. You found them and you put them on."

"Yes, in case the cap fell off. But it didn't. I was lucky there."

"You were lucky, too, that Governor Nelson did not postpone the hanging. You were lucky that Dr. Maurice was away. He might have recognised Luck's features, notwithstanding the damage you had done his face and the distortion wrought by the hangman's rope."

"I took Luck's punishment. And he took mine."

"His body is now decomposing in a pit of lime—in an unmarked grave."

"My back is still scarred from the beating. I was bent double for a week."

"And your face betrays some bruising, I see, now that you have wiped away the powder from your forehead. But you are alive, Sebastian Atitis-Snake. And Achindra Acala Luck is dead. You hobbled out of that accursed prison in Luck's place—your face masked by Luck's make-up, your head wrapped in one of Luck's saris. You escaped Reading Gaol, Sebastian Atitis-Snake. A. A. Luck is forever buried there."

The man blew his nose and wiped his mouth. "Dr. Maurice said you were a clever man and so it seems. When did you have your first clue of this?"

"Did Dr. Maurice also tell you that I am a friend of Arthur Conan Doyle?"

"He did."

"Are you familiar with a story called 'Silver Blaze'?"

Atitis-Snake shook his head.

"In the story, Sherlock Holmes brings to the attention of the detective in the case 'the curious incident of the dog in the night-time.' 'The dog did *nothing* in the night-time,' said the detective. '*That* was the curious incident,' said Holmes."

Atitis-Snake raised an eyebrow.

"On the morning of the hanging," explained Melmoth, "Private Luck did not call out to me. He always spoke to me—every day, without fail, from his cell, at the same time, in the same way. But on the day he left the prison, he did not. I thought of the dog that did not bark in the night and realised that the prisoner who did not speak in the morning could not be Private Luck."

Atitis-Snake nodded appreciatively. He raised his wine-glass to Melmoth one final time and drained it. "I see," he said. He was quite calm. "What do we do now?" he asked, picking up his cheque-book.

"You go to bed—and I take my leave of you."

"You should be grateful to me, you know, Mr. Oscar Fingal O'Flahertie Wills Wilde. I killed the man who would have destroyed you. Luck was a blackmailer, and a determined one. He would have come after you and told your wife all sorts of sordid stories."

Melmoth shook his head. "I cannot be grateful to you, sir. You rid me of an enemy, that's true, but last night you tried to murder me. You sent me to bed with a prostitute— and a dose of your beloved Spanish fly."

"I don't deny it, but much good did it do me. I appear to have got the dosage wrong—for here you are."

"I am here because I did not touch your devilish aphrodisiac. I kept the powder dry, in fact—and, half an hour ago, when I went to 'powder my nose,' I poured your twist of powder—all of it, no half measures—into a glass of champagne. When I returned to our table, I rearranged the glasses and set the poisoned yellow wine before you. I see that you have drunk it all."

As tears filled his eyes, Atitis-Snake began to laugh. "I am going to die," he cried. He looked around the deserted café. "It cannot be." He gazed at Melmoth pleadingly. "Is this true?"

"It is."

"Why? Why must I die?"

"So that the boy, Tom, can live," said Melmoth, simply.

"This is all about the boy, Tom?" cried Atitis-Snake, the tears now tumbling down his cheeks.

"Yes, this is all about the boy, Tom," said Melmoth. "He and I, I realise, are the only ones left who know all your secrets. At Reading Gaol, you made Tom your friend—and your accomplice. Doubtless when he cleaned the cells, he made sure your stocks of poison were not discovered. Once you had murdered me, I think you would have waited for his release and then murdered him." Melmoth smiled and ran his forefinger lightly around the rim of his champagne glass. "On the day of my release, when I had done my shopping and before I caught the train to Newhaven, I took a cab to his mother's address in Whitechapel and I promised her that I would do my best for her son. I have broken so many promises in my life, but this one, at least, I have kept."

Atitis-Snake looked down at the empty glass that stood on the table before him. "What time did you give me this champagne?"

Melmoth took out his half-hunter. "Half an hour ago, at most."

"What time is it now?"

"Five o'clock."

"I will be dead by seven, Oscar Wilde." He laughed and cried at the same time. "Killed—with a dose of my own poison."

Melmoth smiled. "All men kill the thing they love," he said, gently. "Go to your room now, Sebastian Atitis-Snake. And if you have prayers to say, say them. You don't want to die here, at this table. The foot passengers from the paddle-steamer will be coming by in a moment. They are already late."

AFTERWORD

*T*he body of "Dr. Quilp" was discovered in an upstairs bedroom at the Café Suisse on the morning of Saturday, 26 June 1897. According to the brief report that appeared ten days later in the *Gazette des Bains*, the man was *"un inconnu"*—an unknown—who carried in his coat pocket a small packet of recently printed visiting cards bearing the name *Dr. Quilp*, but no other form of identification. His age, nationality, and occupation could only be guessed at, said Dr. Pierre Pollet, the police doctor, giving evidence at the inquest, but what was not in doubt was the cause of death. "This man had poisoned himself with an overdose of cantharides powder. His face was severely bloated, his skin a mass of blisters." According to the coroner, Monsieur Varangeville, it was a regrettable fact of life that strangers would come to Dieppe to avail themselves of prostitutes and take risks with so-called aphrodisiacs. Because, understandably, what little money the man had on him at the time of his death had been taken by the management of the Café

Suisse as a contribution towards his unpaid bill, the coroner had no choice but to order the burial of the deceased in the municipal graveyard at public expense.

Within weeks of Quilp's death, Oscar finished writing *The Ballad of Reading Gaol*. When the poem was published in book form, in February 1898, he arranged for one copy to be sent to R. B. Haldane, the Member of Parliament (and, later, Lord Chancellor) who had visited him at Pentonville Prison at the beginning of his sentence, and another to Major Nelson, the governor of Reading Gaol. The copy that he sent to me was inscribed on the title page:

> *Robert Harborough Sherard: in memory of an old and noble friendship: from the author Oscar Wilde.*

These words were written in ink, but below them Oscar had added, in pencil:

> *In my end is my beginning—from first to last*

And on the final page of the book, again in pencil, he had lightly underlined the first and last letter of each line of the last three verses of the poem:

> *In Reading gaol by Reading town*
> *There is a pit of shame,*
> *And in it lies a wretched man*
> *Eaten by teeth of flame,*
> *In a burning winding-sheet he lies,*
> *And his grave has got no name.*

And there, till Christ call forth the dead,
In silence let him lie:
No need to waste the foolish tear,
Or heave the windy sigh:
The man had killed the thing he loved,
And so he had to die.
And all men kill the thing they love,
By all let this be heard,
Some do it with a bitter look,
Some with a flattering word,
The coward does it with a kiss,
The brave man with a sword!

Knowing my friend's fondness for playing with words, I made a note of the thirty-six letters he had underscored and rearranged them to form a sentence that reads: "Sebastian Atitis-Snake done the dread deed."

Within weeks of completing *The Ballad of Reading Gaol*, Oscar was reunited with Lord Alfred Douglas, the young man whose presence in his life had brought about his downfall. At the end of August, from his favourite table at the Café Suisse, Oscar, now forty-two, wrote to Lord Alfred, now twenty-six: "Everyone is furious with me for going back to you, but they don't understand us. I feel it is only with you that I can do anything at all. Do remake my ruined life for me, and then our friendship and love will have a different meaning to the world."

At the end of September, Constance wrote to her husband from Genoa: "I *forbid* you to see Lord Alfred Douglas. I forbid you to return to your filthy, insane life." But Oscar found he could not obey his wife's command—and so, lost her and his children and the small allowance of £3 a week that she had been paying him. "Nemesis has caught me in her net," he wrote, "to struggle is foolish. Why is it that one runs to one's ruin? Why has destruction such a fascination? Why, when one stands on a pinnacle, must one throw oneself down? No one knows, but things are so."

In the spring of 1898, Constance, who had damaged her back in a fall, had an operation on her spine. The operation failed and she died on 7 April, aged thirty-nine. Oscar was distraught. "If only we had met once, and kissed each other," he wrote. "It is too late. How awful life is." The following year, he went to Genoa to visit her grave: "It is very pretty—a marble cross with dark ivy-leaves inlaid in a good pattern . . . I brought some flowers. I was deeply affected— with a sense, also, of the uselessness of all regrets. Nothing could have been otherwise, and Life is a very terrible thing."

Constance's death brought Oscar £150 a year from her estate, unconditionally. He continued to see Lord Alfred Douglas, but it was not as it had once been between them. After writing *The Ballad of Reading Gaol,* he did no serious work: he travelled, he drank, he borrowed money from friends, he took each day as it came. He could not—or would not—concentrate to write, but when he and I met, over absinthe and cigarettes, he told me stories of his adventures, which I wrote down—promising him faithfully that they would not be published during his lifetime. I asked him if he wanted the story of Atitis-Snake to be published at all.

"Yes," he insisted. "Most definitely."

"But you murdered a man, Oscar," I reminded him.

"Yes," he said, "and I used to play golf—rather well. There is so much more to Oscar Wilde than the public appreciates. In time, they must be allowed to know it all."

"Why did you kill him?" I asked. "Was it part of your desire for experience? Because you wanted 'to eat of the fruit of all the trees in the garden of the world'?"

"No," he answered emphatically. "For once in my life, I did the decent thing. If Atitis-Snake had lived," he said, "the boy, Tom, would never have been safe."

Gradually, my friend's health deteriorated. In particular, his ear worsened. Three and a half years after his release from prison, he died in Paris, of cerebral meningitis, on 30 November 1900. He was just forty-six years of age.

Oscar was given a pauper's burial in a leased grave at Bagneux, a suburb seven miles to the south of central Paris. Nine years later his remains were removed to the French national cemetery at Père Lachaise, where they now rest beneath a fine monument created by the young sculptor Jacob Epstein.

Impressive as is Epstein's monumental winged sphinx in Oscar's memory, for me it does not rival the tomb built for Sir Richard Burton in the graveyard of St. Mary Magdalen in Mortlake, a village seven miles to the south of central London. The Burton tomb, thirteen feet in height, is an exact representation of a desert tent, its sandstone walls sculpted to depict the cloth of the tent rippling in the desert breeze. Oscar in Paris and Constance in Genoa are buried five hundred miles apart. At Mortlake, in their tent-like mausoleum, Richard and Isabel Burton are buried side by side—despite the best efforts of Private A. A. Luck, late of the Bombay Grenadiers.

In 1906, I published *The Life of Oscar Wilde* and included in the biography a chapter specially written by Warder Thomas Martin. When I had completed the book and delivered my manuscript to the publishers, I was sorting through the materials that I had used while writing it and came across a slip of paper that, at first, meant nothing to me. All that was on the paper was an address in Whitechapel—written clearly, but not in Oscar's hand. I asked Warder Martin if the handwriting or the address meant anything to him. He recalled at once that the handwriting was that of Dr. Maurice, the surgeon at Reading Gaol, and the address was that of the mother of Prisoner E.1.1.—the boy Tom Lewis.

I remembered then that it was Oscar who had given me the piece of paper and had asked me, one day, when convenient, to visit the address to find out, if I could, what had become of the boy. I did so, in October 1906. I found the address without difficulty and there, in a tidy terraced house off the Whitechapel Road, I found the boy's mother—living alone. She was a small, bird-like lady in her mid-fifties, with white hair, pink cheeks, and a friendly disposition. She appeared happy to meet me and proud to talk about her son, who, she assured me, had not been in trouble of any kind since coming out of prison eight years before. She saw her boy very little nowadays, but he sent her money every week and she was grateful for that. He ran a restaurant, she told me, near King's Cross railway station, which enjoyed what she called "a very high-class sort of clientele." She had never been to visit it herself—her son discouraged her: "Home is home and business is business," he said—but she knew the address and she gave it to me. I went there that same afternoon. The restaurant turned out to be a café, with, above it, on the first floor, what was undoubtedly a male brothel. I think that Oscar would have been amused. When he had asked me to enquire after the boy, he had said to me, "Remember, Tom Lewis is his name. As names go, it is not very promising. Do not expect too much of him. If only he had been called Oscar Wilde, think what a life he might have led!"

RHS
September 1939

Reading Gaol in the 1890s

Her Majesty's Prison Reading was built in 1844. The designer was the great Victorian architect George Gilbert Scott, who went on to build London's Albert Memorial and the Midland Grand Hotel at St. Pancras station. The design for Reading Gaol was based on the 1842 New Model Prison at Pentonville, which in its turn was based on the design of the 1829 Eastern State Penitentiary in Philadelphia, Pennsylvania. The design was to allow for the implementation of the favoured penal regime of the time, the "separate system," whereby the inmates were kept in solitary confinement and prevented from seeing or speaking to one another. The aim of the system was to allow the prisoners within the "penitentiary" the opportunity for quiet reflection and the true repentance of sins. As a county gaol, Reading also served as the site for executions: the first in 1845, in front of a crowd of 10,000; the last in 1913.

The full history of Reading Gaol is told in *Pit of Shame: The Real Ballad of Reading Gaol* (Waterside Press, 2007) by Anthony Stokes, for many years a senior prison officer at Reading Gaol.

Rules for Prisoners in the 1890s

1. The bell shall ring at the opening and locking up of the rooms and cells, which shall be, from Lady Day to Michaelmas Day, at six o'clock in the morning and eight o'clock in the evening; and in the winter months at daylight in the morning and eight in the evening; and at all times the prisoners shall be locked up in their day rooms before dusk in the evening.

2. No person shall be allowed admission into the prison during the hours of prayer, the time for public worship, or before unlocking or after locking up hours; and no person (except a barrister or solicitor), unless in the presence of the prison Governor or some person appointed by him, shall remain within the prison after hours or locking up, except in the case of sickness of a prisoner, or some other cause assigned to the satisfaction of the Governor.

3. Every prisoner shall attend prayer and public worship, except in the case of illness, or other reasonable cause, to be allowed by the governor or visiting justice.

4. Every prisoner guilty of drunkenness, blasphemy, swearing, or any improper expression, or any abuse or disorderly conduct, shall be punished at the discretion of the governor.

5. Every prisoner shall make his or her own bed, and be washed before nine o'clock every morning, on pain of forfeiting one day's allowance of provisions.

6. No tobacco to be used in the prison.

7. All prisoners who shall not be at work shall be required to walk round the yards, or be locked up in solitary cells.

8. The chambers and cells shall be swept out and thoroughly cleaned by the prisoners every morning before they are left.

9. No wine, ale, beer, porter, or spirituous liquors of any kind, shall be admitted for any convicted prisoner under any pretence whatever, unless ordered by the surgeon in his journal.

10. Every prisoner shall, at locking up time, present himself in the yard, and also at the door of the cell, to the turnkey.

11. Silence must be observed on all occasions by day and night.

12. Every prisoner guilty of any of the following offences will subject himself to punishment:

- Talking, shouting, cursing, swearing, singing, whistling, attempting to communicate by signs, by writing, or in any other way.

- Unnecessarily looking around or about at any time.

- Having in possession or attempting to receive money, tobacco, knives.

- Looking out, or attempting to look out, at window or door of a cell.

- Not folding a bed in the proper manner; being in bed after 6 in the morning or before 8 in the evening.

- Stealing any property of the prison or of a prisoner; trying to take anything left from another prisoner's meal.

- Spitting on, or disfiguring the prison walls and floors.

- Irreverent behaviour in chapel either before, during, or after service.

- Striking, or in any way assaulting or threatening another prisoner or officer.

- Attempting to escape, or assisting other to do so.

- Not folding up clothing in a proper manner.

- Not washing feet twice a week, prior to using the water to clean the cell.

- Not ready to leave cell when unlocked by officer for exercise, chapel.

Prisoners wishing to see the Governor, Chaplain or Surgeon must apply to the officer when paraded for exercise in the morning, who is bound to attend to such applications.

Regulations for the Administration
of Corporal Punishment

All acts of corporal punishments will be carried out in the presence of the governor or warden and of the prison surgeon or chief medical officer.

Standard approved instruments must be used for the administration of all punishments, either birch rod or cat-o-nine-tails.

Each birch rod or cat-o-nine-tails must be used for one punishment only and must be destroyed after use.

Only use a cat-o-nine-tails that bears the seal of the Prison Commission.

For males over 10 and up to 16 years of age, use scale B. For males over 16, use scale C.

	B	C
Weight not exceeding	9 oz	12 oz
Length from end of handle to tip of spray	40 inches	48 inches
Length of handle	15 inches	22 inches
Circumference of spray at centre	6 inches	7 inches
Circumference of handle at top of binding	3½ inches	5 inches
Circumference of handle 6 inches from end	3¼ inches	3 inches

(The Prison Act of 1898 reduced the use of corporal punishment to two types of offences only: gross personal violence to an officer of the prison; and acts of mutiny. In 1906, Colonel Isaacson, by then governor of Manchester Prison, wrote: "In every large prison there is always a small fraction of the population imbued with brutality, to whom dietary punishment is absolutely useless. For these, when they resort to personal violence on an officer, I can see no alternative but the birch rod or cat." Birching as a judicial penalty, in both its juvenile and adult versions, was abolished in 1948, although retained until 1962 as a punishment for violent breaches of prison discipline.)

Executions—the Length of the Drop

The length of the drop may usually be calculated by dividing 1,000 foot-pounds by the weight of the culprit and his clothing in pounds, which will give the length of the drop in feet, but no drop should exceed 8 feet 6 inches. Thus a person weighing 150 pounds in his clothing will ordinarily require a drop of 1,000 divided by 150 = 6⅔ feet, ie 6 feet 8 inches.

When for any special reason, such as a diseased condition of the neck of the culprit, the Governor and Medical Officer think that there should be a departure from the standard procedure, they may inform the executioner and advise him as to the length of the drop which should be given in that particular case.

Letter from Prisoner C.3.3. to the Home Secretary, November 1896

H M Prison, Reading
Prisoner C.3.3.—Oscar Wilde

10 November 1896

To the Right Honourable Her Majesty's Principal Secretary of State for the Home Department.

The petition of the above-named prisoner humbly sheweth that in the month of June last the petitioner, having been at that time a prisoner for more than a year, addressed to the Secretary of State a petition praying for his release on the grounds chiefly of mental health.

That the petitioner has received no answer to his petition, and would earnestly beg that it be taken into consideration, as on the 19th inst. The petitioner will have completed eighteen months of solitary confinement, a sentence of terrible severity in any case, and, in the case of the petitioner, rendered all the more difficult to bear, as it has been inflicted for offences which are in other countries in Europe more rightly recognised as tragic forms of madness coming chiefly on those who overtax their brain, in art or science.

Some alleviations have been granted to the petitioner since the date of his former petition: his ear, that was in danger of total deafness, is now attended to daily: spectacles have been provided for the protection of his eyes: he is allowed a manuscript-book to write in, and out of a list of books, selected by himself and approved of by the Prison Commissioners, a few have been added to the Prison Library: but these alleviations, for which the petitioner is naturally very grateful, count for but little in relieving the terrible mental stress and anguish that the silence and solitude of prison-life intensify daily.

Of all modes of insanity—and the petitioner is fully conscious now, too conscious it may be, that his whole life, for the two years preceding his ruin, was the prey of absolute madness—the insanity of perverted sensual instinct is the one most dominant in its action on the brain. It taints the intellectual as well as the emotional energies. It clings like a malaria to soul and body alike. And while one may bear up against the monotonous hardships and relentless discipline of an English prison: endure with apathy the unceasing shame and the daily degradation: and grow callous even to that hideous grotesqueness of life that robs sorrow of all its dignity, and takes from pain its power of purification; still, the complete isolation from everything that is humane and humanising plunges one deeper and deeper into the very mire of madness, and the horrible silence, to which one is, as it were, eternally condemned, concentrates the mind on all that one longs to loathe, and creates those insane moods from which one desires to be free, creates them and makes them permanent.

Under the circumstances the petitioner prays for his release on the expiration of his term of eighteen months' confinement, or at any rate before Christmas comes. Some friends have promised to take him abroad at once and to see that he has the treatment and care that he requires. There is of course before him no public life: nor any life in literature any more: nor joy or happiness of life at all. He has lost wife, children, fame, honour, position, wealth: poverty is all that he can look forward to: obscurity all that he can hope for: yet he feels that, if released now, somewhere, unknown, untormented, at peace he might be able to recreate the life of a student of letters, and find in literature an anodyne from pain, first, and afterwards a mode by which sanity and balance and wholesomeness might be restored to the soul. But the solitary confinement, that breaks one's heart, shatters one's intellect too: and prison is but an ill physician: and the modern modes of punishment create what they should cure, and, when they have on their side Time with its long length of dreary days, they desecrate and destroy whatever good, or desire even of good, there may be in a man.

To be at length, after these eighteen months of lonely sorrow, set free, for whatever brief space of time health of mind or body may allow, is the earnest prayer of the petitioner.

Oscar Wilde

Letter from Oscar Wilde to the Daily Chronicle, May 1897

On 27 May 1897, from Dieppe, Oscar Wilde wrote a long letter to the *Daily Chronicle* about the conditions at Reading Gaol. He wrote specifically about the case of Warder Martin, "dismissed by the Prison Commissioners for having given some sweet biscuits to a little hungry child," and about the beating of Prisoner A.2.11., Prince, who "had had twenty-four lashes in the cookhouse on Saturday afternoon": "This man is undoubtedly becoming insane." Wilde praised Governor Nelson—"a man of gentle and humane character, greatly liked and respected by all the prisoners"— but concluded: "the system is of course beyond his reach so far as altering its rules is concerned. I have no doubt that he sees daily much of what he knows to be unjust, stupid and cruel. But his hands are tied."

Warder Martin had been dismissed for "gross insubordination." Following the publication of Wilde's letter in the *Daily Chronicle,* the Prison Commission looked again at Martin's case and at the other points raised by Wilde. On 15 June 1897, the Commission concluded that the decision regarding Martin had been the correct one: "He was an unsatisfactory officer and it is not easy to attribute the conduct which led to his dismissal to an excusable motive. Supposing he was a specially tender-hearted man and honestly believed the boy was suffering from hunger, he should have reported this to the governor. To permit warders—

even from humane motives—to distinguish one prisoner from another by kindly acts would obviously lead to very serious scandals, and Martin had previously been suspected of trafficking with prisoners."

R. B. Haldane was a member of the Prison Commission and of the parliamentary committee (chaired by Herbert Gladstone) that had been considering the whole matter of prison reform since 1894. Wilde's letter to the *Daily Chronicle* played its part in the debate and in the reforms that followed. The Prisons Act of 1898 modified the "separate system," allowing prisoners to communicate with one another, abolished hard labour, and introduced the concept of remission for good behaviour.

ACKNOWLEDGEMENTS

Readers of my series of Oscar Wilde murder mysteries frequently ask me the same question: "How much of this is true?" My answer is, "All of it. Or almost all. Certainly, much more than you would think." For example, Colonel Isaacson, Major Nelson, Dr. Maurice, the Reverend M. T. Friend, even Professor Bent Ball and the prisoner Prince: notwithstanding their unlikely names, these are all real people with fascinating individual stories.

I hope that my account of life in Reading Gaol in the 1890s is accurate. It is based on Wilde's own account, of course, and on accounts by others who knew the prison at the time. I am especially indebted to Anthony Stokes, for many years a senior prison officer at HM Prison, Reading, and author of *Pit of Shame: The Real Ballad of Reading Gaol* (2007), who took me on an extended tour of the prison and allowed me to spend some time in Wilde's cell. (Since 1992 Reading has been a Remand Centre and Young Offender Institution, holding males aged eighteen to twenty-one.

Wilde's cell is, of course, no larger than it was in the 1890s, though the prisoner's bed is marginally more comfortable and there is a television to watch. Thanks to that television, the young prisoner I met on my visit to cell C.3.3. knew quite well who I was, even though he had not heard of Oscar Wilde.)

I am also indebted to Isobel Morrow, Independent Monitoring Board, HM Prison, Reading, and to Pauline Bryant, who was Governing Governor at Reading at the time of my visit. My special thanks, too, go to my friend Roger Lewis, who introduced me to the work of Sir Charles Bent Ball, and to Andrea Lloyd, Curator, Printed Literary Sources 1801–1914 at the British Library, who showed me the original manuscript of *De Profundis*, the letter Wilde wrote from Reading Gaol to Lord Alfred Douglas—tear stains and all.

For their continuing encouragement and support, I thank Roger Johnson and Jean Upton of the Sherlock Holmes Society of London, and Michael Seeney and Donald Mead of the Oscar Wilde Society. As ever, I am especially grateful to Merlin Holland, the only grandson of Oscar Wilde and Constance, for his friendship and indulgence. He has been good enough to correct inaccuracies in these books when he has spotted them and generous enough to encourage me in my endeavours. Given that he is certainly the most distinguished Wildean scholar of them all, and that I am making a fiction of his grandparents' extraordinary lives, this is indeed a kindness.

For her sustaining enthusiasm and detailed input, my principal debt, of course, is to my British publisher, Kate

Parkin at John Murray, who has guided me from the outset. I am also much indebted to my publishers in other countries, notably Lauren Spiegel at Touchstone, Simon & Schuster, in New York, and Emmanuelle Heurtebize at 10/18 in Paris. As with each book in this series, I owe considerably more than fifteen per cent to my literary agent, the incomparable Ed Victor, and to his team, including Maggie Phillips, Linda Van, Morag O'Brien, and Charlie Campbell.

This is the sixth book in this series to date. Readers new to the series regularly ask, Which one should I start with? The answer is, Truly, it does not matter. Each mystery stands alone. *Oscar Wilde and a Death of No Importance* is set in 1889 and begins with the first encounter between Oscar Wilde and Arthur Conan Doyle, but it does not need to be read first. *Oscar Wilde and the Dead Man's Smile* is set in the early 1880s, at the time of Oscar's celebrated lecture tour of the United States, and later, when, for a while, he lived and worked in Paris. *Oscar Wilde and the Vatican Murders* begins right back in 1877 when Oscar, as a student visiting Rome, had an audience with Pope Pius IX. *Oscar Wilde and the Vampire Murders* begins in the spring of 1890 and features Wilde's association with the Prince of Wales and Bram Stoker. *Oscar Wilde and a Game called Murder* is an adventure that takes place in 1892, at the time of Wilde's great success with the play *Lady Windermere's Fan*. Please read next whichever of the stories comes most easily to hand.

The third question I am most frequently asked is this: Which biography of Oscar Wilde do you recommend? Of course I recommend *Oscar Wilde* by Richard Ellmann (1987), but, magisterial as it is, the book is riddled with inaccuracies and must be read in conjunction with *Additions and Corrections to Richard Ellmann's Oscar Wilde* by Horst Schroeder (2002). I also recommend, and without reservation, *The Wilde Album* by Merlin Holland (1997) and *Oscar Wilde and His World* by Vyvyan Holland (1966). The two books that, for me, take the reader closest to "the real Oscar Wilde" are *The Complete Letters of Oscar Wilde* edited by Merlin Holland and Rupert Hart-Davis (2000) and *Son of Oscar Wilde* by Vyvyan Holland (1954). For the most complete portrait of Constance Wilde I wholeheartedly recommend *Constance: The Tragic and Scandalous Life of Mrs. Oscar Wilde* by Franny Moyle (2011), and for a wonderfully evocative picture of Dieppe at the time of Wilde's sojourn there, I recommend *60 Miles from England: The English at Dieppe 1814–1914* by Simona Pakenham (1967).

Biographical Notes

Oscar Wilde

Oscar Fingal O'Flahertie Wills Wilde was born at 21 Westland Row, Dublin, on 16 October 1854. He was the second son of Sir William Wilde, an eminent Irish surgeon, and Jane Francesca Wilde, née Elgee, a poet, author, and translator, who wrote under the pseudonym "Speranza." Oscar Wilde was educated at Portora Royal School, Enniskillen, at Trinity College, Dublin, and at Magdalen College, Oxford, where he achieved a double first and, for his poem *Ravenna*, was awarded the Newdigate Prize for Poetry. On leaving Oxford, he settled in London and embarked on a career as a professional writer, critic, and journalist. His play *Vera* was published in 1880 and his *Poems* appeared in 1881.

In 1881, Richard D'Oyly Carte presented the Gilbert & Sullivan operetta *Patience*, satirising Oscar and his fellow "aesthetes." Its success, and Wilde's celebrity, led D'Oyly Carte to invite the young author, aged twenty-eight, to undertake an extensive lecture tour of North America at the beginning of 1882. In 1883, Wilde spent several months in

Paris, working on his play *The Duchess of Padua*, and meeting, among others, Victor Hugo, Paul Verlaine, Emile Zola, and Robert Sherard. On 29 May 1884 he married Constance Lloyd, the daughter of a noted Irish QC, and set up home at 16 Tite Street, Chelsea. Their sons, Cyril and Vyvyan, were born in 1885 and 1887.

Wilde's story *Lord Arthur Savile's Crime* appeared in 1887, followed, in 1888, by *The Happy Prince and Other Tales* and, in 1889 and 1890, more controversially, by *The Portrait of Mr. W. H.* and *The Picture of Dorian Gray.* The first of his successful social comedies, *Lady Windermere's Fan*, was produced in London in 1892, followed by *A Woman of No Importance* (1893), *An Ideal Husband* (1895), and *The Importance of Being Earnest* (1895).

In 1891 Oscar Wilde met Lord Alfred Douglas, the third son of the then Marquess of Queensberry. In 1895 Queensberry left a card for Wilde at the Albemarle Club accusing him of "posing Somdomite" (*sic*) and provoking Wilde to sue Queensberry for criminal libel. The failure of the libel action led to Wilde's own prosecution on charges of gross indecency. On 25 May 1895 he was found guilty and sentenced to two years' imprisonment with hard labour. Released from gaol on 19 May 1897, Wilde travelled immediately to France and spent the rest of his life on the Continent. His poem *The Ballad of Reading Gaol* was published in 1898, and his confessional letter *De Profundis* was published posthumously, in 1905. Constance Wilde died in Genoa on 7 April 1898, following an operation on her spine. Oscar Wilde died in Paris on 30 November 1900. He was buried at Bagneux Cemetery. In 1909 his remains were moved to the French national cemetery of Père Lachaise.

Robert Sherard

Robert Harborough Sherard Kennedy was born in London on 3 December 1861, the fourth child of the Reverend Bennet Sherard Calcraft Kennedy. His father was the illegitimate son of the sixth and last Earl of Harborough and his mother, Jane Stanley Wordsworth, was the granddaughter of the poet laureate William Wordsworth (1770–1850). Robert was educated at Queen Elizabeth College, Guernsey, at New College, Oxford, and at the University of Bonn, but he left both Oxford and Bonn without securing a degree. In 1880, having quarrelled with his father and lost his expected inheritance, he abandoned his "Kennedy" surname.

In the early 1880s, Robert Sherard settled in Paris and set about earning his living as an author and journalist. He cultivated the acquaintance of a number of the leading literary figures of the day, including Emile Zola, Guy de Maupassant, Alphonse Daudet, and Oscar Wilde. He published thirty-three books during his lifetime, including a collection of poetry, *Whispers* (1884), novels, biographies, social studies (notably *The White Slaves of England*, 1897), and five books inspired by his friendship with Oscar Wilde: *Oscar Wilde: The Story of an Unhappy Friendship*, 1902; *The Life of Oscar Wilde*, 1906; *The Real Oscar Wilde*, 1912; *Oscar Wilde Twice Defended*, 1934; and *Bernard Shaw, Frank Harris and Oscar Wilde*, 1936.

He was three times married and lived much of his life in France, where he was made a Chevalier de la Légion d'Honneur. He died in England, in Ealing, on 30 January 1943.

In 1960, in *Oscar Wilde and His World,* Vyvyan Holland, Wilde's younger son, gave this assessment of Robert Sherard:

When they first met . . . they felt they had nothing in common and disliked each other intensely; but they gradually got together and became life-long friends. Sherard wrote the first three biographical studies of Wilde after his death . . . On these three books are based all the other biographies of Wilde, except the so-called biography by Frank Harris, which is nothing else but the glorification of Frank Harris. Sherard got a great deal of his material from Lady Wilde when she was a very old lady and was inclined to let her imagination run away with her, particularly where the family history was concerned; and Sherard, a born journalist, was much more attracted by the interest of a story than by its accuracy, a failing which we can see running through all his books. But where his actual contact with Wilde is concerned, he is quite reliable.

Gyles Brandreth

Gyles Brandreth was born on 8 March 1948 in Germany, where his father, Charles Brandreth, was serving as a legal officer with the Allied Control Commission and counted among his colleagues H. Montgomery Hyde, who published the first full account of the trials of Oscar Wilde in

1948. In 1974, Gyles Brandreth produced *The Trials of Os-car Wilde* (with Tom Baker as Wilde) at the Oxford Theatre Festival and, in 2000, edited the transcripts of the trials for an audio production featuring Martin Jarvis.

Gyles Brandreth was educated at the Lycée Français de Londres, at Betteshanger School in Kent, and at Bedales in Hampshire, where the school's founder, J. H. Badley (1865–1967), provided him with a series of vivid personal accounts of Oscar Wilde's conversational style. Badley was a friend of the Wildes, and their son Cyril was a pupil at Bedales at the time of Oscar's arrest. Gyles Brandreth went on (like Robert Sherard) to New College, Oxford (where he was a scholar, President of the Union, and editor of the university magazine), and then (again like Sherard) embarked on a career as an author and journalist. His first book was a study of prison reform (*Created in Captivity,* 1972); his first biography was a portrait of the Victorian music-hall star Dan Leno (*The Funniest Man on Earth,* 1974). More recently he has published a biography of Sir John Gielgud, an acclaimed diary of his years as an MP and government whip (*Breaking the Code: Westminster Diaries*) and two best-selling royal biographies: *Philip & Elizabeth: Portrait of a Marriage* and *Charles & Camilla: Portrait of a Love Affair.* In 2010 John Murray (publishers of Arthur Conan Doyle) published Gyles Brandreth's diaries covering the years 1959 to 2000, under the title *Something Sensational to Read in the Train*—a phrase borrowed from *The Importance of Being Earnest.*

Robert Sherard's forebears included William Wordsworth. Gyles Brandreth's include a less eminent poet, George R. Sims (1847–1922), who wrote the ballads "Billy's

Dead and Gone to Glory" and "Christmas Day in the Workhouse," and was the first journalist to claim to know the true identity of "Jack the Ripper." Sims, a kinsman of the Empress Eugénie and an acquaintance of both Oscar Wilde and Arthur Conan Doyle, was probably the first "celebrity columnist" and well known in his day for his endorsement of an "infallible cure for baldness" known as Tatcho, The Geo R Sims Hair Restorer.

As an actor Gyles Brandreth has appeared in pantomime and Shakespeare, and, most recently, as Lady Bracknell in a musical adaptation of *The Importance of Being Earnest*. As a broadcaster, he has presented numerous series for BBC Radio 4, including *A Rhyme in Time, Sound Advice, Wordaholics,* and *Whispers*—coincidentally the title of Robert Sherard's first collection of poetry. He has featured on *Desert Island Discs* and is now best known as a regular on *Just a Minute* (Radio 4) and a reporter on *The One Show* (BBC 1). He is a regular on the Channel 4 word game *Countdown,* and his television appearances have ranged from being the guest host of *Have I Got News for You* to being the subject of *This Is Your Life.* With Hinge & Bracket he scripted the TV series *Dear Ladies;* with Julian Slade he wrote a play about A. A. Milne (featuring the young Aled Jones as Christopher Robin); and, with Susannah Pearse, he has recently written a play about Lewis Carroll and the actress Isa Bowman. Gyles Brandreth is married to writer and publisher Michèle Brown, and they have three children—a barrister, a writer, and an environmental economist.

Oscar Wilde died in a small, first-floor room at l'Hôtel d'Alsace, 13 rue des Beaux-Arts, in Paris, at approximately

1:45 p.m. on 30 November 1900. Exactly one hundred years later, at the same time, on the same date, in the same room, Gyles and Michèle Brandreth were among a small group who gathered to mark the centenary of his passing and to honour a most remarkable man, whose greatest play, according to Frank Harris, was his own life: "a five-act tragedy with Greek implications, and he was its most ardent spectator." In 2010, Gyles Brandreth unveiled the plaque commemorating the first meeting of Oscar Wilde and Arthur Conan Doyle at the Langham Hotel, London.

For further historical information and for details of the other titles in the series, and for reviews, interviews, and material of particular interest to reading groups, et cetera, see www.oscarwildemurdermysteries.com.

Oscar Wilde and the Murders at Reading Gaol

In 1895 Oscar Wilde has been sentenced to prison for indecency and eventually lands in Reading Gaol, where must submit to harsh rules for inmates, including no speaking and wearing a hood at all times while outside his cell. He endures this isolation, but when two prison workers die under mysterious circumstances, Wilde must crack the case. This time without the help of Arthur Conan Doyle, long-time friend and crime-solving collaborator, Wilde must identify and stop the killer or risk becoming the next victim.

FOR DISCUSSION

1. Gyles Brandreth narrates his story as Wilde biographer Robert Sherard. Why do you think he does this? What effects did that have on your interpretation of the book?

2. Wilde thinks about the turning points in his life and admits, "I would sooner say—or hear it said of me—that I was so typical a child of my age, that in my perversity, and for that perversity's sake, I turned the good things of my life to evil, and the evil things of my life to good." What do you think he means? Why would he want people to think it about him?

3. Several times in the story Wilde says, "Each man kills the thing he loves," which he also incorporates into his poem *The Ballad of Reading Gaol*. Which characters exemplify this statement? Do you think the statement is true?

4. When viewing Warder Braddle's grave in the prison grounds,

Wilde thinks, "In this life we are all of us are confined in different ways." Consider the ways the prisoners and the prison guards are confined. How is Wilde still confined after his release? How is he a prisoner of his own habits? In what ways do you feel confined?

5. In a conversation with the prison surgeon, Wilde says, "I wrote when I did not know life, Doctor. Now that I do know the meaning of life, I have no more to write. Life cannot be written; life can only be lived." Do you agree or disagree? What does it say about authors?

6. Discuss how the silence rule at the jail affected Wilde and possibly the other inmates. How would react to such a drastic, inhumane rule?

7. Sebastian Atitis-Snake was found guilty of multiple murders, but Wilde found likable qualities in him. What does that say about Wilde? About Atitis-Snake?

8. Review the Rules for Prisoners in the 1890s on page 306. What do you think these harsh regulations are meant to achieve? Compare this to what their actual effects on the inmates are. Wilde thinks, "Prison life makes one see people and things as they really are and that is why it turns one to stone." Does prison life have this effect on both the prisoners and the jailers?

9. Wilde expresses his unabashed dislike of journalists when he states "newspapers today chronicle with degrading avidity the sins of the second-rate, and with the conscientiousness of the illiterate, give us accurate and prosaic details of the doings of people of absolutely no interest whatever." Do you think this can be said of the pursuits and integrity of today's journalists?

10. Reread Warder Stokes's description of the hanging beginning on page 268, chronicling the schedule and procedures. Consider also the Regulations for the Administration of Corporal Punishment on pages 309 to 310. Do you think these methods for killing a man make it more or less civilized? Is government-sanctioned killing a necessary evil? Do the rules and regulations make it easier for people to tolerate the prison system—both those within its walls and society at large?

11. Throughout the story Wilde claims, and indeed seems, to care deeply for his wife and sons, yet his behavior after his release from

prison further hurts his wife and alienates him from his family. What does that say about his affection for them? In the afterword Wilde wonders, "Why is it that one runs to one's ruin?" Why does he?

12. Do you think Wilde redeemed himself by murdering Atitis-Snake in order to save Tom? Did the significance of Wilde's act change for you when you learn that, as an adult, Tom runs a male brothel?

13. How do you think Wilde's life might have turned out had he not been convicted and sent to jail?

A CONVERSATION WITH GYLES BRANDRETH

This is the sixth book in your Oscar Wilde series. Do you feel there is still more for you to write about him?

There is plenty more to write about. Oscar Wilde's life was so extraordinary. There were remarkable highs and incredible lows—the stuff of comedy and tragedy. He knew so many people—writers, artists, actors, princes, poets, prostitutes, politicians; he met a pope and Mark Twain (though not on the same day); he knew all types and conditions of men and women—and he travelled widely, in Europe, in America, in North Africa. The possibilities feel limitless. I have now written six mysteries. In my head, I have plot outlines for at least six more. For example, it turns out that Oscar Wilde was a friend of four men who were among those most often accused of being Jack the Ripper—so it could be that, thanks to Wilde and Arthur Conan Doyle, my next mystery reveals, at long last, the complete (and unexpected) truth about the most notorious and brutal murderer of the nineteenth century. . . .

Your Wilde series has been extensively and positively reviewed. How does that affect you when working on the next title?

The mysteries have been very generously received and that's both wonderful and a challenge. It means that I feel I have to keep raising my game. I want the stories to work as satisfying murder mysteries—in the tradition of the best of Agatha Christie or Dorothy L. Sayers—and at the same time I want my portrait of Wilde and his circle to be as accurate and true as possible. When you meet Oscar Wilde or Arthur

Conan Doyle in my stories, I want you to feel you are meeting the real man. With Wilde there is an extra challenge, too: he was reckoned the greatest talker of his time. Yes, I can borrow some of the brilliant things we know he said, but I have to invent quite a few of my own as well.

This series has been published in twenty-three countries. Have your fan receptions been different in each country?
In some countries, the real Oscar Wilde—poet, playwright, prisoner—is almost unknown. There people read the books simply because they are historical murder mysteries. They assume that Oscar Wilde is entirely my invention! In Russia, they are much more aware of Arthur Conan Doyle than they are of Oscar Wilde, so they are more interested in him than in Oscar—and on the cover of one of the Russian editions I see that they have dressed Oscar Wilde in a Sherlock Holmes deerstalker and given him a Sherlock Holmes pipe to smoke.

You have exhaustively studied the life and personality of Oscar Wilde, a man who was born almost a century before you. Do you view the distance of time as a benefit or challenge to your understanding of the man?
My father was born in 1910, only a decade after Oscar Wilde's death. Arthur Conan Doyle was still very much alive then. Bedales, the English boarding school I was sent to as a boy in the 1960s, was founded by a man—John Badley—who knew Oscar and Constance Wilde: their older son, Cyril, was a pupil at the school. Mr. Badley was still alive when I was at Bedales. I took tea with him on Wednesday afternoons during term time. We played Scrabble and talked about Oscar Wilde. Yes, I knew a man who knew Oscar Wilde. And now, in 2013, I find that I am a friend of Oscar Wilde's only grandson, Merlin Holland. The events I am describing took place more than a century ago and yet, curiously, I feel very close to them. And it's not just the people I feel close to: I feel I know the places, too. With all the books in the series I try to visit the actual locations—and, of course, many of the buildings of the 1880s and 1890s are still with us and some are comparatively unchanged. For example, when I was writing *Oscar Wilde and the Vatican Murders* I had a fascinating behind-the-scenes tour of

the Vatican and, while researching this book, I was privileged to spend time at Reading Gaol. I have sat in the actual cell where Wilde was incarcerated. I have walked along the prison corridors. I have stood in the execution room.

What is the most interesting or striking feedback you have received about your Oscar Wilde series?

Oscar Wilde's only grandson, Merlin Holland, is a considerable authority on his grandparents' lives and the editor of the *Complete Letters of Oscar Wilde*. He has read all the books in my series of mysteries and, as well as being very generous about them, has put me right on details of fact when I have gone wrong. Having his feedback has been invaluable. I have also had generous and helpful feedback from people who knew Wilde's friend Lord Alfred Douglas and from members of the Sherlock Holmes Society of London. When writing these books I want to "get it right." It's a murder mystery: it's historical fiction, but many of the characters were real people (more than you would think) and I want the reality to be real. When this book was first published in London, we held a party at the Cadogan Hotel. The hotel features in *Oscar Wilde and a Game Called Murder* and is the hotel where Wilde was arrested and taken for trial in 1895. At the party the guests included Wilde's grandson and great-grandson; several actors who had played Wilde on stage or screen; the priest from the church where the Wildes were married; and representatives from Reading Gaol, including the present governor and a prison officer who had served in the prison for more than thirty years. He said to me, "The Reading Gaol in your book—it's the real thing." That pleased me very much.

Oscar Wilde and the Murders at Reading Gaol **tackles a darker side of Wilde than the earlier books in the series. A sense of isolation pervades the harsh environment of the jail, but here Wilde also endures the absence of Arthur Conan Doyle, with whom he has solved mysteries in previous titles. How did these more somber, introspective elements affect the writing process for you?**

Oscar Wilde's life was a roller-coaster ride and my series of mysteries must reflect that. To put myself into the right frame of mind for this book, I visited the prison and I reread all the letters we have that date from the time of Wilde's incarceration, including the long confessional letter that he wrote to Lord Alfred Douglas, now known as "De Profundis." At the British Library I was able to read—and touch—the original manuscript of the letter. Seeing Wilde's handwriting on the prison notepaper was a moving experience. I also visited Wilde's grave in Paris while writing the book and—quite as moving—visited the grave of his wife, Constance, in Genoa.

Even more than a hundred years after his death, Wilde's works are widely studied and appreciated. Why do they have this timeless relevance? What makes Wilde such an enduringly fascinating person?

Wilde's works stand on their own merit. *The Importance of Being Earnest* is, arguably, the best comedy written in the English language. It is a play that will stand the test of time. Recently I appeared on stage in a musical version of the play (as Lady Bracknell) and the more familiar I became with the play, the more I admired it. As I get to know Wilde the man better, I don't admire him more, but I do find him ever more fascinating. During his life he went out of his way to make himself a mythic personality—and, incredibly, the myth has endured. The tragedy that followed the triumphs helped, no doubt. And—like Marilyn Monroe, James Dean, and Elvis Presley—he died before his time. He is a wonderful character to write about because he is both touched by genius and flawed. He is somebody you want to meet and, when I am writing these books, I do feel that I am meeting him.

You certainly have extensive experience studying and writing about Oscar Wilde. If you could choose another person as the subject of a historical novel, who would it be and why?

I am happy enough living in the twenty-first century, but if I had to live in another epoch I would choose the nineteenth century so that I could meet the giants of that era who created characters and worlds that are still alive today—characters like Sherlock Holmes and Count Dracula, Dr. Jekyll and Mr. Hyde, Alice in Wonderland, and Peter

Pan. And once I had exhausted the possibilities of the Victorian age, I would move back to the Elizabethan age. Queen Elizabeth I was a remarkable woman and writing about her would be a fascinating challenge. Perhaps I could find a way to team her up with the greatest writer of them all, William Shakespeare. It is strange: Shakespeare knew so much about us and yet we know so little about him. I would like to discover more.

Will your next writing project focus on Oscar Wilde or will you go in a new direction?
I have recently completed *Wonderland*, a play (with music by Susannah Pearse) about Lewis Carroll and a young actress called Isa Bowman who was one of the first to play the part of Alice in Wonderland on stage. I am currently writing a one-man show called *Looking for Happiness* and editing the new edition of the *Oxford Dictionary of Humorous Quotations*. And then it's back to Oscar and Arthur. I think it has to be. One of my forebears was a Victorian journalist called George R. Sims (famous in his day, almost forgotten now): he claimed to be the first man to identify Jack the Ripper. I have uncovered a stash of his unpublished papers. I now know things I feel the world should know.

Wilde was known for his exceptional wit. Can you share one of your favorites of his quotes?
Now did Oscar Wilde say this? Or did I invent it for him to say? I really do not recall, but I like the line because it reminds me why so many of us love a traditional murder mystery: "There is nothing quite like an unexpected death for lifting the spirits."

ENHANCE YOUR BOOK CLUB

1. The book includes an excerpt from Wilde's poem *The Ballad of Reading Gaol*. Read the entire poem and discuss the parallels between it and this novel. How does the poem further illuminate Wilde's frame of mind and experiences as a prisoner?
2. In this book Wilde says, of his life, "I threw the pearl of my soul

into a cup of wine. I went down the primrose path to the sound of flutes. I lived on honeycomb." In honor of his passion for life, set the mood at your meeting by serving decadent hors d'oeuvres and desserts. Elegant teas would make a fitting accompaniment, as would champagne.

3. Explore the five other books in the series. As Brandreth indicates, there is no particular order in which they must be read. To help make your selection, you can peruse excerpts and find reviews on the series website, www.OscarWildeMurderMysteries.com. For further information on Wilde, Brandreth recommends several excellent biographies in the Acknowledgements.

4. Consider throwing a murder mystery party with your reading group members. There are many board or electronic games available online to provide the structure. You can serve murder-themed (or named) dishes or perhaps even have participants dress in Victorian costumes. To further customize the game, incorporate a selection of Wilde's many witticisms into the fun.